HUNGRY

A NOVEL BY

DANIEL PARME

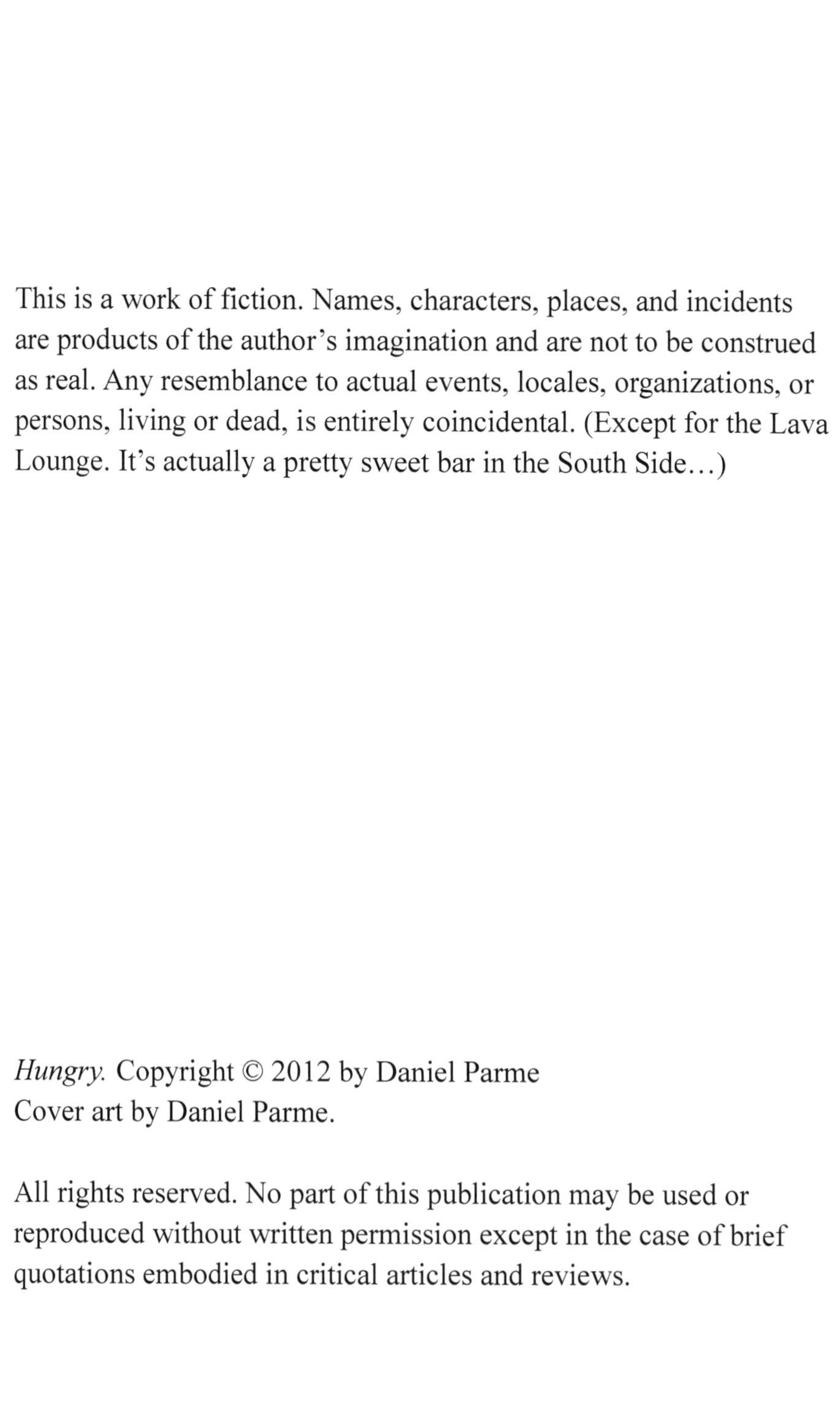

This is a work of fiction. Names, characters, places, and incidents are products of the author's imagination and are not to be construed as real. Any resemblance to actual events, locales, organizations, or persons, living or dead, is entirely coincidental. (Except for the Lava Lounge. It's actually a pretty sweet bar in the South Side…)

For my family.
Eat more people,
but not them, please.

1

The thing about first ascents in the Yukon Territory is that the Yukon Territory is a long fucking way from Pittsburgh, PA. It's a journey requiring many stops and an absurd number of changes in mode of transportation: buses, planes, cabs, helicopters. A ferry. For the first time in my life, I rode a ferry.

The thing about first ascents in general is that there's only one reason to do something so ridiculous as to willingly put yourself hundreds of feet in the air, hanging perilously close to death, nothing more than the tip of your pick piercing the ice and a nylon rope the width of your thumb to keep you from your severely painful doom—simply put, you want to be badass.

Adventure sports are called adventure sports for a reason. If there's no risk of life and limb, then there is no point. I find it's near impossible to impress a woman with a badminton racquet in your hand, both feet firmly on the ground.

Yes, it's all about the badass. Jason, Erica, and I could think of no better way to prove ourselves (to whom or what I'm still not certain) than the first ascent of a potentially treacherous ice route thousands of miles from home.

This was back when being badass was important to me, of course. This was back when my story, the story of Travis Sebastian Eliot, was moving along rather swimmingly. This was back when I was waiting tables, taking people's money with a relentless assault of charm and product knowledge, taking vacations whenever I had the money—long vacations to climb and ride the mountain trails and raft the white waters, to drink the local beer and fuck the local women.

This ice ascending adventure was back when things were simple and life was as easy as all those local broads. I am glad of that time in my life. I fully believe that every man needs, at some point in his life, to know what it feels like to be a bad motherfucker.

This trip was when things were simple.

But the story sometimes takes an unexpected turn, I suppose. Sometimes the characters have no choice but to hold on, white-knuckled, and wait to see how they come out of it.

I came out of this shit more badassedly than I could ever have imagined. I mean, being tough is one thing, but you cross a line that most people don't even know exists when you get into survival cannibalism. There's a constitution there that doesn't seem real to people. It doesn't even seem real to you. Even when you're in the middle of the very real act of cutting the meat from your dead friends' bones, taking a nice big bite of that incompetent fucking pilot, it doesn't seem real to you.

One of the things about being knee deep in such a situation is that you find out what you're made of. I was, after the plane went down, made of broken bones and lacerations. And I was made of fear and dread and pain. And I was made of torment.

I know that this all sounds a little gothic or melodramatic or whatever, but that's the way it was. I mean, they were all dead. My friends were dead, and I was starving. And when I say *starving*, I don't mean it in that way we Americans typically do. This wasn't *I haven't had my three PM McDonald's run yet* starving. This was hallucination-inducing emptiness. This was a searing-pain-in-the-innards kind of hunger.

The thing about a mountain is it's supposed to represent a challenge—this enormous mass of earth and rock, put there by whatever god you see fit, is meant to dwarf you. It's supposed to humble you, remind you that you're small.

Then again, maybe the mountains don't represent a damn thing. Maybe they're nothing more than little fits of rage thrown by our gracious Mother Earth, who doesn't waste her time with small gestures of displeasure. She has no wooden spoon, no need to bother with time-outs or groundings. These punishments carry no weight in a house with billions of children. Instead, she has shifting tectonic plates, volcanic eruptions, hurricanes and tsunamis that swallow entire cities. When that bitch is angry with you, you're going to know it.

You might not know exactly why you deserve this punishment, but hell, sometimes it's better not to know how much of an asshole you really are.

Of course, I can't say that Mama threw her best at me. All I had to deal with was the cold, really. And the quiet. At least, those were the only factors she'd thrown into the equation. She certainly had nothing to do with all the months of planning, saving money, packing all that sub-zero sleeping gear and ropes and spikes. She had nothing to do with our decision to find the cheapest air-fare possible, no matter if the plane looked more like a Volkswagen than a flying craft of obvious genius, no matter if the pilot seemed a little, well, iffy. No, these were all decisions made by three reasonably bright people. Three good friends who wanted nothing more than a grand adventure, their names attached to something awesome.

This was the kind of shit that left me thinking I'd be spending the rest of my life with the arctic night sky as my only scenery, the stars and constellations the only names I'd have to call to. When you get to thinking that you're going to die a slow, painful, lonely death, you begin to see how ancient peoples could have thought the stars were listening to them. Those stars, they're always there. Every night, looking in on you. Why not talk to them? You've got all the time in the world before anyone will rescue you. Or before you die.

2

In the months after they found me, it was mostly questions. People want to know, I guess. They did, after all, discover me unconscious and buried beneath layers of jackets and sleeping bags. They found me with ice in my beard, blood-soaked clothes, and blood-stained cheeks. They found what was left of a shitty little plane buried in the snow that had been drifting for 124 fucking days. They found the faces of my friends.

So they had a lot of questions. Of course they did.

And these weren't even the shrinks. Not yet. These were the orderlies. These were the nurses, nurses' aides, nursing students asking me all these questions. They'd be feeding me—it was months of well-rounded meals of chicken and peas and rice and tall glasses of juice and milk—when one of them would say, "What was it like? I mean, eating your friends? How did you do it? It's amazing."

Or they'd be bathing me. It was months of sponges and averted eyes; of young and beautiful women in scrubs who made you think maybe you were in a porn, only no one told you. Or it was some middle-aged guy who tried to talk about sports or the news or something, anything to keep his mind off the fact that he was giving a sponge bath to another man. They'd be bathing me, and they'd ask, "How did you get through that? I mean, over four months? Where did you find the strength? I'd have just died. It's totally amazing."

They had a lot of questions, but I wouldn't answer them. I was tired. I was emaciated and tired. I was broken. They'd even had to re-break and reset some of me—the parts of me that had already begun to heal without proper medical treatment. In a lot of places, I was broken. Both legs (in different places), a few ribs, one wrist and forearm. They told me I was lucky to have sustained only these injuries. Apparently, people know nothing of luck.

Still, again and again they asked, and again and again I avoided giving an answer. I just couldn't.

Even if I could have, what would I have said? It *was* amazing that I was still alive. Any idiot could have told you that. Plus, I knew there would be plenty to talk about with the shrinks.

"How did it make you feel, seeing everyone dead? Realizing you were lost? Realizing you had no food? Deciding that it would be better to eat your friends than to die there, alone on that mountainside? How did you feel when you finally cut into the rear end of the pilot? Chewed his fat, his muscle, his skin? Swallowed it? And the rest of him? Was he easiest because you didn't know him? And your friends; was it more difficult for you to eat them? Or did it just not matter anymore? How do you feel about it now that it's all over?"

These, of course, were only a few of the questions. People want to know. Those doctors, they want to know *everything*.

But these were my answers: Shocked. Lost. Hungry. Traitorous. Sick to the pit of my soul's stomach. Sick to the pit of my own stomach. A little numb. Full. Of course the pilot was the easiest. Harder for the friends. Of course it mattered. I feel like I got shafted by some invisible force that either forgot about me entirely or wanted to see what would happen if I were forced to decide between cannibalism and death, and that I must have put on a goddam good show, seeing as you assholes want to know so much about it now.

By the end of it, they said they were glad I stopped talking to the stars, lest I developed some sort of split- or multiple-personality disorder. That didn't really make much sense to me, but then, I'm no professional. They also said that I seemed to be a reasonably emotionally stable young man, and that I seemed to be dealing with the unfortunate circumstances leading to the cannibalization of my friends about as well as could have been hoped for. Seriously. That's almost verbatim.

By the end of it, they said I was well enough to go home. They said they thought it would be best for me to continue talking to someone, because you never know what sort of residual effects an event such as mine might have on one's psyche. They said that, soon enough, my memories of the accident would settle down into the muck that is the rest of my brain. It would sink in, and I'd have to get my hands dirty if I ever wanted to really get a good look at it again.

After an unfairly long six months, they said I could go home.

I said thank fucking god and good riddance.

And I went home.

3

As it turns out, while I was in the hospital recovering for all that time, my story had become something of a national phenomenon. It was all over the local news channels at first, giving all those stories about electrical fires and potholes a well-deserved break. From there, it picked up steam and made it to the biggies: CNN, CNBC, FOX News. People all over the place had heard about this guy whose plane went down in the mountains, and everyone else died, and he had to eat them so he wouldn't die.

It was amazing. It was "the most harrowing tale of survival of the decade." It was "this decade's *Alive*." It was all a little ludicrous, if you ask me.

But American society is absolutely fascinated by *harrowing tales of survival*, so I got to be famous. People want to know. They want to know so they can forget about their own lives for a while. Or they want to know so their lives don't seem all that bad.

Either way, I was everywhere. Apparently these kinds of things make for good television. The more outlandish, more gruesome, and more humorous, the more air time, more air time, more air time.

And I have to say, I was surprised by how relatively easy it was to make light of the whole situation. I got a good laugh about *chewing the fat with my buddies* while I was stuck up there. And I had a bit about pulling the pilot's leg—it had been severed, you see, and I'd found it about fifty yards from the plane. Both anecdotes were well-received on Letterman, and then again on Leno. Unfortunately, Jay's first guest was Penelope Cruz, and she seemed none-too-thrilled with all the gory details. In fact, after the show, she took off before I even had the chance to ask for an autograph.

I did get one hell of a nice gift basket for doing the show, though. Expensive shampoos, conditioners, soaps, lotions. There was a mug and a hat. There was a box of the best chocolate I'd ever eaten (dark, smooth, and sexy, the way I imagine Billie Holiday). And there was a slew of other shit I'd never use, but which all seemed pretty pricy.

I gave most of it to the girl who had been taking care of me during my visit to the studio. She was this tiny bit of a thing with dark, dark hair, dark, dark eyes, and toothpaste commercial clean teeth. Hidden somewhere inside of her, a nuclear power plant produced more energy than her little body could have used in a century.

"I met that guy who cut off his own hand when he was here last year," she told me after the show. "Did you hear about him? He got his hand crushed by this huge boulder and he was stuck there, for like, days, and he was out of food and water, so he just took out his pocketknife and started sawing away. God! I couldn't imagine, could you? He was sort of nice. Smiled a lot and said 'thank you' when I brought him a soda." Think about one of those rubber bouncy balls you get from a gumball machine in Wal-Mart, and then imagine throwing it off the wall inside a closed phone booth. That's what it was like listening to her talk, watching her run around the room doing whatever it was her job required of her.

"And I saw you on Letterman the other day," she said. "It was funny. Don't tell anyone, but," she threw a glance at the open door, "I think he's funnier than Jay." As soon as she said it, the walkie-talkie clipped to her belt said something to her I couldn't understand. She unclipped it from her belt, turned away from me, and said something back.

"Maybe you shouldn't have said that," I told her.

"No. That had nothing to do with Jay not being funny. Brad Pitt's coming in tomorrow, so there's a lot of work to do. That was just my boss reminding me to get the pomegranates." She was totally serious.

"Pomegranates? Really?"

"Yeah, really." She said it like she couldn't believe I was surprised. "He also likes to drink this really expensive wine. We order it from Pennsylvania, of all places. I have to make sure to get everything before I go home tonight. No time tomorrow."

"So Brad Pitt's sort of a diva, eh?"

"Not really. He's actually really nice. We just try to take extra good care of all the really big guests that come on the show. That's all."

I couldn't help myself. "So where's my exotic fruit and expensive wine?"

She snatched a clipboard off the table and held it to her chest. "Oh. Well, you're not really a star, so you only get a basket. My boss says that fifteen minutes only gets you a month's worth of personal hygiene products. For some reason, he thinks it's funny."

"Yeah," I said. "That's not funny at all. Still, it is a pretty nice basket."

"It is." She made a quick survey of the room, but I guess she decided she had nothing else to take care of. "Well, I have to go. It was nice to meet you, and thanks for the shampoo and everything. Someone will be here in a minute to see you out. Good luck." And it was like she vanished, poof, into the air that would tomorrow find its way into the lungs of the sexiest man alive.

This was to be my fifteen minutes. Talk shows (late night, prime time, daytime), newspaper articles, magazine interviews. People shaking my hand on the street. It was a wild ride, this fifteen minutes, but it didn't really get me anywhere. All I had to show for my fame was a stack of periodicals, a lifetime supply of shampoos and conditioners, and quite a collection of knick-knacks, trinkets, from NBC, CBS, ABC, FOX. You know: hats, mugs, magnets. That kind of shit.

Other people get these things while on vacation in Atlantic City. Other people get these things as souvenirs. I got these things as payment, which would've been great, if I could have used them as legal tender. But no matter how hard you try, you'll never convince the student loan people that this ball cap signed by Larry King is worth this month's payment. They'll just laugh at you.

They'll laugh at you, but won't accept your payment, which means you have to try to find some way to make money.

I went to publishers. I was sure that I could have written a book, and it would have sold. I did, after all, have my Bachelors in Creative Writing, and if people are going to read Liza Minnelli's autobiography, they'll definitely read about my ordeal. But the book people, they said no. Corporate bastards. "It's been done," they said. "Once you've read one book about survival cannibalism, you've read them all."

Goddam rugby teams in the Andes. Goddam Donner Party.

So no book deal for me. I'd have to find a job. I'd have to go back to the way life was before all the pain and death and fame and parties. But not right away. I always made sure to have a small savings before I went on a potentially hazardous trip, you know, just in case.

I could just go home.

It was an exciting prospect.

4

All my life, except those four years at college in Johnstown, home was Pittsburgh. Biggest small town in the country. Steeler Country. Black and gold banners hanging from the telephone poles. Vendors on street corners, peddling bright-ass yellow shirts that said things like "Cleveland Sucks" and "If You Ain't a Steeler Fan, You Ain't Shit". Pierogies, Primanti's sandwiches, and bottles of Iron City. This was home, and it was the first I'd been back since I tried to go climbing with my friends.

"How was your vacation?" Mr. Hanlon, the landlord, gestured me inside his apartment. "Looks like you lost some weight, kid."

"Yeah, a little." I avoided the question about my vacation.

"Well," he said, "people missed you while you were gone." He crossed the room to a stack of boxes, rested his eighty-six year-old elbow on top. "I'd love to carry them up for you, but I might die."

I laughed. I was allowed to laugh. Mr. Hanlon was perhaps the coolest old guy I've ever known. He'd been a steel worker before WWII, where he suffered some sort of injury. When he got home, he found out his wife had been having an affair with their dentist. "I always knew she'd do something like that," he'd said. He didn't even seem bitter about it.

"Those boxes—that's all mail? For me?"

"That's what I told you, Travis. Good thing you finally got home, or I'd have started throwin' 'em out." The man was frighteningly skinny, like someone had felt bad for a Halloween decoration, pulled it down from the door, and said, "Now be free!"

Mr. Hanlon didn't watch the news. Or read it. Or listen to it. He was skeptical of all things media. "That's why kids are so stupid nowadays," he'd say. "It's because of all those idiots on the television telling lies. And the radio and newspapers, too. If it ain't lies, it's just propaganda. Or else there's subliminal messaging in there. You can't trust any of 'em."

Mr. Hanlon knew nothing of the news, so he knew nothing of the accident. I didn't have it in me to tell him, either. It wouldn't have mattered much. He'd still have to fix my broken bathtub, and I'd still have to pay him the rent on time.

"I gotta try to take a shit," he said. "Get them boxes out of here, if you don't mind too much. Don't worry about locking the door." And he left. To this day I still find myself hoping he had a successful shitting experience.

I grabbed the boxes, three of them, and lugged them to the third floor. I set them on the floor, unlocked the door, and saw my apartment for the first time in what seemed like forever. It was exactly as I'd left it. Finally, something was the way it was supposed to be.

Picasso and Dali prints on the wall, dishes clean and stacked neatly in the cupboards, blanket folded and atop the couch. Oh, it was comforting.

I set the boxes on the kitchen table and went to take a shower. Then I took a nap. And, to me, this was incredibly exciting shit. It's all about perspective.

I woke up and looked at the clock. Five o'clock. Time to eat. To cook in my own kitchen, eat off my own dishes and wash them in my own sink.

This was a Friday, and there's really only one thing for a twenty-six year old man to do on a Friday night in this city: BAR. My bar of choice was in the South Side, on East Carson, down nearer the end of the strip, where most of the halter tops and frosted tips never managed to reach. My bar of choice was called the Lava Lounge; plaster stalagmites and -tites and painted lava running down the walls, threatening all the drinkers without volcano insurance. It wasn't the nicest place in town, but I wouldn't call it a dive, either. To be honest, I never really liked the place. But my friends did, and it's not about where you are, it's about who you're with.

I used to come here with Jason and Erica, and a few other friends, just about every Friday and Saturday night. The thing about going to the same bar all the time is you get to know everyone else who's in that bar all the time. It's actually quite comforting, especially once you get to be good friends with the bartender. There's just something about getting to the bar to find your drink waiting for you, and you didn't even have to ask.

I had to ask this night, though. This was a new bartender, and she made me wait a good five minutes before she closed her copy of *The Amazing Adventures of Kavalier and Clay* and asked what I'd like.

I told her Woodford Reserve on the rocks, and she tilted her head a little and almost smiled. She had black, thick-rimmed glasses and large breasts that were hard not to notice, the way she made them bounce as she walked. Some women simply know how to get your attention.

"He went to Pitt, you know. Michael Chabon, I mean." I put a ten on the bar.

"Um. Yeah. No shit." She picked up the money, but didn't do anything with it. She just sort of sneered at me, but not altogether unpleasantly. "Says so in the bio."

Straight out of the gate I knew I wasn't ready for this. This bitch was *intense*. "Where's Causi? Doesn't he work the weekends?"

"He used to, but he moved. North Carolina, I think." She scanned the bar, but it was still early, and no one needed anything. "Why?"

"I used to come here all the time. That's all."

She looked at me not quite sideways, but close. "Are you... Are you Travis?"

I lit a cigarette. God, it felt good to be sitting at the bar, the burn of bourbon on the back of my throat, the rush of smoke past my lips. "Um, yeah. I'm Travis. I'm sorry, but have we met?" I wouldn't say she was hot, exactly, but she was definitely sexy, and it's hard to forget people who just reek of sex.

"No. I don't think we've met. I saw you on television the other day, in here, and some of the guys said they knew you. That you used to hang out in here." She was still eying me, maybe. Maybe she just always looked at guys that way, like she was thinking dirty thoughts.

I still wasn't used to people recognizing me from television, but I have to admit, it's pretty fucking sweet. "Oh. Right. Yeah, I'm Travis. And you are?"

"Virginia." She held out her hand. "Nice to meet you."

"And you." I tried to sound only vaguely interested. "When did you start?"

She looked up at the neon-bordered Coors Light clock above the bar, which said eight twenty-one. "Four," she said.

I laughed. "No, no. I mean when did you start working here? Like what time of the year? You know?"

She put her head down, laughing at herself. "Oh. About two months ago."

"You like it?"

"Yeah. The money's good. And most of the people are all right."

I knew a lot of the people who came into this bar, and some of them were not all right, so I asked, "And what about all those drunken assholes that constantly hit on you?"

"I don't mind them so much." She took a shot of Jameson, "I know how to handle those kinds of guys. Most of them are just talk, and they know it."

We stalled out. I still wasn't used to normal conversation. For months everything had been about the accident and the recovery and the people-eating, and now I couldn't remember how to keep a conversation afloat. "Yeah, well..."

"What was it like? I mean, if you don't mind, what was it like, being all alone for so long?" Thank god for bartenders and their conversational prowess.

"It was lonely." I took a sip of my drink. "And scary. And hard."

"I can't imagine. Was it pretty? At night, I mean? All the stars had to be completely amazing." It actually sounded like she was jealous.

None of the interviewers ever asked me if it was pretty at night. I suppose it wouldn't have made for good television.

"Yeah. It was gorgeous at night." I studied the burning end of my cigarette before dragging on it. "Actually, some nights it was so beautiful I almost forgot where I was." I smiled for a moment, but then it was gone, and I drained my glass.

"You ok?" she asked as she refilled it. "What's the matter?"

I shook my head. "Nothing really. It's just sort of a shame that every time I see a sky full of stars, I'm going to be reminded of... well... you know."

"Oh. You mean your friends dying and you having to eat them and everything."

I laughed. It's a defense mechanism. "Yeah. That's what I mean."

We heard the door squeak open but paid no attention until—"Yeah, buddy!"

It was Adam, all six-two of him and his long almost-red hair, blue jeans, cowboy boots, and vintage Led Zeppelin t-shirt. He was all smiles as he and his smoke came towards me. "I see you've met Virginia. Hey."

"Hey, Adam. What can I get for you?"

He ordered a Miller Light, told Virginia we'd see her in a little while, and we moved to a table along the wall, about halfway down the bar. A big table with bench seating.

Adam and I had been roommates in college. Ah, college. We were a good match. He was a literature major, and I a creative writer, so there was always at least the potential for a decent and fairly intellectual discussion, unlike with most of the people I'd met at school. This, however, does not mean that the two of us ever shied away from all the healthy nights of drinking and smoking and getting high and getting laid and overturning garbage cans and stealing beer from girls' refrigerators and pissing on the front doors of frat houses. We were, after all, college boys. It's what we did.

Adam was the kind of guy who could say *righteous* and sound perfectly natural. He was also the kind of guy who most of us would love to look like, but he never understood the power of his good looks. Most importantly, though, he was the kind of guy who would feel so bad about dating one of your ex-girlfriends that he wouldn't be able to bring himself to talk to you for months afterwards. Hell of a guy, that kid, even if he was sort of a pussy.

He lit the next link in his never-ending chain of cigarettes and drank half his beer. "What took you so long, man? Get lost or something?"

"I took the scenic route, Adam." I already felt comfortable. Or maybe it was more in sync, like when the windshield wipers and turn signal fall into step for that beat or two.

"So how you doin', brother? Good to be home, I bet." Adam had a gift for hitting the nail on the head, which is more important than most people think.

"Yeah, man. Good to be home. You have no idea how the thought of this stinking city can come close to giving you a hard-on. And man, coming in through the Fort Pitt Tunnels—you should have seen it." I lit a smoke. "All right. Pirate game to the left, skyscrapers all lit up on the right. Only partly cloudy. And then the fireworks from the stadium just as I was coming out of the tunnels. Unbelievable, right? The timing? It was astounding, Adam. Astounding. Like the city was welcoming me home or something. I mean, I guess that sounds kinda cheesy, but what are the chances, you know?" I think it was the first time I was able to string more than two or three sentences together since the rescue. Well, the first time it wasn't about the accident, anyway.

And to Adam's credit, he just let me ramble on, even if I did sound like a fucking idiot. "Wow, dude. That is sort of, uh, freaky." He waved to Virginia, and then looked back at me. "So, how are you?"

I could tell he meant the big *how are you.* "I don't know, man. I—"

"I'm sorry I asked, man. I just... I don't know... I just figured you'd know I'm gonna want to know, so we could get it out of the way. Talking about it, I mean. I'm sure you've already talked about it more than enough, so if you don't want to, that's cool." He fidgeted as he spoke—folded his napkin and unfolded his napkin, ashed his cigarette every couple seconds.

"Adam. Come on. Of course we can talk about it. You think I don't think you want to know? I mean, you're my friend. You better want to know. If it happened to you, you'd better believe I'd want to know." For a moment, an extremely brief and guilt-inducing moment, I wished it would have happened to him. And yes, I felt like a dick about it.

Virginia brought two beers and another bourbon, set them on the table, and stood there too long to have merely been bringing our drinks.

I looked up at her. "You want to hear about it, too?"

Her face told me I was fucking stupid. Her mouth asked me, "Are you fucking stupid?"

"Adam, give this girl a cigarette."

He tried, but she refused, and she sat across the table from me, next to Adam, who put the cigarette back into its pack and turned to me the way he used to turn to a professor at the start of class.

I got as far into it as the plane clipping the summit of one mountain, splitting apart like a florescent bulb, and landing all over the side of another. I told them about the life flashing before your eyes thing being a total load of crap. I thought I was going to die, and I didn't see my family or friends or my cat or my favorite childhood memories. All I saw was a mass of shit flying all around the cabin and smoke and snow and bodies and blood.

Or maybe I knew I was going to live.

I was, in my story, just waking to realize my suddenly dire situation, when a group of blonde girls showed up at the bar. All the same height, same build. All the same hip-huggers and tiny purses.

Adam let out one of those whistles that show up when you realize that a full tank of gas runs you thirty-two bucks, or when you see a man who's nine feet tall. "You have customers, Virginia."

She looked at the girls and groaned. "Oh, shit. It's like they came straight off the assembly line."

"Aren't you going to serve them?"

"Hell no. Not right now, anyway. Besides, they're all going to want fucking apple martinis or something." She was disgusted. "I fucking hate those girls. How do they even tell each other apart?"

Adam was smoking and drinking and staring. "Maybe they don't have to. Maybe they're all clones of the same girl."

I was staring, too. "There's seven of them, right? Maybe Hugh Hefner's in town."

"What?" They both said it, and they both sounded confused.

"He has seven girlfriends, and they're all blonde and look a lot like those girls. I met him at NBC studios." If you've never been able to drop famous names, I apologize. It's a lot of fun.

Adam sat up straight, making him a good three inches taller. "You met Hef? No way!"

"Yeah. In the lobby when I first got there for Leno. He was doing some other show. He said he saw me on CNN. Hef watches CNN. Can you believe that shit?"

Virginia crossed her arms over those spectacular breasts. "That's ridiculous. What did you say to him?"

"I said I was a big fan of the magazine. He said he was, too. Then he said he only eats people if they're alive, female, and well-groomed. He was pretty funny. Anyway, he got my number at the hotel so he could have someone call to make travel arrangements." I was back in the swing of things. Dictating conversation is easier than it should be. I suppose it just took a little booze to loosen me up.

Adam bit first. "Travel arrangements?"

"Yeah, man. He flew me to the Playboy Mansion for two days. Well, one really long day, really. Like I was going to sleep at the Playboy Mansion, right? And man, that place is crazy. All day and all night, those girls—that look a lot like the girls *still* waiting for booze—they were running around in bikinis and half of their bikinis and none of their bikinis. And food and drinks. And, apparently, it's like that every day."

Virginia stood up. "Ridiculous." She went to wait on the Barbie dolls.

Adam leaned in. "Dude, did you nail a playmate?"

I don't know why I didn't anticipate this question. I mean, I'd spent the night in Dionysus's pool house, excess spilling out of the sinks and bath tubs and blooming in the gardens. The walls were built with nakedness and the foundations were solid sex. Of course I'd fucked a playmate. I was, after all, a celebrity, sort of.

So how did I go about telling Adam that I did not, in fact, have sex with a Playboy Playmate? There were options. I could have said I was too busy telling everyone about the crash and partying and hanging out with the Hef, and it just never came up. Or I could have told him I passed out drunk in the garden, a bottle of Jack in my hand.

Then there was the truth: all the malnourishment and stress and mental anguish had an adverse effect on the willingness of my dick to give a damn about anything. The poor little guy was depressed and spent all his time lying down. There was no coaxing him. He was perfectly comfortable all wrapped up in his lethargy.

But none of this would do. Particularly not the impotency thing. "Of course I did, Adam."

"Righteous. You'll have to show me which one." Adam had been a subscriber for six years. Still had every issue. And, to the man's credit, he really did read the articles.

"I don't know if I'll recognize her. I mean, I was pretty ripped, and they all looked so much alike, you know?"

"Awesome."

We sat and drank, watched as Virginia mixed seven drinks that are the reasons every bartender really ought to despise *Sex and the City*. Cosmopolitans and peach/mango martinis. Obnoxious.

I was thinking about the Playboy Mansion, this mythical land of bare breasts and total lack of inhibition. I felt, in some way, like I'd been to Atlantis and could tell of the golden streets and elegant men and women with their smiles and wealth of money and knowledge. I'd been to a place people have heard of, and maybe even imagined, but that couldn't have really existed. It's impossible.

But it's not impossible. This is a real place. Acres and acres of well-kept lawns and gardens. Acres of filet mignon and Cristal. Acres of soft, golden hair, of soft, golden skin. A Neverland for those who dropped their innocence on the sidewalk and simply didn't pick it back up.

I was there, and then I wasn't. The same as I'm no longer in high school or on vacation in Egypt. The same as I no longer speak to childhood friends or remember barely any of my five years of German. The story changes because the character changes. Or maybe it's the other way around.

Even now, when I talk about the women and the nakedness, the partying, the gardens and the mansion, the details are a little different each time. They never stop changing. There's nothing I can do about it.

But let's get back to Adam and me in the bar.

"Duder, that place must have been incredible." He was still stuck on it, too.

"Yeah. But I couldn't handle it all the time, especially now. I mean, I've had enough excitement to last the next decade or so, you know?" I caught my face pulling a somber moment, so I took a drink and asked him what had gone on since I left.

We drank as he told me about the wedding of some old friends from school, and we drank some more as he told me random stories from parties and bar nights. "We've all just been working, drinking, and sleeping," he said. "You know, same as always."

We were in the beginnings of a discussion about why it was that everyone we knew was in the same place they'd been since graduating college: small apartments, not quite full-time employment, and educational loans in deferment, forbearance, or default. It would have been a damned fine conversation, but it never had the chance to get going.

All at once, I was completely surrounded by bar-friends and the realization that I was drunk. No conversation can survive such things.

"Holy shit! Travis! Good to see you, man!"

"How you doin'?"

"Saw you on the news."

"Saw you on Leno. Man, did Penelope Cruz look disgusted, huh?"

"Saw you on The Today Show."

"...on Larry King..."

"...on Channel Eleven..."

"...in *Time*..."

"...in *Newsweek*..."

"...the *Post Gazette*..."

"When did you get back?"

"I'm gonna get you a drink."

"Me, too."

"Me, too."

"Me, too."

I don't know who said any of this, but I'm pretty sure it was all said. It was unrelenting. It was a hailstorm in the middle of the plains and I had no tree to hide beneath. I was assaulted by all these questions, all these people, all at once. All these people knew me through little more than dart games and pitchers of beer, but they still expected me to be glad to see them, to be excited at the prospect of answering all their questions.

I answered them all at once by dropping the glowing butt of my smoke into the ash tray, standing up, and walking to the bathroom. It may have been more of a mad dash than a leisurely stroll, really, but the bathroom was so far away, and some of them were following me. I mean it. Following me.

I locked the door and sat on the toilet. I blew my nose and read the graffiti on the stall walls. "Tom gives good head." "God is dead." "You are dead!" "Oh, shit! I'm dead?" "This place is shitty."

The last one made me laugh. I took a leak, washed my hands, splashed some cold water on my face, and decided to crawl out the window and into the alley behind the bar.

The window was barred and nailed shut.

My seat was open and my beer was full and my cigarette was lit and handed to me by some ownerless hand. No one said anything to me, though. They watched as I sat, drank, and smoked. They watched. That's it. Watching and murmuring to each other, like they were all afraid to take that first bite. I got through about half of a cigarette. It was absurd.

"Will someone play some fucking music already?" I snapped it out there like a whip, and they all jumped, startled, and looked around at each other. Some kid I didn't know left the back of the crowd—yes, the crowd—and put a five in the jukebox.

"So," I cracked my neck and took a sip of beer. "What's up, guys?"

Apparently nothing was up. Ten-thirty on a Friday night in the South Side, and nothing was up. The tables were now taken, the fun in full swing, and nothing was up.

I rolled my eyes and cleared my throat. "Go ahead."

After the initial barrage of questions had settled, while they were reloading, I told them this was going to have to be more like Kindergarten. I'd call on them, and then they could ask their question. All this mayhem had to stop.

And it did. One question at a time, they were satisfied. Essentially, all I had to do was repeat everything they'd already heard me say on television. Maybe they needed to hear it in person before they could believe it. It's not like they had to touch the holes in my hands and my side or anything. They just wanted to know.

5

Virginia poured a cup of coffee and buttered an English muffin, brought them to the table, and set them down next to my head, which was resting on my folded arms and throbbing something fierce. "You really don't remember anything?"

I groaned. The speaking was going to be difficult. "I remember answering a bunch of questions and doing a bunch of shots, but that's about it." I didn't dare shake my head. It would have made me sick.

She stretched her back, hands clasped over her head. I thought she was going to fall over backwards, her back arched so much.

"You a dancer?"

She straightened up. "Twelve years of ballet. Of course, you'd never know it to look at me."

"I knew it."

"Yeah, but you saw me stretch. I mean if you just looked at my body." She cupped her breasts. "These fucking things ruined everything."

"They look all right to me."

She rolled her eyes and sat down. Her bottom teeth were a little crooked and her lips were a little thin, but something about their shape was crazy attractive. Her eyes, there in the middle of those super-thick frames, were a light blue/grey sort of color with star-like patterns in the irises. The whites were a little bloodshot.

She sipped her tea, which she'd found as she was looking for the coffee. "You ever seen a ballerina with tits like these? I don't think so. They're all skinny and tiny and flat. Dance companies don't want my body. Fuckers."

"Well, if they don't want your body, I'm sure they'd kill for your personality. Very classy."

"Eat me." Smiling.

"It is a shame about your chest, though." And I meant it. I don't really understand why women aren't supposed to be built like women anymore. Think about all those Renaissance paintings of women with their bellies and thighs, their hair hanging down over their breasts. *Those* are women, soft and soothing.

I wasn't about to go into all that with her, though. "So, what did happen last night?"

She blew steam off the surface of her little Earl Gray ocean. "Oh, nothing really. It was almost two by the time all those assholes stopped asking you about everything. Didn't they see you on all those shows? Anyway, you were smashed by then. You just sat there smoking, staring at nothing. I told Adam I'd drive you home in your car. Then we came back here and I put you to bed."

I tried to take a bite of my English muffin, but there was no way. "Well, I'm glad I didn't do anything stupid."

"No," she said. "Nothing stupid."

There was a quiet, awkward moment, but she figured a way out of it. "You think you can take me back to my car? I have to work in a couple hours."

"Sure. At the bar?"

"No. I tutor math for extra cash."

I asked if I had time for a quick shower first. She said there was plenty of time, so I went upstairs and washed the stink of the bar off of my skin, and steamed the hangover most of the way out of my head.

I came downstairs to find her in her own clothes (she'd been wearing one of my t-shirts and a pair of my boxers) and drying the mugs. "You didn't have to do the dishes."

"Eh. I was bored."

On the way back to the South Side, I learned that she tutored algebra. She had her Bachelor's in Higher Mathematics, which she studied when she lived in Florida, "where it's not so fucking cold all the time." She lived there with a boy—three years of seemingly easy, blissful love—before moving home to Pittsburgh. "Four years and ninety-thousand dollars so guys can stare at my chest while I pour them shots."

I thanked her for everything and told her I was sure I'd see her soon.

"I hope so," she said. "Maybe next time you'll do something stupid."

I went home and went back to bed.

6

The thing about spending a few weeks on television is you're always seeing all these people who know you. The problem is you don't know them. People on the street, stopping you, taking pictures, shaking your hand, telling you stories about their cousin or whoever, who once saw an avalanche while on vacation in the Alps. People asking for your autograph—yes, your autograph—on the bill of a hat or a receipt from the CBS gift shop.

The thing about spending a few weeks on the television, and in the papers, and the magazines, is you actually get fan mail. Fan mail. Unbelievable.

All those boxes from Mr. Hanlon were *full* of fan mail. There were also, of course, quite a few bills (credit cards, gas, electric, school loans—you get the idea), but mostly it was letters from people who had seen me that night I was on with Conan O'Brien, doing that sketch when I pretended to be stuck in the elevator with Tom Arnold, and we had to cut off his leg and eat it before we were rescued. Or they were from people who were distant relatives of the Donner Party or some other such nonsense. People are crazy.

I'm not exactly sure how these people were able to find my address, and I suppose it's not that important, although it does make me uncomfortable in a Big Brother sort of way.

It was pretty fucking awesome, though, opening all these letters. They all said they'd seen me on television. Most of them said something about me being so brave and they couldn't imagine. Some of them included phone numbers and *call me* with stars or smiley faces as punctuation.

There were even a few letters that included pictures, dirty

naked pictures. Those were nice. I mean, here I was, just some guy who was in a plane wreck, just some guy with a Creative Writing degree and a few dead friends, just some guy, and I was getting Polaroids of naked women on motorcycles, sprawled over the bed, in interesting positions with showerheads. People are crazy.

I wasn't about to respond to any of these people, though. They could have been anyone. I mean, people are psychotic, or they can be. And if you're crazy enough to track down my address, write me a letter, give me your phone number, or send me dirty pictures, all because I ate my friends and just so happened to be on television, you're going to have to be crazy on your own time. My life was weird enough already.

I kept the pictures in a shoe box in my bedroom closet. And a few of the death threats, too. It would appear that there are those to whom cannibalism is, shall we say, frowned upon. But I must say there's a certain satisfaction that comes with offending people to the point they want to kill you.

I threw all but one of the letters away. It had no return address and was printed on heavy, high-quality paper:

Mr. Eliot,

I am deeply sorry to hear about your unfortunate experience. To lose your friends in such a dreadful manner is something that must be horribly difficult to come to terms with.

I am the acting president of an organization with great interest in certain aspects of your ordeal, and I would like to invite you to attend one of our meetings.

I understand that you may be quite busy once you return home, so if you are interested, you will be able to find me at the James Street Tavern every Thursday night.

I will almost certainly be the only one-armed man in the smoking section, and I look forward to meeting you.

Sincerely,
Walter Synchek

I couldn't get rid of that one. I read it over a few times and left it on the coffee table, where I'd be able to look at it a thousand more times and try to decide whether or not meeting this man would be a good idea.

I called Adam, who invited me over to his place. "Just me, you, and Dave," he said. "I think we'll have a better time that way."

"Yeah. I don't feel like giving another drunken press conference. And I haven't talked to Dave in a long time."

Dave was Adam's roommate, and another friend from college. He had a penchant for collared shirts that were a little too tight, and blue jeans that were a little faded, maybe a hole at the knee. Brown hair that's been spiky and disheveled since before spiky and disheveled was cool. He could be a little bitter sometimes, but it was really just his sense of humor. Mostly, Dave's thing was music. Some would call him a snob. He was never one to be shy about a roll of the eyes or a sigh/groan kind of thing if someone had chosen a CD he didn't agree with. The problem was that most people have never heard of most of what Dave listened to, so you could never make the man happy.

But it didn't take much to make him smile; all I had to do was show up at the door with a case of beer and a few of the pictures I'd received from my adoring fans.

"You gotta be kidding. What the hell's wrong with these women?" Now, just because he was bitching does not mean he wasn't enjoying the pictures. Quite the contrary, in fact. We had to yell at him to put them back in the envelope I'd brought them in. The envelope also held that mysterious letter, which he pulled out when he couldn't quite get the pictures to fit. "What's this?"

"Read it."

Dave read to himself while Adam packed a bowl. If I haven't mentioned it yet, Adam and Dave both smoked a good bit of marijuana. Adam was the kind of guy who would call it grass, and Dave was the kind who would call it pot. It's amazing what you can tell about a person merely by how he refers to the reefer.

"So, is this guy serious?" Dave handed the letter to Adam, who handed me the bowl in the same motion.

"I don't know, Dave." I hit the pipe. It was the first I'd smoked in a really long time, and I took a moment to appreciate how sweet it tasted. Not like cigarette smoke. Not like burning nylon to stay warm smoke. Not like burning oil on the snow smoke. Like reefer smoke. Like candy.

Adam folded the letter and handed it to me. "You should go."

"I don't know. I'm not sure I can handle any more crazy shit right now. I just want some nice, boring routine to fall into. Nothing exciting. Nothing new. Just, well, auto-pilot, I guess."

Dave choked on his cigarette. "Yeah. Right. Wasn't the *plane* on auto-pilot when you hit that mountain? Isn't that what they said on the news?"

"Fine. But you know what I mean."

Adam took a hit, held it, his hands out like he was meditating, and spoke in that holding smoke in your lungs voice. "You should go."

Dave chimed in. The thing about being a group of three is that one is easily outnumbered. It's not necessarily a bad thing, but sometimes you're really not in the mood to get gang-raped, you know? "You should go, man. Ever since college you've been talking about how you need to get out and experience weird shit. How could you ever be a writer if you just sat around and did what everyone else does, right?"

I tried to explain to him that I was tired, too tired to mess with some supposedly one-armed man in some tavern on the North Side who wanted me for something he was unwilling to write about in the letter. I also tried to explain that I'd long ago given up any serious aspirations to become a writer, and I hadn't written anything in months and months.

But he wasn't buying. "So the fuck what, man! How can you honestly say you're not interested in this at all? Not even one tiny little bit? You think anything like this is ever going to happen to you again? Take advantage, man." He took a hit of the pipe Adam had been trying to hand to him for at least two minutes. "I mean, shit. What's the worst that could happen, right?"

7

I'd been to the James Street Tavern once before, well before I'd ever had any bright ideas about going ice climbing in Canada. This was when I was a counselor at a Lutheran summer camp, teaching Bible studies and conflict management skills to kids. The first time I'd been to James Street, I was leading a group of high school juniors on an urban service mission: helping in soup kitchens, babysitting kids of drug-addicted parents, etc. And no, the kids were not there illegally; the place was just as much of a restaurant as it was a bar.

This was when I was all gung-ho about helping people. This was when my biggest concern was staying out of the pants of sixteen year-old girls. This was when my life was relatively normal.

The story changes, I suppose.

But not for the James Street Tavern. The place was exactly the way it had been when I was there for the first time, seven or eight years prior. The sign on the front wall was the same dim, almost-but-not-quite neon red. The lights inside were just as dim, and had a subtle red tint, as well. The smoke hanging in the air could well have been the very same smoke from all those years ago, for all I know. Even the band was the same (Five Guys Named Moe, although there were only four guys in the band, and none, to my knowledge, were named Moe), playing the same covers of Coltrane and Davis. I was instantly sorry I hadn't made a point to hang out in this place more often.

You could feel the air in this place. As you walked, the sounds of jazz and the smells of various tobacco smokes and expensive French cuisine filled your wake as though you were walking through water.

I found the smoking section easily, as there was no non-smoking section, and I found Synchek just as easily. He was, as he'd promised, the only one-armed man in the place, and was easily seen as such because of the folded sleeve at his left shoulder. He would have been easy to spot even without his disability; the man was gigantic. In every way, he was gigantic. Fat, tall, wide. There would have been no way to miss this man. It was mildly disappointing, actually. I'd half-hoped I wouldn't have been able to find him and would have been able to go back to Dave and Adam and say he wasn't there, but at least I went to check it out. Turns out Adam wasn't the only pussy in our little group.

I thought about turning around, walking out, and lying to my friends about it, but I thought about it for too long. He turned his head around, maybe looking for the waitress, and spotted me. His right arm shot up, and he began waving me over, calling, way too loudly, "Mr. Eliot! Mr. Eliot!"

So I went over to him. What else could I have done, right?

He stood up, way up, and had to tilt his head down significantly to look into my eyes as he spoke. "So good to see you, Mr. Eliot. I was beginning to think you weren't interested in meeting me."

"Well, here I am." I didn't bother to make it sound like I was excited.

He offered his right hand and, by the sad state of that handshake, I gathered that he must have been left-handed.

"Have a seat, Mr. Eliot." He watched as I sat, and then he flagged down the waitress. "I'll take a Grey Goose martini, up and dirty. And for my friend, here..."

"Woodford Reserve on the rocks, please."

"I'm sorry, but we don't carry the Reserve." She wasn't sorry. You could tell.

"Knob Creek, then?"

She nodded and walked away, and I was certain she'd be returning with a glass of Jim Beam, or, if I was lucky, Maker's Mark.

Synchek sat down with a big old grin on his face. I couldn't tell if it was genuine or if he was selling me something. "So good to meet you, Mr. Eliot."

I was already annoyed with myself for coming to meet this man. One should be wary of any man who says your name more than twice in two minutes. Of course, I didn't have that rule in place when I met him; he's the reason for its inception.

"So, what's this about?" I suppose I should have been a bit more polite, but I was so angry with myself that I just didn't have it in me.

He paused. I don't think he wanted the conversation to go this way. What was supposed to happen was, he was going to bullshit for a few minutes, break the ice, establish a good rapport, sucker me in the way a telemarketer would. Or maybe a good cult leader.

"Well, Travis—do you mind if I call you Travis? Well, Travis, as I said in my letter, I would like to invite you to be a guest speaker at the next meeting of an organization of which I am the acting president."

I wondered if he always spoke this way, with grammar that was uncertain at best, and forced. I wondered if anyone in the world could speak to him for more than five minutes without wanting to smack him square in the mouth and scream, "God dammit! Speak like a human being!" I gathered not.

I asked him what, exactly, this group was.

He straightened up. "We are an organization of folks who have had experiences similar to your own. We've been following your story with great interest and feel that you may have a lot to offer to our ranks."

"Excuse me?"

He looked puzzled, like he didn't understand what I couldn't grasp. "We feel that we could take quite a bit from your tale, that you have a lot to offer to those who have been in similar circumstances, and that we may have a good bit to offer you in return."

This was a painful conversation. "What, like a support group? Thanks, but I'm finished with therapy."

"No, no, Travis. Not at all like therapy. We're not a support group. We're merely a small group of people who have this one relatively odd thing in common. I was involved in an accident, too, you see." He rolled his left shoulder, his stump in tiny circles. "So have many of the others."

"So this is like a club? What, like survivors of ungodly accidents?"

"Exactly like a club." He nodded to the waitress as she placed our drinks on the table.

I took a large swallow of my bourbon and was pleased to find that it was, indeed, what I'd ordered. "So, what? You guys have ice cream socials and everything? You get group rates on Kennywood and Pirate tickets?"

"Nothing like that, Travis. We just get together and talk about our experiences. Well, sometimes we have events that somewhat resemble ice cream socials. We're merely a group of people with similar interests. It just so happens that our interests are a trifle more unique than those of most people."

"So, all you want me to do is come and talk about what happened, huh?"

"That's what we want, Travis. And, while you're there, perhaps you'll meet a few people and think about becoming a member. We don't like to pressure anyone into joining; most discover for themselves that they enjoy our meetings and events, and they become members with very little encouragement." He sipped his martini as punctuation.

I sipped my Knob Creek and thought about it. "I don't know..."

He smiled. "We can pay you five-thousand dollars."

8

The night I was at Adam and Dave's apartment, I'd mentioned that I needed to find a job, and Dave said that his uncle may have been looking for some help. In the morgue. With dead people.

I was a little hesitant. I mean, it's the morgue for Christ's sake.

"Think about it," Dave had said, "they're all dead, you know? You said you don't want a job where you have to deal with customer relations or anything. You know, no more waiting tables or calling people while they're eating dinner."

"Come on, Dave. The morgue? Don't you think that's sorta creepy? When people ask me what I do for a living, I'm going to have to tell them I work at the morgue."

"Just think about it. I mean, it should be full-time. Benefits. And you could be as much of an asshole as you wanted. It's not like dead people are going to complain to your manager, right?"

He'd made a strong enough argument that the following Monday I found myself on the bus, headed downtown to my interview with the head of the city morgue. I wish I could say I took the bus for some honorable reason such as reducing air pollution or doing my part to ease our dependence on foreign oil, but in reality I just didn't feel like paying a quarter to a meter that only gave me seven-and-a-half minutes in return. It's not that I'm cheap. It's just that I happen to have strong beliefs about certain things, and one of those things is that nobody should ever have to pay that much for parking.

Besides, there's something to be said for the morning commute, with the other morning commuters and their morning commuter faces. It's always an interesting mix of briefcases and backpacks, suit coats and leather coats, sneaks and dress shoes, novels and newspapers, CD players and mp3 players, coffee and Red Bull. It's like a cosmopolitan casserole. The guy next to me (backpack, leather coat, sneaks, coffee, and *walkman*) even smelled like those crunchy onion things on top.

It was a nice ride. Reminded me that even though my world had been more than a fucked up over the last year, the rest of the world went right on doing what it does. I felt like I could slide right back into that little niche I'd created before my accident.

I got off the bus and made it to the morgue. The reception area, if you could really call it that, was this small, square, grey room. Grey. They'd actually painted it grey. Who does that? There were four chairs side by side along the wall to my right, also grey except for the chrome legs, and nothing else. No posters. No pamphlets. No magazines or newspapers. Nothing.

At the far end of the room (and I only mean *far* as in *the other side*; it was only about fifteen feet away) was a counter with a sliding glass window separating the "waiting room" from the filing cabinets and computer and incredibly pale and skinny guy who was at work. At work in the morgue.

"Can I help you?" He looked exactly the way a guy who worked at the morgue looked when he was merely a figment of my imagination. So pale. So skinny. His eyes were, not big, but wide. Open. And he didn't blink as much as a person should. His hair was black and thin, and thinning, from what I could tell. He even had those thick-rimmed glasses and that nervous twitch that comes along with creepy jobs.

Just looking at him was enough to convince me that this would be among the most interesting of all my employment debacles. And I'm not going to lie about it: I was a little excited, even if I was pretty creeped out.

"Yeah. I'm supposed to be meeting Richard Pearson." I glanced around that horrible, boring room, that valium/thirty-years-to-life themed room, and hoped I wouldn't have to wait. "Is he in?"

"Do you have an appointment?" No blinking. Just staring. "Or are you just dropping in for tea?"

"For tea? No." Weirdo. "I don't really have an *appointment*, though. I was just supposed to come in sometime this morning."

He folded his hands on the counter. "Come in for what?" Still no blinking.

"An interview, if you really have to know."

BLINK. But only one. "He's busy. You can have a seat, and I'll go tell him you're here. Name?"

"Travis Eliot."

The creepy little bastard nodded, slid the glass shut, and disappeared through a door to his right. I sighed and took one last look around the room before resigning myself to taking a seat and fidgeting with a quarter I'd found in my pocket. I tried doing that thing where you flip the coin from knuckle to knuckle, across your hand, and then back again. I tried it, with no success, for a long time. Ten minutes, twenty, forty-five, who knows? I didn't own a watch, had left my cell phone at home, and there was no clock on the wall. I imagined what it must be like to be in prison, and then figured it must be a lot like waiting to see the head of the city morgue, in a tiny room with nothing to do and no way of knowing exactly how long this doing nothing was taking.

After a while, I fell asleep. I know how bad it is to fall asleep at a job interview, but I couldn't help myself. Those walls were like that machine in *The Princess Bride* that sucked the life right out of you. That thing made Westley mostly dead, and he's at least twice the man I am.

I jumped out of my seat when I felt a hand shake my right shoulder, and the owner of that hand nearly fell over when I jumped out of the chair and out of his grasp.

"You must be Travis." He offered his hand. "I'm Dick."

It took a second, but I remembered what was going on here. Job interview. Right. "Oh. Shit. I was asleep, huh?"

He laughed as I shook his hand. "Yeah. You were. Don't worry about it, though. People fall asleep in here all the time. Especially when Eli doesn't let me know there's someone to see me. He's not the best with customer service."

"Yeah. I noticed."

He looked at his watch. "How long have you been waiting?"

I told him I had no idea and that he really ought to think about getting a clock, maybe something to read, and a few gallons of paint. Bright paint of any color at all.

"We've thought about it," he said. "But we find that all this dull grey, well, it has sort of a calming effect on people, as you've already noticed. It's strange. It's sort of like the lack of color..." He stopped, searching.

"It doesn't seem real."

"Exactly." He seemed pleased that I was able to finish his sentence. "A lot of the people who come in here are here to identify bodies, so they're usually pretty, well, distraught. The grey sort of takes them out of the reality of the moment, so there's a lot less breakdowns when they realize that this dead kid is really their son, you know?"

I just raised my eyebrows and nodded. What was I supposed to say to that?

"It doesn't always work, but most of the time." He looked at his watch again. "At any rate, I hope you weren't waiting too long. It's about eleven o'clock right now."

"Eleven? Hmm. It's been about an hour, then."

He opened the door next to the sliding glass window and gestured me inside. It was polite, to be sure, but also pointless, as I had no idea where to go and he would only have to maneuver himself around me to lead the way. "What did Eli say when you told him why you were here?"

"He said you were busy."

"Well, I was in the middle of something, but I had plenty of time. It's not like the dead have anywhere to be, so they tend to be fairly patient." He laughed at his own joke. I gave it a little chuckle, too. It was funny, considering.

We got to his office, and he sat behind his desk and held his hand out in the direction of the sofa against the wall. The red sofa against the white wall. The first bit of color, maybe the only real sign of life, I'd yet seen in this place. I heard a bird chirp and looked up to see one of those clocks with a different bird where each of the numbers should have been. I guessed the song was different every hour, too. Eleven AM appeared to be the hour of the lark, no matter what Shakespeare said.

Pearson put his feet up on his desk. "So, David tells me you're a bit of a celebrity."

"I guess you could say that." Don't ask why. Don't ask why.

"He said there was an accident or something. I remember hearing something about it on the news, too. Must have been a pretty bad one if it made you famous."

"Yeah. It was pretty bad."

He took a cigarette out of a box on his desk, lit it, took out another and offered it to me. "If you're famous, why do you need a job?"

I suppose this is a common misconception, that fame equals money. "Well, I only got half of that whole *rich and famous* thing."

"Hmm. That's interesting." He tossed his lighter to me. "Did David tell you anything about this job?"

"Well, no. Not really."

"It's nothing too difficult, really. I won't be asking you to do much with the bodies. Just to help move them every once in a while. And even then, they'll usually be in body bags, so you won't really have to touch them."

"Well, that's good, I guess." I figured I'd already touched all the dead bodies I'd ever need to.

"I'll mostly just need you to do a lot of paperwork for me. Filing and whatnot. You'll mostly be in the front, where you met Eli."

"Wait. Aren't you going to ask me any questions? Like, what my qualifications are or anything like that?"

"Well, David said you're a smart, hardworking, trustworthy guy. I figure that's good enough for me. Just as long as you can show up on time."

"Actually, I'm sort of an early person."

"Good." He smashed out his half-smoked cigarette. "The only thing about this job is it gets to people sometimes. You know, seeing all these corpses all the time. The last guy, well, it sort of ate him up, if you know what I mean. But I figure if you've gone through what you've gone through, and you're still fine, you should be able to handle it."

9

I walked out of the morgue and into a cool breeze that blew trash down the street and messed the thin white hair of the old woman in front of me. A cool breeze on a hot, bright, summer day can stir one to do something completely mad. Something like walking all the way home instead of taking the bus.

I crossed all the necessary crosswalks, adjusting my steps so not to become entangled with the lunch hour traffic and dragged back to work after a bagel sandwich and a cup of coffee.

At Forbes and Grant, I lost control. There was a sandaled foot involved, and its owner was suddenly lying on my back, her breath heavy on my ear, reminding me of the last time a woman's mouth had been so close to any part of my head. It had been quite a while, I'm afraid.

"Oh my god. I'm sorry. I should have—Oh. Hi, Travis."

I rolled over onto my back, there on the pavement, to find Virginia's hand coming down to meet my own. "Hey. Fancy running into you down here." Sometimes they just sneak out like that. They have a mind of their own, you know?

"Did you really just say that? I had no idea you were such a fucking dork." She raised her eyebrows and sort of smirked at me. It was insulting, but not really. It was more fun than mean.

"I am, indeed, such a fucking dork. I have my membership card in my wallet, if you'd like to see it. It's been, oh, seventeen years. They give you the Star Wars trilogy after your first five, an autographed picture of the guy who played Bones after ten, and in another three I'll get my bronzed pair of Buddy Holly glasses. They look a lot like yours, actually."

"Aren't you funny. I hope that's working out for you." She was damned cute, this one. "What are you doing down here?"

Hmm. "Leaving a job interview. At the morgue."

She moved her hands to her hips. "Bullshit."

"No. Really. I start Friday." I was right. It was strange, telling someone I had a job at the morgue. It didn't sound right.

She scrunched up her face. "That's kind of gross."

"Yeah, I guess." I glanced at her chest, her belly, her long hippie skirt, her ballerina feet. They weren't bad feet, as far as feet go, and I've always hated feet. "And what are you doing down here?"

"I was playing chess at Market Square. Just on my way home."

"Chess? Really?"

"Yeah. Chess. That ok with you?"

"It's fine. Sorry. I just –"

"Didn't expect a girl to play chess?" She tilted her head to one side and went to move her hands to her hips, but was exasperated to find them already there. I knew they were there. I kept looking down at them and thinking that the last hips I'd had my hands on belonged to Erica, and they weren't good hips like Virginia's. Nor were they very good eating.

The meat around Virginia's hips could have lasted me at least two days, if I needed to stretch it.

"Hey. Take it easy. I just don't know any girls who play, all right? At least, not any who'd be playing at Market Square on a Monday morning. I'm sure you're great." I decided to push my luck. "I mean, chess is all about scheming and deception. You women are pretty good at both."

"Fuck you. Not all women are like that, you know. I fucking hate—"

"Relax, dear. Relax. It was just a joke. I know most women aren't like that." I couldn't help but smile. She was downright hot when she was fired up.

"Asshole."

We walked past the county jail, which gave me an excellent opportunity to tell her an amusing story about the only time I'd ever spent the night in a holding cell, with twenty-some other guys, three of them coming down off of heroin, taking turns on the one toilet. The full version of that story also involves doing coke off one of the benches in the cell, but since there's really only one way for someone to sneak cocaine past the guards who search you when you're brought in, I left that part out. I figured a story about doing butt-coke was not the best way to impress a lady, no matter how crass that lady might be.

"So, what's the point of that story?"

"Um. I guess it's just to be really polite to your arresting officer. Maybe he'll let the fog of pot smoke in your car slide, and you won't get charged with driving under the influence, or with possession."

"So, you got arrested for switching the plates on your cars, huh? Are you retarded or something?"

"Maybe a little."

She looked at me. "You love telling that story, don't you? You get all animated when you tell it."

I did, in fact, like to tell that story. I was sort of proud of that night, although I couldn't tell you exactly why. "I don't know. Not really. I mean, just as much as any story, I guess. It's not like—"

She grabbed the back of my arm. "No. It's cute, you getting all excited like that. Do you have any more of those stories?"

We'd stopped walking and were now across the Tenth St. Bridge, on Carson, between Tenth and Eleventh. She was facing me, smiling, with her head down just enough that she had to look up to see me. They all know that look. I don't know where they learn it, but they all know it, and they all use it, and it works every fucking time. It made me nervous.

"No," I said. "I don't really have many good stories. I've always been sort of boring, actually."

"Yeah. It sounded like it from what you said on Leno. Or maybe it was Oprah. I don't know. I guess everyone's gone through what you've gone through."

I narrowed my eyes. "You know, they say sarcasm is the weapon of a weak mind."

I think I hit a nerve with that one. She took a deep breath through her nose, crossed her arms, and said, "You know, I don't really give a shit."

And that was that. She turned and walked quickly down Carson. It wasn't quite storming off, but her steps were certainly not happy ones.

10

The thing about being stranded in the mountains is that you have no one to talk to, so you talk to anything. But the other thing is that once you start talking to one inanimate object, there's really no reason not to talk to more. (You might have a problem if they start responding, but I'm no professional, so whatever.)

The other thing is that you can no longer get it up.

And this is a serious fucking thing.

Serious enough that you start talking to your dick. You give little pep talks. "Come on. You can do this. I've seen you do this. You know you can do this. Just focus. Focus. Visualize yourself getting up for this game, making all the big plays, and then fucking do it! Do it for pride! Do it for the love of the game! Do it for me! JUST FUCKING DO IT!"

I'd been having these conversations with Little Travis (LT, to his friends) ever since we left the hospital. But he wasn't into it. Didn't care. If I hadn't been so attached to him, I'd have told him to get lost. You're not welcome here anymore. Sure, we've had some great times together, but what have you done for me lately?

But, no matter how difficult, I still loved the little guy. So, inspired by my chance encounter with Virginia, I decided to give him one more chance.

It went down like this:

"Ok, buddy. You have to snap out of it. I know, I know. You've been through some pretty tough shit. It's amazing you survived. And I understand how hard it is to get over it. Believe me. Who knows better than I do, right? I was right there with you, beside you. It was me and you, brother. I know this is hard, but it's been long enough. It's all over now. You can go back to your old self. Remember that guy? Easily excitable, curious, anxious, even a little over-zealous sometimes? You remember that guy? I remember that guy. I loved that guy. And, as your friend, I feel I should tell you that this new guy you've become, well, he sucks. I miss our time together. Even our alone time. Especially our alone time. We were always there for each other, remember? Anytime you ever needed a helping hand, I was there to give it to you. And I was always happy to be there for you. Now, I can let that Playboy Mansion thing go. It was still too soon. I understand that. But it's been long enough, my friend. You have to get your shit together. You can't go through the rest of your life this way."

But LT, he wanted nothing to do with it.

So I gave up on the words. Instead, I closed my eyes and thought about women. All about women: the thin hair on the forearms, the smooth slope from ear to shoulder, the soft curve of the underside of the breast, the small of the back, backs of the hands. Everything. I imagined that wonderful journey up the inner thigh, the way you can feel the rising temperature as you get closer, the way the scent gets more intense as you get closer. The taste and the heat of Her on your lips, dribbling down your chin. I thought about it. I thought really, really hard about all of it.

But that little bastard, he didn't budge.

There was nothing I could do.

Finally, I gave up. I was exhausted.

And then, an epiphany: I was forcing what I wanted onto him, and maybe this wasn't the best way to bring him back to life. Maybe I had to relinquish my control of the situation, let him take the reins, forget about my needs and let him focus on his.

So I did. I just closed my eyes and cleared my head. I just drifted, and let whatever came into my head come into my head.

What came into my head was Erica, my dead friend, my first. She was naked. She was just lying there, naked. Naked and dead and pale.

This is what I saw.

This is when LT sprang back to life.

This is when I completely freaked out, left my apartment, ran to the first bar I could find, and drank until I couldn't remember where I was.

11

I've never been a man who's claimed to possess what people commonly refer to as a sense of style. Ever. I like my earth-tones solid and my pants to have cargo pockets, and that's about as far as I take it. It never really mattered that most of my clothes were nearly identical to most of my other clothes because I spent most of my time in dark, dingy places that reeked of cigarette smoke, places you'd have to be worried about getting some sort of funky-smelling stain on whatever it was you were wearing.

Style, I'd found, was a waste of my time. Too much effort and too much money are required to maintain a keen fashion sense. I've read that Einstein kept a bunch of identical suits hanging in his closet so he didn't have to waste any brain-power deciding what to wear. And that man was a fucking genius.

I, however, am not now nor have ever been a genius, which I think goes a long way towards explaining a great many of my decisions. But I digress.

The point of all this fashion talk is that Synchek was picking me up soon. Tonight I would meet his group, and I had absolutely nothing to wear. I owned one suit, but I didn't think this was a suit and tie kind of affair. Beyond that there were jeans and khaki cargo pants and a few not-so-ratty button-down shirts. As we've already discussed, I like pockets and solid earth-tones. Cargos and blue button-down it would be.

I looked at Synchek's letter, still affixed to the fridge, and I started to get an uneasy feeling, as though I'd just smoked a ton of weed and was now incapable of going to the bar with all those fucking people. The feeling didn't last long though, as it was interrupted by my phone.

It was Synchek. He was here, waiting in his car out front of my building.

Fan-fucking-tastic.

I got outside to find a behemoth of a black Caddy, recently waxed, with tinted windows and a man I'd never seen before opening the back door. I wouldn't have been able to pick him out of a lineup, but I'd recognize that limp a mile away.

"Mr. Eliot," he said as he gestured for me to climb in.

"Uh, thanks," I said. And in I went.

"Travis! So good to see you." Synchek sat on the driver's side of the back seat, his newspaper folded on his lap. "Are you excited about this evening's festivities?"

"Sure am," I said. I even managed to put on a pretty good fake smile. Sometimes the skills you learn in the food service world come in handy in the rest of the world as well. I was most certainly *not* excited.

"Excellent. We are all looking forward to it as well, aren't we, Malcolm?"

Malcolm, it would appear, was the driver, the gentleman who opened the door for me. "We sure are, Walter. We're all very excited."

I didn't know what to say. "Well that's good then." Like I said, not a genius.

"Travis," Synchek continued as he reached into his breast pocket, "this might seem like a bit of an odd request, but you must understand that many of our members are people of high-standing in the community. We prefer the location of our meetings to be, shall we say, discreet."

"Discreet?" I know when somebody's getting euphemistic on me.

"Secret, Travis. Our members value their privacy, and so I need you to do something before we continue any farther."

"First off, I know what discreet means. And what would that

something be?"

The thing he had taken from his pocket was in his hand. He lifted it and allowed a long, narrow strip of black fabric to dangle there in front of me, like some raven-haired Rapunzel inviting me up to her dark tower.

"Seriously? A fucking blindfold?"

"I know it seems, well, probably a bit frightening. A man you don't know driving the car. A man you just met asking you to voluntarily put on a blindfold. On your way to a mysterious destination. But you are free to say no, of course. We're not kidnapping you. I know it's a difficult decision, but I ask that you trust us, if for no other reason, then simply because we are giving you the option in the first place." Apparently, he'd had this conversation once or twice before.

I took the thing and tied it around my head. "I'm going to be severely pissed off if I take this off and find myself in some remote cabin about to be chained to a bed with a nasty old mattress and some dude named Buck licking his lips. Like, seriously pissed off."

Malcolm chuckled. "I like this kid, Walter."

"Yes, so do I, Malcolm. Even if he is a bit crude."

"I'm in a blindfold here, man. How about some slack?"

"You're right, Travis. I'm sorry. Now, we'll be arriving in about twenty…" His phone rang. "Excuse me for a moment, please Travis."

"Sure." This was fucked up. I'd just let myself do a really stupid thing, and I knew it. I told myself not to trust them, and I didn't, but I still tied that black strip of fabric around my head. And now I was in the back of a black Cadillac, unable to see but perfectly capable of listening to Synchek on the phone.

"…no, Angel. I told you. You have to mash the pills up *and* mix in some of the wet food. Otherwise Donner won't eat it. He hasn't defecated in four days, that's why. Ok. Good. Yes, you're coming, and I won't hear another word about it. Just make sure you pet him for at least fifteen minutes before you leave. He'll get cranky and claw at the sofa if you don't. I will not! He'd be defenseless! I know he's a house cat, but what if he gets out?"

I mean, come on, how can you mistrust someone with that much love for his cat?

We talked some small talk about the weather and the Steelers and fireworks, and then, out of the blue, "We've arrived, Travis. You can remove the blindfold now."

I took it off and rubbed my eyes. It was twilight, so the shock of the light wasn't too intense. I looked at the building. It was a warehouse. Just a warehouse. I looked around to try to get a sense of where we might be, but there was nothing else nearby except a field and some trees in the distance. No signs. Nothing. "Well, at least it isn't a cabin."

"Ha! Very good, Mr. Eliot. I shall very much enjoy listening to you speak tonight, I'm certain. And I know it's not much to look at, but it is what is at the heart of a thing that matters, Mr. Eliot."

From the looks of it, the inside of this building had better have been trimmed with gold, its floors carpeted with some sort of fine Italian fabric, and original paintings by Van Gogh and Klimt hanging on the walls. The wall with the front door was old white paint, peeling down to the ground in some places. I'd have thought it was just some abandoned warehouse, maybe a crackhead or two huddled on the floor inside.

After some serious fumbling of his keys, Synchek got the door open and let me inside. The hallway inside didn't exactly give me high hopes about the rest of the interior. It was a long, straight hall with florescent lighting and vinyl flooring. A small table, almost a podium, sat inside next to the door, with a black register closed on top of it.

"You're right, Walter. This looks much better than I thought it would." I found it easy to jest at him. For some reason it seemed he didn't quite understand sarcasm, and it's impossible not to be sarcastic around people like that.

He didn't respond. He locked the door behind him and led

me down the hall, past a door on the right that had too many locks to count at just a glance. I let myself wonder what could possibly be behind this door. Curiosity, as it turns out, likes to fuck with more than just cats.

But this door was not to be opened, and I was left to let my mind dwell on what was back there until we reached the door at the end of the hall. No locks on this one. Just a simple white door with a simple silver knob that would turn simply to the left and allow me simple passage to a much more difficult life than I could ever have guessed.

It's a shame I didn't think about it that way then, that I walked right through, as one typically does with an open door. Then again, I suppose that at that moment there was no reason to be suspicious of anything that may have been hiding behind that door. It would just be a room. I'd been through many doors, and up to this point none of them had fucked up my perception of life.

"This," he said, holding the door open for me with his foot, extending his arm to present me with the room, "is where we meet." He seemed to enjoy gesturing with that arm. I think maybe he was trying to make up for the fact that he no longer had his left arm. Can't really hold it against him, I guess.

"Wow. This is quite a room." And it was. The walls were papered with a majestic deep maroon and trimmed with what appeared to be oak. There was a bar at the back which seemed to be stocked solely with bottles of red wine. Eight tables, with six seats each, were set for dinner with fine silverware and china and wicked gorgeous centerpieces of lilies and some other flower. Closer to the door, to us, a table was set up with coffee dripping into a pot and stacks of simple and elegant mugs. The front of the room boasted a sizeable podium facing rows of black, cushioned folding chairs, lined up like a battalion ready to take orders from whichever general happened to be speaking. There was even an almost comically gigantic crystal chandelier hanging from the ceiling. "Seriously, Walter. This is impressive. I almost forgot I was standing inside a dingy old warehouse."

He looked pleased. "Thank you, Travis. I'm quite proud of it."

"It's a bit empty, though, isn't it? When's everyone else supposed to get here?" I was under the impression that we were cutting it pretty close.

"Oh, they should be arriving shortly." He looked at his watch. "We'll begin in roughly half-an-hour."

Hearing the words 'half-an-hour' brought out my nerves. It was like a countdown had begun, and not to the start of something awesome like the space shuttle launch, either.

"What exactly will I be doing, here?"

He put his hand on my shoulder. It was too paternal for so young a relationship. "You've no need to be nervous, my young friend. It's nothing you haven't done before. I'll get up to the podium, welcome everyone, and then introduce you."

This thing, this thing with him never really answering any of my questions, was starting to bug me. "And what, exactly, will you be introducing me to do?"

"To tell your story, Travis. That's all. To tell your story and," he scratched the tip of his nose, "if you're comfortable taking a few questions, I'm certain everyone would be grateful."

I really wasn't in the mood for questions, but hell, I'd been answering so many questions already that I was beginning to feel like a fucking Oracle, only without the perk of receiving all those offerings. It seemed people were lined up for miles, wanting to know. Everyone wanted to know. I could handle a few more questions, sure. Especially for five thousand bucks.

"Yeah. I could answer a few questions."

"Excellent." He looked again at his watch. "I have a few things to attend to before everyone arrives. Feel free to fix yourself a cup of coffee or a glass of wine from the bar. I'll return shortly." And off he went, through a set of double doors across the room from the bar.

I mad-dashed it to the bar, got open a bottle of wine. It smelled of merlot, sort of. Had the color and the body, too, but there was no label. There had to be fifty bottles of the stuff. I was still unsure about what I'd gotten myself into but figured a glass of wine, or maybe two, would calm me. I downed my first in one gulp and poured another. It was good, this wine, and I made a mental note to ask Walter what it was. Actually, I felt a little ashamed of myself for taking it down so quickly. I'm sure there are those who would have been appalled at my behavior. I should have been sipping slowly, getting a good sense of its nose and whatever else you're supposed to do when tasting wine. But when you're scared, no matter of what, it seems you have no time for anything at all.

This time I happened to be correct. I heard the door and looked up to see a group coming in, and coming in, and coming in. They must have rented a bus. Or, from the look of these people, maybe it was a super-sized limo. Most of the crowd were men, all dressed up in suits that were probably worth more than any car I've ever owned. Their hair was slicked, and not one of them had any facial hair. I could feel the power coming off of these men, like they were radioactive or something. About a third of the group were women, also dolled up, covered in diamond bracelets and necklaces and earrings, their faces obviously Botoxed at some point in the recent past. I could smell their perfume all the way across the room, and it was easy to guess what they were wearing: MONEY. They absolutely stunk of money. Most of these people looked to be in their thirties and forties, although at least a handful were pushing sixty and seventy.

I felt underdressed in my khakis and blue button-down shirt, both purchased in discount stores. I found myself finishing my second glass of wine and pouring my third. I found myself sweating a little, shaking a little. I wasn't expecting people like these. I didn't even know people like these existed in Pittsburgh.

But apparently they did. And as I was standing there, behind the bar, staring at this rich mess and pouring my third glass of wine, a few of the gentlemen managed to make their way to the front of the bar.

"Two glasses," ordered the tallest of the three, resting an elbow on the bar and turning to face the other two.

I poured the wine and set the glasses in front of him. "You know, it's customary to say 'please'."

He whipped his head around and glared at me. "Excuse me?"

"I'm just saying, most bartenders would appreciate a little common courtesy. Of course, since I'm not the bartender, I don't really give a shit."

There's a nerve, somewhere deep inside of me, that has always enjoyed pushing the buttons of the over-privileged.

There is also a nerve, somewhere not so deep inside the over-privileged, that detests the pushing of those buttons.

"And who are you to lecture me on etiquette?"

I took a sip of my wine, looking him square in the eye. "Nobody special, I suppose."

"And why are you here, behind the fucking *bar*, if you're not the bartender?" He crossed his arms and straightened up, trying to intimidate, I imagine.

"Oh. My name is Travis. I'm behind the bar because I have no problem pouring my own drinks when I get thirsty. And yours, if you haven't noticed. And I'm assuming you haven't, since you've yet to thank me." Ah, alcohol. The quickest route to candor.

The guys behind him, both a little shorter and a lot more Italian (although I'm willing to bet they had the same sixty-dollar boxers and solid gold business card holders), exchanged a look of recognition. One of them tapped the asshole on the shoulder. "He's the young man who had the accident, Jim. He's speaking for us this evening, remember?"

He paused for a moment. "Oh. Is that so? In that case, I'm terribly sorry, sir. I had no idea." He extended a hand, dropping the snobby rich guy routine. "I'm Jim Stearns. This is Tony Conicella and Michael Cansellini."

Each of them nodded, in turn, at the mention of their names.

Tony said, "We're all very excited to hear you speak."

Michael said, "Yes. Very excited."

"And you are right," Jim held his glass in the air, "I behaved rudely. I am truly sorry. I hope you'll forgive me." Asshole or not, he sounded sincere enough.

"Don't worry about it," I said, touching my glass to his. "We all have those moments."

He smiled and nodded. "These two are right. People here are very excited about your little visit."

After this point, the conversation gets fuzzy. All three of them were in sales—inside, outside, who knows? All three were married, and so each had a glass of wine for himself and one for his wife.

It's difficult to say about much else. I hadn't really been paying attention. I was still a bit overwhelmed by the sight of these folk, by the feeling that something was amuck here, and all the wine wasn't making it any easier, either.

I nodded my head and offered those nuggets of sound that pass for conversation when the conversation is one-sided. And this was definitely a one-sider. Some people simply don't have it in them to stop talking. I think those people feel like they have to justify their very existence every time they open their mouths. It must be exhausting.

This exhaustion must have been why they were all quiet and staring at me like I had something they wanted. Maybe some insider trading tip or something.

Conicella shifted his weight to his left leg and said, "Well, what do you think about it, Mr. Eliot?"

It seems that one of them, or maybe all three of them, had asked me a question. "Oh. Sorry, guys. I sort of zoned out for a second there. What do I think about what now?" Sometimes, you just have to be honest about not paying attention. It'll be ok. Most people don't really care if you're listening anyway.

"About tonight's menu?" Stearns was all wide-eyed excitement about it.

I, however, was unaware of any menu. I suppose I could have guessed food was to be a part of the evening's festivities, what with all the tables and place settings and centerpieces.

The three of them eagerly awaited my opinion. The food at these things must have been great.

"Sounds great to me." I know I should have asked what was being served, but I really didn't care. I was getting bored with these guys and hated the thought of having to hear them say anything more. "I don't think I'll be staying for dinner, though. Places to see, people to do, you know?"

They laughed. Stupid bastards.

Cansellini thought I should know what I was missing. "That's too bad. The chef is head chef at a wonderful little place downtown. The man is an absolute genius in the kitchen." He looked like he just remembered something, spun around to look at the crowd, and then turned back to me. "I should really get this wine to my wife. She's probably waiting."

The other two nodded.

"Yes. Alana isn't exactly a patient woman, either. I should get back over there." Stearns shook my hand again. "It's a shame you can't stay for the food. I'll remind Walter to pack a doggie bag for you."

I was amused at the sound of such a rich, snobby fucker saying the words 'doggie bag', and I laughed aloud. They all gave me kind of a sideways look, but I was fairly certain they didn't know what I was laughing about. They walked away with their wine. With their wives' wine. They walked away in single file, back to the pow-wow near the coffee machine.

I stood dazed for a moment, trying to process that whole conversation, but not really getting anywhere. It was going to be one of those nights, I thought, that I'd be able to talk about later, but only the way I can talk about some movie I saw once, a couple years ago, and I was so very high.

I stepped out from behind the bar and studied the group, which was a little intimidating. These people, they should have been on Wall Street, or maybe Mars. Stearns and Co. had rejoined their friends, and many of them were now turning to get a look at me as I took my sweet old time weaving through the dining area.

I don't know how *real* celebrities do it. All these people looking at me all the time was something I still couldn't get used to. I can't imagine what it's like to be Brad Pitt, Mr. Pomegranate himself, trying to sit and enjoy a meal or go Christmas shopping at the mall, swarms of looks flying around his Sexiest Man Alive face, teenage girls and grown women alike shrieking and crying and screaming, "Can I have your autograph? Your picture? Your babies?" Shit. It's like that all over the world for him. The poor bastard.

Me, well, I was only sort of famous, and not even once has a crowd of girls gone bat-shit crazy as I walked down the street. It would have been great to have been able to sign at least one breast, but I was merely a Pittsburgh celebrity, which only really counts if you play for the Steelers, or if you happen to find yourself at a meeting with a bunch of people you don't know, who want something from you that you're also unaware of, so they can get their rocks off about something they won't let you in on.

All the same, I did get a bit of a thrill from knowing that I was the buzz, and the buzz was only growing louder with each step I took. Of course, the buzz may have actually been the most-of-a-bottle of wine flowing through me. Either way, the nerves were settling.

If you stop to give it some consideration, it's really quite amazing how little time is needed for a change in outlook. Or maybe it's inlook. Or even attitude adjustment. Whatever it is that changes, it's big and astoundingly quick.

In the twenty or so steps I'd taken from the bar, I'd set down my discomfort and dropped my apprehension. Somewhere along that path, I'd stumbled across a heaping pile of self-confidence and, conveniently next to it, a pile of fearlessness. It was one hell of a timely find, even though I can't give you a scientific explanation for its sudden appearance. It was like that wine bottle secretly housed a genie or something. It's all about the wine.

"Hey folks. How's everybody doing?" My cheeks were burning, but my smile cooled them nicely.

And then these rich people, they were all over me. Hello's and Hi's and Nice to meet you's. Handshakes and nods of the head. The chaos was that of the hive stirred by a child with impeccable aim, and they all buzzed for me.

There were so many of them that I can't really remember meeting any of them. When I try to picture one face, it never fails to morph into the most generic face you've ever seen. Grey, even. Like the walls in the morgue waiting room. The kind of face you can only stereotype, much in the way that people describe extraterrestrials as having egg-shaped heads and large black eyes.

I know I shook more than one prosthetic hand, though. That was a new experience for me.

Well, I do remember one face from that crowd, I suppose. And, as should always be the case when you can remember only one of many, this face was striking. Beautiful, slap you in the face kind of striking. She had fair, smooth skin, huge (and I mean HUGE) blue eyes, and full pink lips with curves like a *real* woman's hips. When she got close, it was slow motion like the first day Nikki Sinopoli walked into my third grade classroom, guaranteeing me a life of heterosexuality.

But she didn't stand out because she was lovely. There was a sort of innocence somewhere in there that didn't seem to fit in with all these other people. The rest of them had the look of someone who had stolen something and didn't feel the least bit bad about it. I doubt she'd ever taken so much as a boy's well-meant sweatshirt on a cold day.

We didn't get the chance to exchange hellos, but I did get to look her in the eye and shake her hand. It was a good start.

I could tell I was some form of entertainment to the rest of them, but something about her face (or her aura, or vibe, or whatever) led me to believe she wanted something else from me. What that something was, I couldn't tell you, but such is the way it goes with angels.

As I was about to speak to her, Synchek appeared at the podium and asked "if everyone would please take a seat, everyone please." In the scuffle to get to the good seats, I lost her. It was like being thrown into an adult version of musical chairs.

I was left standing near the coffee table, a mostly empty wine glass in my hand and an obviously struggling look on my face. People don't run for their seats like that, I thought. They meander toward them. They take their time. They're polite about it.

What is going on here, in this warehouse banquet room, with all these demons and only one angel?

And then it was explained to me, at least partially, by Synchek, who now addressed his army.

"Hello, friends. I'm glad to see that so many of you could make it this evening. As many of you know, this is the two-hundredth meeting of PEP, which I'm proud to say is something of a milestone." And a milestone it must have been, judging by the applause.

"We are lucky to have with us this evening a special guest, Travis Eliot, who is going to tell us first-hand about his unfortunate accident and the harrowing tale of his survival."

I was beginning to tire of this whole "harrowing tale of survival" crap, but that was hardly Synchek's fault. It was the right phrase, at least for those who had never gone through anything like it. Personally, I'd have gone with "hellish tale of pain and despair", but it wasn't up to me.

"Mr. Eliot is also kind enough that he has agreed to take a few of our questions once he has finished. And, as per usual, dinner will be served at nine-thirty, followed by drinks and a few hours to socialize. And with that, my friends, I would like to introduce..."

Me. Little old wine drinker me. Bewildered, lost, confused, and a tad drunk.

Me, the most famous bloke in the room.

Me, the guy who ate his best friends.

Me, the guy who couldn't get it up without the mental image of a dead girl.

Weren't these people lucky, eh?

I didn't know where to start my story, but I figured I couldn't just stand there with a glass of wine in my hand and a curious urge to piss myself, so I decided to walk up to the podium. They were all watching me walk. They looked like they wanted to tear me apart, but not necessarily in a bad way.

So I got to the podium, grabbed the sides and rested my weight onto my elbows, and I began to speak.

I have to be honest, here. Public speaking has never been high on my list of entertaining activities. I hated it when I was a kid, giving book reports about Charlotte and her web, and had grown only slightly more comfortable with all eyes and ears on me by the time I finished college. I'm not saying I would vomit or break out in hives or anything, but I'm sure more than one person had noticed the nerves rattling around in my mouth like marbles.

But this time was different. No nerves. No panic. No triple-checking to make sure my fly was properly flied. And, most importantly, no sense that the room was closing in on me.

This time, I controlled everything. I could have brought the ceiling down with little more than the mention of my desire to do so. I had become powerful up there in front of all those suits and diamond-studded heels. I felt it in my fingers, wrapped over the edge of the podium. I felt it in the small of my back. I felt it in my lips, throwing words like solid balls of epiphany at the ears of all these strange strangers. And I felt it in my eyes, open and cold and blue, turning them to stone as though I were a sexified Medusa.

My eyes, which locked for at least a moment with every other pair of eyes in the room, could have driven those people to any point I wished. I knew it halfway through my story.

Well, I knew it about all but one of them, anyway. My tiny angel did not look at me the way the rest did. She paid close attention, but she didn't have her pretty little mouth agape the way the rest did. She listened to me, but that was all.

The rest of the crowd seemed to imbibe every syllable the way they did their wine, and they would have gone on drinking this oft-repeated tale until their bodies could hold no more and it spilled out of their mouths, noses, ears.

She would have her fill after only one sip. Just for the taste.

The rest were obviously excited. She, though, seemed saddened.

And her sad face snapped me out of whatever world I was in. Something about the way she looked at me made it clear to me that something was seriously wrong with the way everyone else looked at me. They shouldn't have been listening with so much intensity. They shouldn't have wanted so much from me.

I shouldn't have given it to them so freely.

I stared at her through the last twenty minutes of story time, which ended with what I felt to be an inappropriately enthusiastic round of applause, and then the hands went up. It was time for the Q & A.

"When and how did you finally come to the decision that you had to eat your friends? And how did you convince yourself that it was ok, given the circumstances?"

I took a deep breath. "About ten days after I ran out of food, which was about two weeks after the wreck, I realized it was very possible I would starve to death. So I had to eat them. There wasn't really a decision to be made about it. I would have died. That's why I thought it was ok."

"Do you think your friends would have been ok with it? Would you have done the same if you knew they wouldn't approve?"

I had been nervous about answering the questions, but these didn't seem too bad. "I think they'd have been ok with it. Even if they weren't, how would they have stopped me, right?"

"Did you enjoy the taste?"

That one shook me a little. It's hard to believe, but nobody had asked me that question yet. Not the doctors, not the interviewers, not my friends. I guess everyone thought it might have crossed some sort of line, asking that question. And I didn't really want anyone to ask that question because, "Once I let myself forget they were people... yeah, I guess it tasted pretty good."

"Have you ever thought about eating anyone else?"

That one shook me to the core, and I froze. Perhaps the questions were a bad idea. I searched the crowd wildly for the blonde girl, but she had somehow slipped out without me noticing. If she had been there to help me with her peaceful grace, I may have been able to avoid passing out and falling forward into the podium.

I'd fainted/passed out only once before. It had been a combination of too little food, too much pot, and too much steam in an ex-girlfriend's shower. I remember the steam. It was like inhaling some space-aged concrete that only hardened once it found its way into your lungs. I remember heading for the window, but I never made it. When I woke, naked and wet, comfortably lying on the porcelain, I found poor Liz wrapped in a towel and kneeling over the edge of the tub, tapping at my cheeks and repeating my name. She looked so scared. "What's the matter, babe?" I'd asked her. "I'm fine. But why am I laying in the tub?"

This current lapse of consciousness was a similar experience, although thank God I was clothed this time. Still, I couldn't figure out how I'd gotten to the floor, my head resting on a fur coat. My bewilderment was furthered by the unfamiliar faces huddled around me, murmuring, "He's awake. It's ok. He's awake."

And you know, the phrase "bewilderment was furthered" may have been poorly chosen. I should have said that the shock of this moment scared me right off the floor, my head turning violently in all directions as my heart revved into the red and my nostrils flared like a demon bull snorting evil smoke. Yep. That ought to do it.

"It's all right, Mr. Eliot. You fainted, that's all."

My lost little head, which had been so verbose and eloquent only minutes before, could only come up with, "Huh? What happened?"

"You passed out at the podium, Travis." It was Synchek, sitting cross-legged in one of the folding chairs. "Onto the podium, actually." He pointed to the splinters of wood that used to tell the group who to listen to. They were all over the floor, except the few that were stuck in my skin.

My cheeks must have gone as red as the wine I'd apparently spilled all over myself. "Ooh. Sorry about that, Walter."

"Make no mention of it, my friend. I've been toying with the idea of getting a new one anyway. This is not a pine room. This," he said, with another of those grandiose hand gestures, "this is an oak room."

I noticed that everyone was still there, near my point of impact, silent and interested. The interest presumably stemmed from a general concern for my well-being, so it was welcomed. The silence, however, freaked me out.

"I think I need some air." A path showed itself in the crowd like an old friend, and I took advantage of it in much the same way. In a moment I was outside, cursing myself for listening to Dave and Adam.

I'd used the old need-to-get-some-air line the way it is meant to be used (that is, to get me out of a situation that had become less than cozy), but it seemed that the air had thought me an honest man. It was cool out there, amidst the BMWs and Jaguars, and a few deep breaths managed to straighten me out pretty quickly.

Good thing, too. After a few seconds, Synchek poked his presidential head out the door. "Are you feeling any better, Travis? Dinner is going to be served, and you really ought to eat something."

No way did I want to go back in there. No way, no how, brother. "You know, Walter, I think I've had about all I can handle today. I mean, thank you for the offer and concern and everything, but I think I should call it a night."

It was the first expression of anything other than pride or contentment I'd seen him pull. He looked sincerely disappointed, considering all I'd done was to pass on dinner.

"Well, I suppose I can understand that. It is a shame, though." He sighed and gave a shrug. "At the very least, allow me to pack up some food for you. It's really quite delicious."

I agreed to take some of the food (I mean, everyone had been talking it up so much that it had to be good, right?) but told him I'd prefer to wait outside, if he didn't mind. He didn't, and after a few minutes, he handed me a white styrofoam box.

"We hope you'll come again, Mr. Eliot. Everyone appreciated your story."

"Well," I started, knowing full well what I was about to say, but for some reason unable to stop myself, "let me know when, and we'll see." I wanted to say no. Why didn't I just say no?

Synchek beamed. "Excellent. Have a pleasant evening, young man. Malcolm will be out to take you home shortly." He turned around and walked inside.

But I remembered something and caught the door before it swung all the way shut. "Wait. Walter. Who was that cute little blonde girl?"

"Cute little blonde girl?"

"Yeah. Fair skin? Big blue eyes?"

He thumbed his chin. "I don't know. Sometimes it's difficult to know who shows up. But, if she was here tonight, there's a good chance she'll be here again." He handed me the blindfold and went inside.

12

It was still early, and it was Thursday, and I knew that Virginia worked on Thursdays. That meeting, with all the talking and the passing out and everything, had me in the mood for a few more drinks.

I had Malcolm drop me off at Carson Street News so I could pick up a pack of cigarettes and walk the handful of blocks to the Lava Lounge. I walked through the door a few minutes past ten to find the place about half full. I recognized a few of the faces, but no one I wanted to talk to, so I pulled up a seat at the bar.

"Here." Virginia slammed a drink down in front of me as if she knew exactly how much force it would have taken to break the glass. She'd obviously had practice with this.

"What's this?"

"Woodford Reserve. What do you think it is? I may have a weak mind, but I'm smart enough to remember what you drink." She was cold, but something about it seemed playful.

"You still upset about that sarcasm remark? It's not mine, you know. I stole that line from somebody. Don't remember who, though."

She poured a drink for someone while she spoke. "Doesn't matter. Whatcha got there?"

"Food."

"No shit, asshole. What is it?" She enjoyed this sort of patronizing conversation. It was easy to tell. You're only good at it, balancing on the fence between fighting and flirting, if you like it.

"Actually, I'm not sure. Someone packed it up for me." I opened the box. "Looks like some sort of steak, potatoes, and green beans."

She leaned over the bar, her dream-defeating breasts smashed between her weight and the dark, cool wood, and she took a whiff as I sliced a hunk from the steak. "Smells kinda funny."

"You smell kinda funny." I sniffed the air above the box. "Smells fine to me."

She snatched the first bite right off my fork and threw it into her mouth. She chewed it, a pensive look on her face. "Pork?"

"I don't know. I haven't had a bite yet."

Some guy got her attention and ordered six Long Island Iced Teas. "So eat it, then," she said before making for the liquor.

So I ate it. Devoured it, actually. One, I was starving, and fainting hadn't helped. And two, it may have been the best meal I'd ever eaten. The potatoes, well, they were good, but still just potatoes. But the green beans were amazing—crisp and juicy and with just the right amount of garlic. As good as the beans were, though, they couldn't hold a candle to the meat. I'm talking tender, juicy, succulent bite of Heaven, here. After one bite, I could have sworn my forearms were about to triple in size and battleships were about to set sail on my biceps. I yam what I yam, and I yam a man who thoroughly enjoys a good steak.

"Holy shit, Travis. Hungry?" She took the empty box, held it upside down for a moment, and tossed it into the trash. Then she turned to grab a glass of water from the counter behind her.

She was wearing those tight black pants that some bartenders and most waitresses have to wear, and her ass just about sent me to the floor. It was smallish and round, and I would eventually come to make a habit of watching this cute/sexy little bum any time I had the chance.

This was my first really good look at it, though, and I wasn't the only one who noticed. Little Travis had finally awoken from his coma and was thrashing about in his just over six-inch hospital bed, tearing hoses from his nose and tubes from his arm. "That's enough!" he screamed. "Let me the fuck out of here! Now, goddammit!"

And by God, I would have. Right there. I'd have thrown her against the wall, sending bottles of rum and tequila crashing to the floor, and let the poor little guy announce his presence with authority, like that pitcher from *Bull Durham*.

This sudden rush of blood to the head left my own head a touch oxygen-deprived, and I had to steady myself by grabbing the bar with both hands.

"Whoa. You all right, Travis? That's your first glass, right?" Virginia placed her right hand on my left and gave a gentle squeeze.

I looked her in the eye, but I might as well have simply said to her, "I want you naked. I want you naked and sweating and screaming. And I want it now."

And she gave that shit right back to me. This look was nothing if it wasn't pure, dirty, raw sex. This look took the Lava Lounge and all its customers into its lungs and breathed them out as a fire that engulfed all of the South Side. The smoke could have been seen from Cleveland. Not that people from Cleveland even have a word for smoke that doesn't rise from the flaming river…

This look was extinguished by the cool water of Adam's hand slapping me on the back, startling me enough to knock my drink off the bar, and Virginia enough to let out a shriek.

"Sorry, guys. Didn't mean to interrupt." The kid was so genuine you almost wanted to hit him. "Who won?"

I shifted on the stool, working LT into a slightly more comfortable position. Hard-ons are a bitch to hide unless you happen to be carrying a chemistry book, which I hadn't done in years. "Who won what?"

"You were in the middle of a staring contest, weren't you?" That's just the kind of place Adam's head was, you know? I mean, *staring contest*?! What the fuck?

Virginia jumped all over that the way she would have jumped all over me if Adam hadn't shown up just then. "We were, and I would have won. You, Travis, wouldn't have known what hit you."

It is innuendo—not opposable thumbs, the use of tools, or the mental capacity to understand the concept of numbers—that sets us apart from the animals.

She poured a beer for Adam and went to do what bartenders do.

Adam sat down, and we did what friends at the bar do. "So I guess you decided not to go to that thing tonight, huh?"

"No. I went."

He lit two cigarettes, handed one to me. "Really? It's over already?"

Sometimes, conversation gives me the same feeling I get when I look at a sink piled high with dirty dishes. I know I should wash them now, get it over with, make them disappear into their respective cupboards. And sometimes I do just that. But not usually. "Yeah," I said. "It's over already."

"Well? What was it?"

I hit my cigarette twice before answering. "I'm not really sure. I think they're called PEP. I don't know what that stands for, though. And the people there were weird, man. They were rich, or at least *very* well-dressed. And they were a little older. Like in their forties and fifties, a lot of them."

"I guess that's sort of strange."

"I know, but..." It was going to take a moment to get this right. "They all seemed a little bit, well, *off*. I don't know. They all seemed like they wanted something. The same thing. Like they were hungry for it." I shook my head and took a sip of my drink. "I don't know. It's hard to explain."

"Yeah. Sounds like it."

"It was weird."

"Sounds weird. What did you have to do?"

"Oh. I just talked about the accident and everything. Then I answered some questions." I didn't want to talk about the questions leading up to my collapse. I wouldn't have been able to make Adam understand why they made me so uncomfortable, and I didn't want to try. I was having enough trouble trying to figure that out for myself. "I left around nine-thirty and came here."

"Righteous." Adam tilted his glass towards mine, we tapped them together, and we finished them off.

Before we had the chance to set the empty glasses on the bar, Virginia showed up with one more for each of us. We both looked surprised.

"What? I'm a good bartender. You should know that by now." She winked and smiled at what could have been me, or Adam, or both. She was a tough one to figure, all right. But the wink and the smile were just as attractive no matter who they were meant for.

I already had every intention of staying until last call, waiting for her to wash the glasses and wipe down the bar, then taking her home and tearing the shit out of her. It had been *my* idea before I saw that wink. After that wink, though, I had no say in the matter. Sure, the results would have been the same, but sometimes it's how you get those results that counts. I liked the idea that this girl—excuse me, this *woman*—was my choice. Maybe it's a power thing. I don't know. But that wink shifted the power into her hands. Or maybe her pants.

When it all boils down, though, this feeling that we were two unstable gasses wafting towards each other, eventually to meet in a violent explosion of noises and smells—I was totally into it.

"You, Virginia, are a *fine* bartender." I wanted to wink, but held it back.

"Yeah, well, you better give me a much better tip than you did last time, then." She raised her eyebrows and waited for a response.

"Wait. He didn't tip you last time?" Adam leaned away from me. "That doesn't sound like you, man. Even when you are blacked out."

Virginia laughed. "Oh, he left me enough money last time." Then she walked away. She had a real talent for closing the chapter with just the right words to make you want to keep reading.

Unfortunately, she was the book, and it's difficult to read any book that up and decides to walk away.

Adam threw an elbow my way, which I caught with my ribs. "What was that, duder?"

It was not easy to answer him, my entire body taken over by the thunderous pounding in my chest. I'm surprised I heard him at all. "I don't know what that was, Adam." I leaned over the bar to get a better look at her ass. "Don't you worry, though. I'll find out."

"I'll drink to that." And he did. We both did. And we kept drinking.

The next few hours brought with them a good number of shots along with a slightly smaller, although equally as good, number of beers. Enough of each that there was no keeping track. Enough of each that we had to call a cab for Adam, right after I sent him to the ATM so we could pay the tab. I can't believe he made it there, remembered his PIN, and made it all the way back without severely injuring himself. All of Adam's sheets were in the wind, blowing around like enormous pieces of confetti.

I, however, had my sheets neatly stacked and under my arm. A few of the pages were wrinkled, one or two of them maybe even torn a little, but they were all there. I should have been slurring and stumbling, swaying on my stool. But I wasn't.

I couldn't figure it out, but the alcohol didn't affect me the way physiology and conventional wisdom say it should have. It couldn't touch the energy that swelled inside me, filling my veins and my breath, my heart, my head, my libido. I was a juiced-up lion, ready for all the ladies in the pride, and maybe of the neighboring pride, as well.

And I still wasn't sure if it would be enough for Virginia. It seemed she could eat kings of jungles for breakfast and be angry when she found there were none left for lunch.

"You sure did a number on Adam tonight." She rested her elbows on the bar, her chin on her hands. "How are you?"

I said the first thing that came to mind: "How much longer

till I can get you out of here?"

She smiled, but tried to hide it. Or, maybe, she tried to make it look like she was hiding it. Those women, they're a wily bunch. "About twenty minutes. You want another drink while you wait?"

"Who said I was willing to wait?"

"You've been waiting since you got here. You think I've been bending over at the waist all night for nothing? It's bad on the back." Clever minx. "Boys are way too fucking easy. I almost feel like I'm cheating." And away she went, to pour another glass of whiskey.

I worked my drink as slowly as she worked the bar quickly. I paid close attention to her every move, although I couldn't tell you what she was actually doing. It was as if her closing duties were merely the music she danced to, the glasses and rags nothing more than excuses to extend her smooth arms, the lower shelves a reason to bend. It was all beautiful curves and lines. It was all a dancer's grace.

I was all surging testosterone and throbbing, uh, heart.

The twenty minutes went by quickly. "Let's go, daddy."

And we went, barely saying a word to one another as she drove her beat up forest green Jeep Cherokee to her place in Wilkinsburg.

I followed her up her front steps, through the front door. I started to follow her up the stairs, but couldn't take any more. I grabbed her waist from behind, spun her, and threw her to the floor. Those tight black pants didn't have a prayer. I was rabid, foaming at the mouth crazy, and after a bruising round of bites and slaps, I needed a break.

"What do you think you're doing? I'm not finished with you yet." She actually looked pissed.

I could barely speak. "No, but I need a break."

There was a flash in her eyes that the dark had no hope of hiding. "No. You don't need a break. "You..." she whispered into my right ear, "need..." into my left, finishing it with a bite of the earlobe, "me." She pulled me back inside of her, and as it turned out, she was right. Breaks are for the weak. And, for this night if none other, I was not the weak. I was king of the jungle, dammit. I was goddam Superman. And LT, well, he was back to being LT.

We went three times before we even made it all the way to her bedroom, and twice more once in the bed.

"Now that," she bit my chest, "was a good tip."

13

The thing about having a whole lot of sex is it's not enough. Never enough. Especially if you haven't had any for, oh, let's say over a year. And it's not even the lack of sex, really. It's the lack of the ability to have sex. To make love. To fuck. Whatever.

There was a time, a long time, years and years, when you had no control over yourself. You remember those days of untucking your shirt and walking with your books held down below your waist. You remember those days when you'd be doing your geometry homework, trying to remember the Pythagorean Theorem, and he'd just stand up and say hello for no good reason. You remember those days. You can't forget those days.

You can't forget those days because these days there's no saying hello. They say you don't miss something until it's gone, and they're right, except it's not gone. It's there. You see it every day. You use it every day. It's there; it's just not working properly. And God, you miss it.

The thing about suddenly having a lot of sex is you don't ever want to stop. The last time you stopped, look where it got you. The last time you stopped, you couldn't start again.

The thing about suddenly having a lot of sex with Virginia is that it's good sex. Violent sex. Get all that frustration about the last year—the pain and loneliness and sense that you're eternally screwed—let it all out kind of sex. And she loves it. Screams things like "Fuck me, Daddy!" and "God, yes! Fucking hurt me!"

And you do, and you love it. You fuck her and hurt her until you've forgotten all about your dead friends and their blood the only thing that's kept you alive. You fuck her and hurt her until you've forgotten all about the nightmares that come from knowing what you've done, whether it was for survival or not. You fuck her until you've forgotten about how you used your memories, your dead friends, to get on television, to get famous. You hurt her until you go numb from it, numb from all of it. And you wish you never had to stop so you'll never have to feel any way about any thing ever again.

If it meant you'd never have to think about those things again, you'd do anything.

And that's what I did for three days. Nothing but fuck Virginia. Nothing but hurt her. And it was great. It was great because she loved it. No harm, no foul. Of course, I never told her why I was so into it. I never told her that, although I did truly dig her, I was also using her as my whipping girl. My escape. My own little therapy session.

I never told her, and she never asked. She just took it. Again and again she took it.

And I never asked her why, and she never told me.

We did, of course, have a few actual conversations during those days. I mean, you can't have sex twenty-four hours a day, no matter how much you want to.

And these conversations, they were pretty run-of-the-mill. We talked about family (or her lack thereof—"Most people don't have decent families anyway, so I really don't mind.") and friends and college. About exes and jobs and pets. We talked about all those things that don't make for a good story, so I'm not going to try to make a story of it. The end result, though, was that I really liked her.

The only problem was that she was difficult to read. Other than the sex, I could never tell if she enjoyed my company. There was a lot of biting sarcasm in her voice, and sometimes it was hard to take.

The thing about having a lot of sex with Virginia is that you don't really pay much attention to anything else. Not even your new job at the morgue, which, you might think, should be more than enough to hold your attention. All those dead bodies, normal dead bodies. Bodies dead from sickness or old age or all the regular things that kill bodies. All those dead people, and their families crying in that sad grey room. All those dead bodies should have been more interesting than they were in those first few days, even if you didn't really work with them, even if you spent most of your day on the phone or filing paperwork.

The thing about having all that sex with Virginia is you don't even notice the way you've been looking at those dead bodies, even if you haven't really been working with them. You don't even notice how you stare at them. Longer each time. You stare at them and get lost. Zone out. You go to work and you look at these dead people, and you don't realize the effect they're having on you because you're too wrapped up in forgetting about everything.

The thing about having all that sex with Virginia is that after those three days, you don't have all that sex anymore. In fact, you don't have any. It just stops. It stops because LT, he's regressed. He's back on his couch, watching TV and completely ignoring your pleas to get up and do at least a little work around the house.

And Virginia, she notices. And Virginia, she is not pleased.

One morning, the third morning, you wake up and say to her, "I have to go to work."

And she says, "Ok. Bye." And she goes back to sleep.

And just like that, she's done with you.

14

The morgue was full of shiny tools and the smell of chemicals. It was clean. Sterile. The front desk, where I would spend most of my time, housed a computer and drawers filled with writing utensils and all manner of things you would expect to find at a front desk. The wall behind the desk was lined with filing cabinets.

The back of the morgue was surprisingly similar to the front desk. There was a desk with a computer and writing utensils and everything you'd expect to find at a desk. There were a couple sinks for washing hands and tools, two tables for autopsies and whatnot, a cabinet full of all sorts of chemicals with familiar and unfamiliar names and smells. And the back wall was lined with filing cabinets, refrigerated filing cabinets, full of people rather than paper.

After my first few days, I started showing up early. And when I say I was early, I mean I was *early*. Forty-five minutes, an hour. I wasn't having sex anymore, so I had plenty of time to show up early.

I started showing up early because I was becoming fascinated by the dead bodies, sleeping completely covered in pale blue blankets that almost matched the skin. I studied the bodies. The way a woman's breasts would hang down to the sides, into her armpits. The way the fingers and toes never really looked relaxed, or tense. The way veins would show up in the oddest places, like holding a flashlight up to and egg.

I studied them because, well, I'd never really studied dead bodies before. I'd only eaten them.

One of my first early days, I found myself alone. Dick was out, Eli was out. It was just me, in the morgue, with two new bodies in the back. I'd already gone over the paperwork: a forty-seven year-old woman who'd had a heart attack, and a kid, sixteen, who'd been shot in the chest.

I couldn't help myself. I had to do it.

I slid the woman out of her drawer and looked for a moment at the sheet covering her body. It reminded me of a loaf of bread covered by a dishtowel, cooling on the kitchen counter. The only real feature was the little tent at the bottom, pitched with the poles of her feet.

I pulled the sheet, folded it up, and set it on the examination table a few feet behind me. The loaf of bread took shape: round, pale, cold. A transubstantiation the Catholics would go ape-shit over. (Thank God they don't burn people at the stake anymore. Although I'm sure this sentiment is quite capable of landing a few protesters on my lawn.)

The muscles had grown tired of holding all the fat and skin in their proper places, and the fat and skin hung at the sides. The breasts had slid to rest on the arms, a mudslide brought on by the rains of death. The fat belly had flattened, or migrated, so the fat sides were now really fat sides. It went the same for the meat of the arms and legs, the way topsoil is pushed aside to make room for the expanding gas chamber of a volcano threatening to blow.

This woman, though, she would never blow anything again. Not the steam from a spoon of hot soup or the candles on a birthday cake. Not a fat line of cocaine or an entire paycheck at the mall. Not her husband or her lover.

She was done. Everything building up inside her, everything ready to explode—it all just stopped. All that power that had taken years nearing the surface, it was all trapped. She could never let it out. She was a false alarm, and I felt sorry for her. Or, more accurately, I felt sorry for all that stuff she'd never be able to let out.

I imagine that as she was dying, clutching at the arm they say hurts when your heart gives out, she was sorry for all that stuff, too. There was so much of it in there, and now it would rot away with the stretch marks on her hips and the cellulite on her ass. She had to have thought about it, that poor woman. Knowing there's more in there than what you've been able to set free in the last half-century. If her heart hadn't already failed her, I'll bet it would have broken at the thought.

I looked at her face, and I had myself convinced that she had moved her mouth. Or tried to move her mouth. Like I could see the muscles trying, trying so hard, to get those lips open. To tell me something. To let something out.

The mouth, that's where all the power is. The gateway to what's inside. Breathing, eating, drinking, speaking. It's the mouth that allows all of it. At least, that's the way I thought about it then.

All these bodies used to be people, people with strength and some sort of power (or soul, or spirit, or aura, or whatever), and now, because the mouths were out of order, this power was forever stuck in there, in those fleshy sarcophagi.

I'd once read that certain tribes (in the South Pacific, mostly, although probably in other places, too) believed that a dead body still contained the strength of the person who had inhabited it while alive. The warriors would eat their defeated enemies and absorb that strength. This same book also said that some cultures were known to eat the flesh of their dead relatives. They believed they would carry the soul of their dearly departed grandfather around in their veins until their own grandchildren ate them. And so on. And so forth.

I learned all this in an Anthropology class in college.

This was when I didn't pay too much attention to theories about Big Namba or Small Namba tribal culture. This was when my biggest problem was trying not to show that I was in class hung-over and fighting my need to vomit.

I learned about this in college, and I hadn't thought about it since. Now, standing over this woman's corpse, I thought about it again, and it made sense.

I poked and prodded like a farmer looking over a pig, deciding if it is good enough, fat enough, healthy enough, to serve to my family for Christmas dinner.

I poked and prodded, comparing the feel of the thighs to my recollection of Erica's. Erica's thighs were thin and athletic, muscular, great to look at and easy to chew, like the most tender of human filets. These thighs, you could tell they'd be chewy, fatty. Slow roasted, like a nice prime rib, they would have been fantastic. But raw, not so much.

You might think I'd have caught myself thinking about all this and stopped because it was disgusting and twisted and wrong. You might think I'd have thrown that sheet right back over that loaf of cold bread, walked back to the front desk, called Dick Pearson, told him I quit, and run out the door.

I guess maybe I should have.

Yes, I did realize that the goings-on in my head were a little, well, off the mark. And no, I did not believe that eating this woman would somehow allow her, or those things trapped inside her, to live on. I'm not fucking crazy.

Sure, I thought about what it would be like to cut her up, cook her up, chew her up, swallow her. I thought about which ways to cook which cuts. I thought about what it would be like to eat her, but in that way you'd imagine what it might be like to fuck a chicken.

I did *not* think about what it would be like to *actually* eat her.

So my mouth watered some. So what?

I was squeezing the right triceps when Eli showed up. "New one?"

I dropped the arm, which bounced off the table and fell swinging over the edge. "Holy shit, Eli. Don't sneak up on me like that. You could give someone a heart attack."

"Like her, huh?" He stepped in for a closer look. "She's a heart attack, right?"

"Did you look at her file?"

He cracked his neck, then his fingers, out in front of him, like an arthritic pianist. "No. I can just tell most of the time."

"That's creepy."

He smiled. "Yeah. Comes with the territory." He picked up the folded sheet from the exam table. "What are you doing back here, anyway?"

Hmm. "Nothing, really. Just looking." Looking, yes. Sweating now, too. "Thinking about what it's like to die."

He seemed to buy it and walked to the side of the table, looking the woman over slowly from feet to head. "You're new. You won't think about that anymore, not after a while. After a while, you'll forget they're even people. Of course, they're not people. Not anymore. The people part is gone. Poof. And all that's left is this." He punched her in the stomach, and she farted. She farted, and Eli laughed. "Ah. That'll never get old."

I covered her back up, slid her back into her drawer, and went to spend the rest of my morning filling out and filing paperwork. To spend the rest of my day thinking about why I was thinking about whether a cabernet or a merlot would go best with a nice, tender rump roast.

15

The thing about working at the morgue is it's a new experience for you, full of interesting and oddly exhilarating sights and sounds and smells.

The thing about not talking to, or sleeping with, Virginia anymore is that now you have all sorts of free time to indulge in your new interests. You get yourself into a new routine, which goes something like this: wake up, eat, shower, drive to work (speeding, rolling through stop signs because you simply can't get there soon enough), check out some corpses, go home.

Life is all about routine, especially when you don't share your life with other people. And the routine doesn't stop just because you're home. Maybe you'll red-up your apartment a little (tidy up, if you're not from the 'Burgh). Maybe watch some television or read a book. But usually you'll sit at your computer and spend some time in Jeffrey Dahmer chat rooms, or type C-A-N-N-I-B-A-L-I-S-M into search engines, you know, just to see if anything interesting pops up, anything you can learn.

You learn, for instance, that you are—by definition—a cannibal. Or a recovering cannibal, at any rate. You learn that the technical term for cannibalism is Anthropophagy, and that your particular practice is recognized under Anglo-American law as a necessity defense under something called the Choice of Evils Doctrine. It is formally known as Survival Cannibalism, for obvious reasons.

You learn about other forms of cannibalism, as well. The Aztecs practiced ritual religious sacrifices and ate war captives, strangers, and enemies. This is known as Exocannibalism because, you know, it's outside the tribe.

You learn that the Celts and Aboriginal Australians would eat their dead friends and relatives as a way to release the soul from the body (and you're proud of yourself for remembering that from college). This is called Endocannibalism because it's inside the tribe. They do say that it's good for families to sit down to a nice meal together.

You read case studies of serial killers, crazy fuckers who would decorate their houses with body parts. Skulls on bedposts, shrines of bone and preserved genitals. They'd keep heads in the freezer, heads in their beds. They'd prefer little boys, or little girls, or ethnic boys, or they'd prefer the taste of virgins.

You learn that these people are fucking crazy. Even when they explain themselves, they're really only telling you that they're completely gone, off their rockers, the lights in their attics all smashed bulbs on the floor, which is covered in beautiful, hand-crafted, human-skin rugs.

You learn these people are crazy.

You learn you may be crazy, too.

You learn that you're developing an unhealthy obsession. Survival is one thing. You can't feel bad about doing whatever you had to do to survive, even if you do.

Survival is one thing. Pleasure is another. Compulsion, curiosity, desire—all others.

You learn that you're crossing into dangerous territory here, letting yourself learn about all this, letting yourself become more and more interested with every word you read.

You're crossing into dangerous territory, letting your mind wander like this. And oh, it wanders. It wanders over every inch of skin, every muscle. It wanders through every vein and in and out of every organ. The liver, heart, brain. Even the spleen. The pancreas. None of the body escapes these sick new fantasies.

You learn you're definitely crazy.

But you're still sane enough to know you're crazy, and that's something. You're sane enough that you're not murdering people and bringing them home. Or bringing them home and then murdering them. You're not cutting them up, making milkshakes out of their flesh. You're not replacing the carton of Rocky Road with a head full of grey matter.

You learn you're crazy, but not totally.

You wonder if anyone is keeping an eye on your internet usage. Is *cannibalism* red-flagged? *Jeffrey Dahmer*? *Albert Fish*?

You wonder if anyone is going to come for you, but you only wonder for a moment because you're only a little bit crazy, and you know that you're allowed to learn about anything you want to, as long as you don't start practicing.

So you make rules for yourself.

No killing.

No dismembering.

You can't believe you're making these rules, but they seem like pretty good rules to live by anyway, so you continue.

No stealing any bodies from work.

No eating.

No talking about this with anyone. Ever.

16

In all fairness, it's wrong to say that I'd fallen out of favor with Virginia due to lack of physical performance. She loved the sex, no question, but there was more to her than selfish little nympho.

When you can't get it up, you start to think that you're no good for any woman, so how could she possibly want anything to do with you? It's really nothing more than an insecurity issue.

I hadn't talked to her in a couple weeks, but that was hardly her fault. I was embarrassed, you see. And then I got all wrapped up in my new hobby. There just wasn't any time.

"So how's work?" She was pouring a drink for me and was perfectly friendly.

I expected her to be colder. I thought it was her nature. "It's work. Dead people aren't very exciting, but at least they don't give you any shit."

"Really? Dead people aren't exciting?" The sarcasm knew to come out of her mouth the way baby sea turtles know to head for the ocean.

I was in no mood for it, though. "Yeah, really."

The thing about sarcasm is you really can't fight back. How do you fight with a tone? You might as well take a swing at the fog. Sure, you can try to fight, but you're usually met with either "Oh, relax. I was only kidding," or "You misunderstood my tone." Then there are those with a preternatural gift for sarcasm, born with a sense of bitter, passive-aggressive humor. You'll never come out on top with them. At best you'll hear, "You need to learn how to take a joke."

I was in no mood for it, so I just sat there, quiet, looking at my drink.

"Oh, what? Can't take a little sarcastic remark?"

Sarcastic people also have trouble understanding why some people don't handle it well. It's not their fault. They just didn't grow up on the same side of that fence.

"Listen," I said. "I'm a little embarrassed about, well, you know. That's all."

She put her rag down and positioned herself across the bar, where she crouched down to my eye-level. "I don't mean anything by it. It's just my tone. You can't help your tone, you know? I'm not mad or anything. I don't mean anything personal. I just pick on people I like. I totally destroy the rest."

"Like a six year-old putting gum in a little girl's hair, huh? At least you're mature about it."

She smiled. "There, see? Like that. You can do it, too."

I wasn't about to tell her that even though I sometimes had a problem dealing with her biting remarks, it was also kind of a turn-on. "I just don't think sarcasm is an all the time thing."

"Yeah, well, I'm not sarcastic all the time." She took a sip of her water, or maybe it was whiskey. I couldn't tell through the red plastic of the cup. "How's that going, by the way? With your little guy, there?"

And there *that* was. "Not so good, actually. I can't figure it out. I mean, after the accident, up until that night with you, I couldn't. I figured it was the stress and the malnourishment and everything. And then there were those days with you. And then nothing again. I can't figure out why it's happening. Or *not* happening, I guess. It's really starting to piss me off."

"I can understand that. It's pissing me off, too." She pulled some goofy-looking ballet stretch and cracked her knees. "Ahhhh. That's better. I wonder what snapped you out of it then."

"Yeah. So do I." I sucked down the rest of the drink.

I wondered why I was talking to her about this. I couldn't bring myself to talk about it with anyone else. Not the doctors or shrinks. Not Adam or Dave. I think it may have been because they were all men. I didn't want them to know. Yeah, it was sort of childish.

"I don't know," I said. "That night I was here, Little Travis just suddenly—"

"Wait." She let out one laughing breath. "You call him Little Travis? That's retarded. If you're going to name him, you might as well actually name him. You're more creative than that, aren't you? Than 'Little Travis'?"

It took everything in me not to get defensive. "I don't know. You got any better ideas?"

"I do, actually. I was watching *Bull Durham* the other day. That night you first came to my place, Little Travis there, he announced his presence with authority. Maybe you should call him Nuke." Amazing. I mean, what woman is going to say you should name your pecker after a character from the greatest baseball movie ever?

"Anyway," I continued, "I got here that night, and *Nuke* just sort of woke up. Out of nowhere. I guess I was just too excited about it to give it any thought."

The phone rang, and rang again.

"Well, you should think about it. Maybe it's something you can do again." She answered the phone, told whoever it was to hold on, and went back into the office.

I rested my head on my hands and started to think about what could have possibly charged my sexual appetite that night.

Then, as so often was the case, Adam showed up, smiling and bumping my thoughts right off the track. "What's going on, brother? Haven't seen you in a while."

Virginia reemerged from the office and got back on the phone to tell whoever was on the other end "Wednesday." Then she noticed Adam. "Adam, how do you always show up out of nowhere like that?" She brought him a beer.

"I'm one quarter ninja," he told her. "You didn't know that?"

I lit a cigarette for him and asked what he'd been up to.

"Nothing much, man. You know, working and sleeping." As long as I'd known Adam, I don't think I'd ever once known him to be up to anything much. I think that might be why he was always in such a good mood. "What about you? Go to any more of those secret meetings?"

Virginia's ears went up with that one. "Secret meetings? What? Are you part of the Illuminati or something? Scheming for world domination?"

"Well, I've always been scheming for world domination, but I prefer to work alone. Those Illuminati bastards, they always manage to fuck everything up." It was a feeble attempt to avoid any more questions.

And yes, it failed.

"So what are these secret meetings, then?"

I looked at Adam and wished I could sock him a good one for spilling my beans like that, but he didn't know he had a hold of my beans, so I couldn't really be all that angry with him.

"I've only been to one meeting, and I'm not really sure what it was all about, actually. Best I can guess is they have something to do with surviving accidents. They asked me to speak for them a couple weeks ago."

"What night was that?"

"The night we had to call a cab for drunkie-boy, here."

Adam shrugged. "I don't remember that night too well."

"Oh. *That* night." Virginia blushed, and I couldn't believe it. "*I* remember that night."

"Yeah. That night. Anyway, they were really strange people. And they were all loaded. Rich, I mean, not drunk. I didn't know what they were about when I agreed to speak for them, and I didn't really learn much." I knew it sounded ridiculous. How could I not know anything?

Virginia knew it, too. "You don't know anything? That's ridiculous. Do you at least know what they're called?"

"Yeah, I think. PEP, but I don't know what it stands for." I took a sip from my refreshed beverage and turned to Adam. "The main guy, he said he'd get in touch with me to tell me when the next one is."

"You gonna go?" I couldn't tell which of them said it first.

"I don't know. Maybe."

And then, we drank.

17

I got to work and told Eli he could leave and that I would sign him out at his normal time, like always. He told me about our over-nighters: two simply got too old, and the other was an overdose. He left the paperwork out for me. Then he left.

I should have slept another hour. This was a waste of my time. The old people with their pale raisin wrinkled skin and brittle bones and the drug addict with his pale bruised skin and near-atrophied muscles did not interest me. I wanted my dead bodies the way I wanted my women: meaty. It could be muscle or fat, so long as it was substantial. Substantial, but not obese. The very fat and very skinny seemed equally weak to me. It was strength I was after.

Still though, I gave the corpses a look. I would have given them a physical exam, too, if it wasn't like looking at three skeletons, either exhumed or discovered frozen in an iceberg. Nothing to prod. Nothing to poke.

So I put them away in much the same way I put their files into their respective drawers.

I managed to get the bodies put away without dropping any of them to the floor, but I can't say the same about their files. I dropped them all. On their way down, they opened, and their innards spilled all over the floor and under the desk.

I scraped the mess that was out in the open into a quick pile and stuck the upper half of my body in the space made for your knees. I got my right hand on the last few sheets and used my left to steady myself against the bottom of the drawer above me, where I found a key stuck to the desk with a magnet.

We're curious, people. We can't help ourselves. Look at

Socrates. Look at Adam and Eve. We all want to know. Sometimes you better your life and the lives of others, and sometimes you fuck it up for everyone. It can go either way. But whichever way it does go, at least now you know.

I knew this key unlocked Dick's office. I knew I had almost an hour before anyone else came in. I knew I was bored.

Other than a box of cigarettes and a bird clock, I didn't know what Dick kept in his office. I didn't know much about Dick.

I couldn't help myself. I went to his office and stood in the middle of the room, looking around for what I wanted to molest first. Filing cabinets, bookshelves, end-table drawers, a closet. So many choices. I settled on the desk. People are always hiding things in their desks—liquor or little black books, pistols or records of dirty deeds.

Everyone who has a desk has something to hide in that desk. Everyone except for Richard Pearson. The most exciting thing I found in any of the four drawers was a novelty pen. When you turned it upside down, the upside down woman in her underwear turned right side up, and her underwear fell to her feet. I got the sense that this would not be a productive exploration.

Disappointed, I leafed through the stack of papers sitting neatly on the polished oak. (It was quite a desk to have in a coroner's office. It could have belonged to the CEO of some huge, money-grubbing corporation.) Nothing interesting there, either. Just the autopsy reports of all the unclaimed bodies we'd had in the last two weeks.

I grabbed a pencil from the golf bag, held by a six-inch caddy, on the desk. I started doodling on a pad of blue post-it notes and noticed indentations on the paper. I shaded lightly over the entire square, like they do in detective movies, and found a note now written in the dead space.

Six for Friday the tenth. Call W tomorrow.

This wasn't much more interesting than the nudie pen. I peeled the note from the pad, folded it in half so the glue was inside, stuck it in my wallet, locked the door on my way out, and wondered if Dave knew he had the most boring uncle in all the land.

18

It was hot outside, and because I had time now, since my regression back into the world of the perpetually flaccid, I spent most of that time in my air-conditioned apartment, reading books and watching documentaries. I had all the time in the world to read the pixilated words of people who were *really* obsessed with this cannibalism stuff. I was merely taking a tour of the grotesque mansion in which these people lived, this house decorated with bloody gruesome paintings and severed parts preserved in yellowish liquid in jars on the mantles.

There were rooms I couldn't get into without a password and a credit card (turns out you truly cannot go anywhere without your American Express card), and rooms I wouldn't dare enter. Sometimes you have to know when to leave a door shut, you know?

Even so, too much of my time was given to exploring this house. When I did manage to force myself to go out, I'd find myself sitting at the bar, sizing everyone up. Which of these would Fish have picked? Or Dahmer? If I were stranded again, who would I want to be there with me? Which of these boozing, smoking twenty-somethings would be of greatest nutritional value?

These games were moderately effective substitutes for what was once known as my sexual desire. I still checked out all the women, but not because I wanted to fuck. I eyed their legs and breasts and bellies and asses, all the same parts I used to, not because I wanted to touch them but because I wanted to eat them.

Before this gets out of hand, I have to tell you something. I was afraid. I knew I was getting too far off the path. I knew it was somewhere nearby, but I was beginning to lose track of which direction I had to go to find it again. I felt like a child in the woods at night, with an enormous amount of fear and a little sense of adventure. I was scared because each step meant one of two things: either I was closer to where I should have been, or I was farther away. I found myself praying on more than one occasion that it was the former, but every now and again I'd have been ok with the latter. Still, I didn't want to get too deep into these woods. I didn't want to do the things you'd have to do to survive in this forest of the damned.

To make matters worse, I couldn't stop thinking about Synchek and his pseudo-cult. And about Pearson's note, which had since been moved from my wallet to the fridge, right beside Synchek's letter. Something was up. If Pearson had nothing to do with it, it was of no matter. Those PEP people, something wasn't right about them, and I felt a strange attraction to whatever it was. A connection. I couldn't figure it out, but for some reason, I was drawn to them.

I was curious. I wanted to know.

I hadn't heard from Synchek, so I didn't know when the next meeting was. I *needed* to know when the next meeting was.

Conveniently enough, this was a Thursday, and Thursdays were One-Armed-Man Day at the James Street Tavern.

"Mr. Eliot! So good to see you!" Synchek stood as though he was being pulled up by tiny wires at the corners of his smile, like some puppeteer was in the ceiling, controlling everything. "Please, have a seat. Let me get you a drink."

I sat across from the blue suit with its arm folded and pinned to the shoulder. "When's the next PEP meeting?"

He laughed. "So, we made an impression on you then? I trust it was a good one." He sat and looked pleased with himself for a moment, then continued. "What won you over?"

I didn't dare tell him anything about my newfound love of research, or about how I felt connected to his group of, uh, followers. I searched my head for a reasonable response. "The food. It was unbelievable."

Ah, truths that are lies. And lies that are truths. God bless the subtleties of the English language.

"I told you, John Gregory is quite the chef, is he not?" He knocked back the rest of his martini and looked for the waitress, who was taking an order a few tables away. He lit a cigar. "Well, Travis, the next meeting is scheduled for next Saturday. The eleventh. If you're serious about coming back, you'll need to know the password."

I thought about a clubhouse with a crayon-scrawled *no girls allowed* sign on the door, kids inside stockpiling porno mags and fireworks. "Really? A password?"

"It's more of a pass-phrase, I suppose. 'I should have been a pair of ragged claws, scuttling across the floors of silent seas.' T.S. Eliot. Hmm. Eliot. Isn't that a coincidence?" He thought it was clever. I thought it was stupid and didn't crack a smile.

"Why Eliot?"

He stared into the lit end of his cigar. "Oh, I don't know, exactly. I've just always enjoyed that line. And a password has to be something, does it not?"

"I guess so."

So that was that. Saturday, August eleventh, I would go back to that warehouse and learn what was what.

19

Smoking cigarettes is bad for me. I know it. And my parents knew it, and some of my friends know it, and my dead grandparents all know it first-hand. Smoking is bad for me, and by this point in my life I'd been doing it for almost a decade. There was an eighteen month period when I'd quit, not had one cigarette, even if I was drinking, even after sex, but I'd since started up again. I knew I had to quit then because the stairs were beginning to look more like Everest every time I approached them, and the balls of phlegm that I coughed up in the morning were growing larger, a little more discolored. I knew I had to quit because eventually you realize that things are getting worse, and someday they'll be irreparable. You know that someday a doctor will tell you that you have cancer, emphysema, whatever. He'll tell you you're going to die, and you should have stopped before it got to this point.

And the bitch of it is, he'll be right.

Surgeon General's Warning: Cannibalism can lead to such horrifying diseases as Kuuru (or the *laughing death*, as it's referred to by tribes in New Guinea, which is sort of like the Mad Cow Disease of humans). It can also lead to jail-time or, more likely, a death sentence.

It says so right there on the box.

There are many ways to quit smoking. There's the gum, the patch, the rubber-band around the wrist, the hypnotherapy, the acupuncture therapy, the twelve step programs. They call them aides, helpers, crutches.

I call them crap.

The only way to quit doing anything is to *quit fucking doing it*. Just stop. No aides. No crutches. If you think you have to stop eating so much, then don't put all that food in your mouth. If you have to stop drinking and driving, don't drink, or don't drive. If you have to stop smoking, stop lighting things on fire and sticking them in your mouth. You get the idea.

If you have to stop wondering what it would be like to have people as your main source of food, as a preference rather that out of necessity, then you have to stop reading about it. You have to stop watching your documentaries. Stop sitting around your apartment with all that access to cannibalism websites. It would help if you could stop going to work at the morgue, too, but a man has to work, and the benefits are a major plus.

But the thing is, you have to stop doing all these things NOW, before the doctor tells you your nervous system is completely shot and soon you'll collapse, trembling onto the floor and losing your ability to speak, before you start breaking all those rules you made for yourself only a couple chapters ago. Before the police catch you with body parts in your freezer, you have to stop all of it.

They call it cold turkey.

I call it way more effective than all that other crap.

I woke up one morning, a couple days after meeting Synchek at James Street, and the first thing in my head was, *I wish I had to work today. I want to feel-up another dead person*. If I'd become this addicted to the *idea*, just imagine what the actual practice would do to me. Finally, my conscience recognized this as a very bad thing. I was killing myself, like with the cigarettes, and one form of slow suicide is plenty, thank you. At least the cigarettes don't hurt anyone else. At least the cigarettes don't mean you've completely lost your senses of humanity and of right and wrong.

So I decided to quit. Cold turkey. No crutches. If I could survive months of being alone and starving and broken in the mountains, in the snow, in the tragedy and death of that fucking accident, I had to be strong enough to stop myself from getting deeper into this addiction.

I disconnected my computer, threw my books into the incinerator in the basement, returned the documentaries to the library, and I quit. Just like that.

The thing about working at the morgue is it's much more difficult to quit your addiction to dead people—eating them, thinking about eating them, or otherwise, if you swing that way—when you have to be around them all day. It's like an alcoholic carrying a full flask in his jacket pocket, like a gambling addict moving to Vegas.

I should have quit my job.

But I didn't. I decided I would just have to deal with it. Piece of cake. I spent most of the time at the front desk anyway, an entire hallway separating me from my vice. I could bury myself in paperwork, reorganizing files, cleaning.

And I did. Come August ninth, I hadn't even looked at a dead body. I kept busy answering the phone, ordering chemicals and new tools, scrubbing the waiting room floor. I kept busy by whatever means necessary, and it was working. And it certainly didn't hurt that nobody seemed to be dying. At least not in the city.

August ninth, and Pearson came out from the back. "So much for the undertaker always having work, huh?"

I was busying myself, putting new labels on the file folders. "Yeah. I guess so."

He sat on the corner of the counter, picked up a couple of paperclips, and started bending them up, sculpting. "You feeling all right, Travis? You seem like you're getting a little too involved with all this cleaning up out here."

I pulled a faded yellow label from its plastic holder at the top of the folder. I-J, it said. "Yeah, I'm fine."

"I noticed you've been coming in early. That's good. It shows you care about your work." He looked down at the paperclip figure in his hand, curled his lip, and went back at it. "Seems like you're settling in nicely. That's good, too. Sometimes this place makes people a little weird."

"I guess I'm doing all right. I like it well enough." I stuck a nice, new, bright orange I-J label on the folder and slid it back into its drawer.

"Are you interested in any overtime work? There's something I need to do tomorrow night, and I think I'll need a hand."

This was perfect. A few more hours at work, and actually working, would help me hold my focus. I'd stopped going to the bar because I was still having trouble looking at women as anything other than sexy sides of beef hanging in the butcher's window. I'd spent the last few nights hiding out in my apartment, smoking dope, eating Mac 'n Cheese, watching television, and playing video games. Puzzle games. With no blood. I knew I'd held onto my NES and The Legend of Zelda for a reason. I'd been avoiding phone calls, allowing voicemail to politely lie for me. "I can't answer the phone right now," my voice would say, "Leave a message, and I'll get back to you." It must be easy to keep a straight face when you have no face. Lucky voicemail.

"Sure, I can help you tomorrow night. What are we doing?"

He stood back up. "We're going to deliver a few bodies to a place in the South Side. Unclaimed bodies. Or unidentified. For research."

Oh, grand. "Yeah. I can do that."

"Good," he said, pitching his botched wire sculpture in the trash. "It'll be much easier with two people." He started towards his office.

"Hey, Dick. It's your job to do that?"

"What's that?"

I stood up. "To deliver the bodies. That's your job?"

"Oh. No," he said. "It's just something I do. I know the head of the research department. He's doing great things, or trying to anyway. I like to stop in and see how things are going." He headed for his office again, but stopped, this time of his own accord. "Since you're helping out tomorrow, and nobody's dying, how about you take the morning off. I'll still pay you for it."

"Sure thing." I wasn't positive staying home was going to be a good idea, but a day away from such easily accessible corpses couldn't hurt, particularly if I'd be handling body bags stuffed with the tasty morsels all night. I was sure I'd be able to find something to keep me busy. Maybe I'd pay some bills, go through my fan mail box. Maybe I'd just sit around and look at porno mags all day, wishing I could masturbate, thinking about how Virginia could very well have been the last girl I'd ever sleep with.

Maybe I'd get back to thinking about my poor dead friends and their poor grieving families. Maybe I'd get back to writing. After all, I now had plenty of material. I could do what the doctors said I'd have to do. I could get my hands dirty digging up all the memories I'd been trying not to think about. It would be the perfect distraction, the ideal way to keep myself from thinking about this new thing I was trying to keep out of my head.

I could get specific, down to the blood stain on Jason's jeans that looked almost exactly like South America. Down to the way the snow drift, steadily growing over the plane, threatened to swallow the entire scene. Down to the details of how I'd built myself a shelter out of ski poles and scraps of metal.

Nothing takes you out of reality like a good day of creative self-wallowing.

I pulled the K-L file from its place in the drawer. "What time should I get here tomorrow?"

"Be here at six."

20

After a gluttonous amount of sleep—imagine wine, grapes, and naked girls with fans—I was up and alert like I'd woken up to an eight ball on the nightstand, only without all the talking and fidgeting, without the numb teeth and nosebleeds, without the constant need to do another rail.

I cooked, ate, cleaned, showered. I looked at the clock every five or ten minutes, and the clock seemed to have some sort of problem with me because it wasn't moving. Stubborn fucker. It was only 1:30, and I had nothing to do before meeting Pearson back at work. Sure, it was only four-and-a-half hours, but it felt like an eternity. I had too much energy to have nothing to do, and it was good energy, happy energy, the kind of energy that motivates you to do something, anything. Maybe it was more like doing coke than I thought.

I needed time to move faster. Or maybe I needed a time machine.

But since time moves to the beat of its own drum and time machines are hard to come by on such short notice, I figured I'd go to the bar. The bar was safe in the afternoon. There would be no women there, plump or otherwise, to get me salivating. My only temptation would be the booze, and I've never been much of an afternoon drinker. Not to mention, I had to go to work. I couldn't let myself get drunk. But the drive to the South Side would kill some time, as would all the circling to find a parking spot. And if I got bored, I could always walk around and check out all the little shops.

Twenty-till-three and Virginia wasn't working. She never started before four, which worked out quite well for her and her snooze button addiction.

Dominic was working. He was this queer little Italian guy, and I couldn't tell if he was actually queer, or Italian for that matter. The two of us were friendly, but by no means were we friends. He was a decent bartender, and I was a decent tipper, and that pretty much covered the essence of our relationship.

Since I couldn't let myself get drunk, I ordered a beer. "Is Virginia working tonight?"

"Yep." He threw his dishrag over his shoulder with a flamboyant flair. "She doesn't start till eight tonight."

He was bored. You could see it in the way he walked the bar, lifting ash trays and rubber mats, wiping the cool and already clean wood beneath them. You could hear it in his voice, which, masculine but with a hint of lisp, was much less playful and energetic than usual. It sounded like he'd rather be, well, anywhere, doing anything else.

I, too, was bored. Already, I was bored. I watched Dominic as he searched for something to do, the way you look for anything to do when you've done nothing all day. On the television, some guy was talking about marinating techniques as he carved up a drool-inducing cut of pork, which, I've heard somewhere, is the closest to the flesh of a man. I'm pretty sure it was in a Scorsese flick. I guess it's not important.

I watched my drinks drain themselves like water down mostly-clogged pipes, slow but steady. I never managed to see the grain of the wood through the bottom of my glass, though, as Dominic topped off each glass before there was any reason for that half-full, half-empty debate.

Not that we'd have had that debate anyway; there was no conversation. Just two men killing time in a bar, picking up the occasional tip for keeping your chicken juicy or your angel food cake spongy and moist.

I tend to drink more when I don't talk. I always need to be doing something with my mouth, particularly when I'm so full of energy.

Five o'clock came with a heavy, red-headed Italian guy promising his secrets to a "heavenly dish of lamb and eggplant" spiced with something or other and served with something or other. I was too drunk to pay close attention.

After one more drink—a free drink meant to keep Dominic company on this slowest of days—I left a twenty on the bar (I'd been paying as I went, but he only charged me for half of my drinks), thanked him for his excellent service, and headed for the morgue by way of the Tenth Street Bridge.

I hoped the walk would sober me enough that Pearson wouldn't fire me. Since we were coming back to the South Side, I figured I'd pick up my car at the end of the night.

The trip into town took only twenty minutes, leaving me with about an hour to let the late afternoon sun sweat the drunk out of me. I walked to the Point, the confluence of the Allegheny and Monongahela, the beginning of the Ohio. I watched the boats cruising up and down their respective rivers, and then a coal barge, massive and lumbering toward the Mississippi, all of its hard carbon stretching thirty yards ahead of the engine.

I stank. I could smell it over the scents of flowing water and summer breeze. I could smell it through the mist of the fountain, behind me, with its tower of water. I could smell it, and it almost made me sick.

Dick would surely smell it. He would tell me not to come back to work tomorrow. He might even tell me to go home tonight. Whatever he might do, he might do it soon. It was almost six.

He smiled and said hello as I walked through the door, five minutes late. "What's that smell?"

"Uh, what smell?" I tried to say it like a joke.

"Did you bathe in cologne?"

I had, in fact, very nearly bathed in cologne. The stench of me was so foul, at least in my drunken assessment of the situation, that I thought cologne-stink was better than alcohol-stink. Alcohol-stink will lose you your job. Cologne-stink will merely prompt a question or two.

"I spilled it all over myself before I left. I never wear it, but I'm going out later and thought I'd put some on tonight. Maybe hide the smell of death some. I guess that's what happens." God, I'm a horrible liar when I'm drunk.

"Yeah. That's pretty potent stuff, isn't it?" He was at the paper shredder, shredding away, julienning thin white lettuce into the salad bowl of the garbage can. "Good thing I'm the only one here who can smell anything." He tossed his thumb towards the back. "Eli has no sense of smell. He says it has something to do with some stupid thing he did when he was a kid. Lucky bastard."

"Where is Eli?"

"In the back, putzing around. I'm not exactly sure, actually."

I made sure not to get too close to him. Although on my way to work I had managed to find a store that carried cologne, the place didn't have any breath mints. Not even any gum. "Destroying the evidence?"

"Yeah, right," he said. He grabbed a piece of paper from the counter. "Here's a list of who we need to grab. If you want to start taking them to the truck, I'll be in to help in a few minutes."

So I took the list and went to the back. Eli was nowhere to be found. Focusing on the small print was still a bit of a challenge, but I managed. I bagged two of them, loaded them onto two gurneys, and wheeled them out to the truck, which was little more than a moving van rigged up with shelves enough to hold a dozen bodies. I bagged the next two and loaded them up, and then the last two, with no help from Pearson. I could have used it, too; these were not small people. They were each around two-hundred/two-hundred-fifty pounds. Four men, two women.

The lifting and moving seemed to do me some good though, as I felt more sober after all the physical exertion. The sweat, though, had begun to peek its head through the curtain of Brut I'd shrouded myself with, and again, I almost got sick.

After strapping everyone securely to their shelves, I lit a cigarette and leaned against the cool metal of the Deathmobile.

"Wake up, Travis. We have work to do."

I wasn't really sleeping, but I had let my smoke burn most of the way to the filter without hitting it once. This was going to be a long evening. I shook my head, a sleepy dog shaking loose visions of Milkbones and mailmen, and climbed into the cab.

"Sorry about not helping load them up," he said, or groaned, as he pulled himself up to the driver's seat. "I had to make a quick phone call."

I told him not to worry about it and made use of the headrest. He turned on the radio. Light jazz. Light jazz and the low roar of the engine. I didn't have a prayer.

He was kind enough not to wake me until we'd reached our destination, wherever that was. "I don't normally let people sleep on the job, you know."

"Sorry."

"Don't worry about it. It's not like we were working. Just driving." He opened his door and stepped onto the pavement.

We were in an alley or small side street that I didn't recognize. He had backed the truck up to a loading dock, and a large garage door exposed what looked like, well, someplace that might have a loading dock.

"Well, let's go," he said.

I thought it odd that no one was there to meet us, but it seemed that Pearson had done this a hundred times, and that nobody ever met him at the door.

I hadn't thought to load the gurneys, so we carried each body in one by one, Pearson at the feet, and laid them on tables in a very cold room. I could see my breath.

"This place used to be storage for some meat-packing company. This cooler is almost a hundred years old." Dick seemed awed by this cooler. People are into whatever they're into, I suppose.

After setting the last body on the last table, Dick told me he'd be out in a minute. The way he said it, I knew he meant for me to wait with the truck, so I did. As interested as I was about what sort of research lab would be housed in a meat locker, he was the boss.

I smoked another cigarette, really this time, and took note of the way my head was clearing out. My thoughts were less fuzzy around the edges, and I didn't get dizzy when I stood up after tying a shoelace that had come undone. I was glad to be sobering; it was a cool evening with a clear sky and the hint of a breeze. It would have been a shame to waste the entire evening, working or not, in that place between drunk and not quite devoid of alcohol.

As I pulled my foot off the remnants of my cigarette, Pearson came outside, followed by a very tall, very bearded man. "Travis, this is Gregor. He's the head of research here."

Gregor gave me a healthy handshake. "Nice to meet you, Travis." His voice was deep, low, the kind of voice that would have been perfect for telling bedtime stories.

I returned his hello and asked exactly what he was researching.

"It's complicated. Essentially, we're studying and comparing the vitamin, mineral, and nutritional values of humans to those of cows."

Yeah. I was interested. "The nutritional value of humans? Seriously?"

"Seriously." Gregor lit himself a clove cigarette, the sweet smoke a nice break from the smell of death. "It started because of Mad Cow disease, actually. I was curious to see if this was something that could happen to other species. And well, the most unique and complex species on the planet is people." He elbowed Dick. "It's amazing. The government will give you a grant for just about anything."

"Wait," I said. "What about Kuruu?"

They both looked at me like I knew some secret I shouldn't have.

"The laughing death? How do you know about that?"

"Internet."

"Oh. Well, this is a little more complicated than that. I have work to do now, but maybe the next time we meet we'll talk about it some more."

That satisfied me for the moment, but I still had another question. "How many people do you, uh, study?"

"We have sort of a deal with the coroner's office," he answered. "People who die—I mean, if someone dies and there's no relatives or friends or anybody else who claims the body, Dick brings them here for us to study."

"Normally," Dick said, "we'd just cremate them or give them to a medical school."

"Why do you bring them at night?"

Gregor said this was sort of a side project for him. During the day, he worked at some lab in Oakland, amidst all the other medical buildings. "This," he said, "is more of a personal interest, so it's almost like a private endeavor. I don't get paid for it. It's just a hobby, really."

"Interesting hobby."

Dick agreed, with a strange inflection in his voice and a knowing look on his face, and wished Gregor good luck with his work. "I have to get home," he said. "I promised the wife we'd catch a late movie."

Gregor thanked us and went back inside, and we climbed back into the truck.

I was so focused on what sort of purpose Gregor's research could possibly serve that I forgot to ask Dick to drop me off at my car. We'd already woven through the back streets of the South Side and were across the Tenth Street Bridge, near the jail. "Oh, shit. Hey, Dick, could you let me out? I'm parked on Carson."

He laughed, but not at me, really. "You should have told me that before. I guess you were too worried about whether I'd notice you were drunk, eh?"

I went red. "Yeah, I guess I was."

21

"What the hell are you talking about?" Adam was on his way to needing another cab this evening.

Luckily, he had Dave with him to drive. "Mad Cow? Nutritional value of people? That's crazy, man. Where is this place?"

"I'm not really sure. I told you, I slept on the way there, and I was sorta preoccupied when we left, so I didn't pay attention." I shook my head and took a drink. "I think it's somewhere in the twenties. Like, twenty-third-ish, maybe."

"I can't believe you don't know where it is." Dave stole a cigarette from Adam's pack.

I couldn't believe it either. This was one of those things that you ought to remember in every detail, especially when it happened no more than an hour ago. I felt a tinge of humiliation somewhere in the heat of my face, and I tried to recover, well, something. Some sense of not being a total waste of space, a total idiot. "I am going to another one of those meetings, though. Tomorrow night."

Adam's face lit up. "Really? Awesome. What time?"

"Seven-thirty. They have a password and everything. It's fucking crazy, man."

"What's the password?"

I figured that Adam, the lit major that he was, would appreciate it. "'I should have been a pair of ragged claws, scuttling across the floors of silent seas.'"

"Eliot. Nice. That's a good one. How'd they come up with that, I wonder." He actually stroked his chin.

"The guy, Synchek, he says he's just always liked that line, so why not."

I suppose I should have, but I didn't feel like I was betraying anyone's trust. Yes, it was a secret society kind of thing, but it's not like I was a member. And I only told Adam because he'd get a kick out of it. Besides, what harm could possibly come from Adam knowing the password?

If I were ten years old, and if this were that little clubhouse with the *no girls allowed* sign, there's no question that my membership would have been terminated following this slip of the tongue. An honor exists among children that is somehow lost as we get older, and I am ashamed to say that I too have been affected by this phenomenon.

I didn't think about it like that at the time, and neither did my friends. Why should they have?

"Maybe I'll stop by," Adam said in that joking manner that suggests a hint of seriousness. "Think they'd mind?"

I let out an exaggerated breath, not quite a laugh, and tried my hand at some of Virginia's acutely skilled tone. "No, I don't think they'd mind at all. Seems to me like they're pretty much open to the public."

"Awesome. Where is it?" This was a serious question.

I was about to tell him the truth, which is to say I was going to tell him that I honestly had no idea, but we were interrupted by a group of college kids, three of them, and their recognition of "that guy who ate those people in Canada." Two of them appeared to be brothers. I would have even guessed they were twins, were it not for the height difference and the striking difference in the widths of their noses.

It was the taller one who set the shot in front of me. "Holy shit," he said, "I can't believe you hang out in here."

I shook my head at Dave and Adam. "Neither can I."

The unrelated one stood behind the brothers, his cap down, almost hiding his eyes. "Do you mind signing my hat?" He took it off his head and held it out between the heads of his friends.

Adam stifled his amusement by going after his beer. Dave,

well, Dave wasn't the stifling sort.

Neither was I. I laughed right out loud, right in the kid's face. This might as well have been a night at the Improv. "Really man? An autograph? On your hat? You're kidding, right?"

He looked confused. Wasn't I famous? Don't famous people sign things? It was obvious he'd never been out of Pittsburgh.

If I hadn't been so wrapped up, so lost in the absurdity that was becoming my life, I like to think I'd have been a little more polite. "No, man. I'm not signing your hat. That's fucking stupid."

He covered his head back up, and the brothers laughed at him the way you're allowed to laugh at your friends. "Smooth, dipshit."

I held up the shot glass full of clear liquid. "What is this?"

"Grey Goose." The tall one looked really proud of himself.

I slid it over to Adam. "Thanks for the thought, guys, but I'm not a vodka man."

"He's a whiskey man," said Virginia, who'd been serving drinks at the other end of the bar the way they throw bread to refugees crowded around relief effort trucks. She set a big fucking bourbon in front of me. "It's still on them," she said before hurrying back to the poor starving bastards dying for a drink.

"Thanks, boys." I raised my rocks glass.

We took the shots. "We figure anyone who went through what you went through deserves a shot." It was the short one, and he caught his mistake all on his own. "A lot of shots, actually."

"Amen to that. Thanks, guys." I nodded to them, which was, in effect, my way of shooing them off with a wave of my hand. Only they didn't get the hint. "Um, I'm sort of in the middle of something here, boys. If you don't mind."

Heads down, they found themselves a table, and Adam rolled his eyes. "He asked you for your autograph. Unbelievable." He paused a moment, then took a few sips of his beer. I think he was trying to pick up where we'd left off before my celebrity pushed the conversation to the back, but he was getting drunk, and to my relief, he gave up.

He did stumble across something during his search, though. “So, what’s up with you and Virginia?”

I checked to make sure she was out of ear-shot. As luck would have it, she wasn’t even behind the bar. “Nothing, man.”

And then I stopped. I thought about telling him everything, the way you think about admitting to cheating on a test (if you’re a conscience-driven person, that is). The way I’d thought about telling the shrinks that I sort of enjoyed the taste of my friends. The way I thought about telling anyone about my inner conflict concerning my newfound interest in cannibalism.

I thought about it in the same way, which is to say that I thought it would be a bad idea.

As it turns out, I didn’t need to tell him; Virginia was standing behind us, holding a tray loaded with dirty glasses. She told him for me. “We fucked for a few days, and then we didn’t anymore.”

I shot her a look that I hoped would either shut her up or knock her unconscious. It did neither.

“You have to be honest sometime, Travis,” she said, and then continued, looking at me while she spoke to Adam. “We were fucking, but then he went back to not being able to get it up, so we stopped.”

At that moment, I was closer to hitting a woman than I’d ever been. Instead, I gave her my best *fuck you* face, finished my drink, and went home.

22

My buzzer buzzed, and when I opened the front door, there was Malcolm. "Are you ready to go, Mr. Eliot?"

"Yeah. And you can call me Travis, by the way."

"Oh. Ok, Travis. I see you've learned about what kind of people we have in our group."

He meant my clothes, and he was right. I didn't want to show up in my other duds this time. I wasn't about to buy a new suit for these bastards, but I had to step it up at least a little. I'd had time to go out and pick up some black slacks and a nice shirt and new tie.

"Nice tie," he said, and he handed me the blindfold. We walked down to the car.

"Again with this? Really?"

"Sorry, but Walter insisted. And you understand. We need to protect ourselves."

"Protect yourselves from what?"

"Hah! 'Protect ourselves from what?' You're a pretty funny guy there, Travis."

He opened the door for me, and I got in and put the blindfold on again. Malcolm got in and started the car. He called someone to let them know I was with him, and we were on the way.

My phone rang.

"Hey Malcolm, do you mind if I pull this blindfold up a little to see who's calling?"

"No. Go ahead. We're still in the city."

I lifted the blindfold off my right eye and saw that it was Adam. I didn't ask about answering it.

"What's shakin', duder?"

“Hey man. I was just pulling up to your place because I was close by and I thought maybe you’d want to smoke a little, and I saw you get into a car with some guy in a suit. I was right behind you until a minute ago. Who is that guy?”

Fucking Adam.

“Oh. Uh, I have an interview at KDKA.”

“An interview? I thought you had that meeting thing tonight. That’s why I thought you’d want to smoke. Keep you calm so you don’t pass out again.”

“Yeah. Well…”

“Wait wait wait. That guy’s giving you a ride to the meeting, isn’t he?”

“I’m kinda in the middle of something, man. Can I call you later?”

“I’m totally gonna follow you.”

Fucking Adam.

“And how are you going to do that?”

“You guys just got off the Fort Duquesne Bridge. 279 North, baby. I can catch up.”

“Adam, please. I’ll just call you later, all right?”

“You better, man. I want to know what their deal is. Peace.”

Fucking Adam.

I put my phone back in my pocket.

“You’re doing an interview with KDKA?” Malcolm scared the shit out of me. Adam got me all worked up, and I’d forgotten the man was up there, driving. “That’s interesting. It must have been a lot of fun doing all those shows after your accident, eh, Travis?”

“Fucking blast, Malcolm.” I suddenly wished I hadn’t told him to call me by my first name.

The rest of the way, he asked me questions about people I’d met in L.A. and what were they like and a bunch of stupid shit like that. I honestly don’t remember the conversation very well because, even though I was 99% sure Adam wouldn’t try to catch us and also 99% sure he wouldn’t be able to find us even if he did decide to try,

Adam had sort of a knack for giving you the unexpected. I gave Malcolm the auto-pilot answers as I calmed my thoughts.

And then we were there. My blindfold was off, and I was somewhere north of the city. I looked back the drive to make sure Adam's dumb ass didn't follow us up. I stooped to untie and retie my shoe, just to give it an extra minute.

"I should have been a pair of ragged claws scuttling across the floors of silent seas." Malcolm had walked past me and given the password. And the guy inside opened the door.

"Come on, Travis. People are already here."

And in I went, a few paces behind Malcolm. I said hello to the doorman, or guard, or whatever it was they considered him to be, and I walked down the hall. I wanted so badly to give a good shove to the door of many locks, but I knew it wouldn't have opened anyway.

The door at the end of the hallway opened easily, though, although it was difficult to walk through. I had a feeling, as I watched myself open the door, much like the feeling I'd had when Jason and I took stab at cliff diving some years earlier. I stood there, atop a monster cliff, high above some big body of water, and I didn't move a muscle. Even with Jason's coaxing, I couldn't bring myself to jump. Bastard had to push me.

This time I jumped, and when I landed I ditched Malcolm and went straight for the bar, expertly avoiding two circles of conversation that threatened to pull me into their orbits. I made sure to make no eye contact, to get to the booze before anyone noticed me.

And I very nearly made it, too.

"Hello, Mr. Eliot. Nice to see you. Tony Conicella. We met at the last meeting, briefly."

Handshake. "Oh. Right. How are you, Tony? Where are your friends?"

"They're here somewhere." He looked for them, straining his neck and getting up on his toes to see over and around my head. "I don't know. They may be in the back, helping Walter or John Gregory with something."

"Hmm. I need a drink." I tried to use a tone that would let him know I didn't really want to talk. Either I'm no good with that tone, he didn't get the hint, or he just plain didn't care. He followed me to the bar and kept talking.

"I enjoyed your story, by the way."

"Most people do," I said into my ever-increasing serving of wine.

"I'm sure they do. No matter what they say, most people are fascinated by cannibalism. They just can't embrace that interest. Taboo, you know." He smiled at me and filled his glass. "You should get acquainted with some people. Follow me."

I reminded myself that I was there to find out who these people were—what they were—and I followed him.

He introduced me to Damien Rogers and his wife, Elaine. He was a lawyer with a firm that specialized in malpractice claims, and she was his wife. "I see no reason," Damien told me through his thin lips, "that we should both work. I make more than enough. Not to mention our investments." Elaine smiled and kissed him.

I was also introduced to Larry something and Bruce Rienhart, also attorneys, although I never learned for which firms. Larry was short and fat and balding. He snorted more than spoke, and he was sweating just standing there. Bruce was also a portly fellow, although his height thinned him out a bit. His moustache, like all good moustaches, gave him the look of a pedophile, but I have to say he gave me no indication that this stereotype fit him.

"We were just talking about the market." Larry raised a stubby hand to my shoulder. "How's your portfolio, Mr. Eliot?"

"Nonexistent. Yours?" There was a time I'd have gone along with this conversation. There was a time I'd have just kept talking because I knew he'd appreciate it.

Damien lit a cigar the size of a Louisville Slugger. "You should think about investing, Travis. People think that money is power, which is only true to a certain point."

Synchek snuck into the group. "Indeed. It used to be that those with money and land were the powerful. Now, the power is held by those who own the big businesses. Even if only in part."

Elaine Rogers worked her plastic face into a smile. It looked painful. She giggled. You could tell she was brought up with money and had no reason to outgrow the role of rich fifties housewife. "You boys and your power. You'll do anything to make yourselves feel like you're in control."

"Enough, Elaine." Damien shot a look at his wife. "Isn't that why you're here? Didn't you say it makes you feel powerful?"

"You're right dear." She left her head down for the rest of the conversation, which was neither very long nor very interesting.

At least, not for me. The rest of them were deep enough into it that I was left to listen to stock market babble: points, quarters, selling, mergers, and a slew of other words that I knew, but could make no sense of.

As I paid less attention to them, I paid more attention to the growing number of people filling the room with this exact conversation.

This was a power-hungry group. Power suits and ties all walking around, shaking the hands of other power suits and ties. I could see the Lexus key chains resting on the marble tables of the foyers. I could smell the money oozing out of their pores. I could have reached out and grabbed hold of their desire to have more. Not more money or more stuff, although I'm sure they'd have been more than pleased with both; they wanted to *be* more than everybody else. They wanted to be higher on the food chain, to be the lions that the rest of the creatures on the savannah feared.

It was scary. As cordial, as polite, as friendly as they were, they all had the look of predators. It was scary because I could identify with them, even if I couldn't understand them.

Synchek noticed my silence. "Mr. Eliot, I'm glad to see you." He pulled me a few steps away from Larry, Bruce, and Damien,

Attorneys at Law. "Enjoying yourself, I hope."

"I guess. To be honest, I'm not really sure why I'm here. It doesn't seem like I have much in common with these people."

He looked me up and down. "At first glance, I may have to agree with you. But you have more in common with these people than you might think."

"Well. If you say so." I looked around, but not for anything in particular. I think it made me feel better to look like I was searching for something. "Is anyone speaking tonight?"

"Not tonight. We only have guest speakers every so often. It's not always easy to find people of interest to our group, and most of us already know each others' stories. We come mainly for the sense of, well, fellowship, I suppose."

The word *cult* came to mind. Big, bold, flashing red letters.

"We're not like a cult, though, Travis. I don't want you to get the wrong idea. We're simply a little social club."

The doorman entered the room, shouting for everyone's attention. "Does anyone know a Thomas J. McGovern?"

There was no answer. He repeated the name. Still no answer. He thanked everyone and told them to go back to their conversations, then came over to Synchek. "Walter, we might have a situation, here. This guy out here isn't on the list."

"Why did you let him in, then?" Synchek looked annoyed.

"He knew the password."

El Presidente sighed and turned to me. "If you'll excuse me, I have to take care of this." He bowed his head and went out into the hall.

The door hadn't even closed behind him and the buzz was buzzing, beginning slow and quiet but picking up speed at an impressive rate, zero to sixty in six seconds flat. Between sips of wine, the name Thomas J. McGovern hovered over the rims of the glasses, the finger that makes the crystal sing.

"I don't know him," they said. "Nope. Don't know him. Nothing to worry about, though. Walter will take care of it."

Some pulses sped up. I could almost hear the racing beats of all these greedy hearts. It was a drum circle, the dreadlocks replaced with hair gel, the patchouli with Chanel. The energy of the room swelled like the plastic bag attached to the vaporizer I'd bought a couple years earlier, when I decided that *smoking* the pot was bad for me. You could see it in dilating pupils and beads of sweat dotting foreheads and upper lips.

I nudged Conicella. "Hey, Tony. What's the deal with this McGovern guy? Why does everyone seem so excited about him if nobody knows who he is?"

Conicella's smile seemed like a nervous one. "Apparently, he's not on the list. So somehow he found out about us and is trying to sneak in."

"So don't let him in, then. What's the big deal?"

"It's not that simple." He looked at me like he couldn't figure out why I couldn't add it up. "We can't just let him leave, go tell someone about us. If word got out, we'd… well, it wouldn't be good."

I was about to ask why it wouldn't be good, but a tap on my shoulder clasped its hand over my mouth.

"Nice to see you, Travis." It was Dick. My boss. Dave's uncle. Dick was there, grinning big.

"Dick? What are you doing here?"

"I'm a founding member. Almost twenty years now. What do you think?"

I didn't know what I thought. "Why weren't you here last time?"

"I was away on business. I'm sorry I couldn't hear you speak, by the way. They tell me it was fascinating." He, like everyone else, had his glass of wine, his cigar. He also had his suit, although it didn't look like Armani or whoever. My guess would be Sears. "So, what do you think of the place?"

"It's great."

"Yeah. We're proud of it. It's really grown from when it

started." He looked around. "Well, I just wanted to say hello. If you gentlemen will excuse me, I have to help Walter give this McGovern character the grand tour."

He and Conicella laughed. I couldn't find the joke, but laughed anyway. For some reason, I felt the need to fit in.

Once Dick left, I asked Tony what was included on this 'grand tour'.

"Oh," he said, "I'm sure he'll gain an intimate knowledge of our kitchen facilities." With that, he excused himself and went off to find his friends.

I refilled my glass and snuck to the front of the room, where a new podium, solid oak and imposing, had taken the place of the pine I'd shattered on my previous visit. A pattern of grapevines was carved into the front. It was excellent work. Not to say that I know anything about woodworking, but it looked good to me. Meticulous, even. Down to the veins in the leaves and a split grape here and there, where there was too much imaginary water for the imaginary skin to hold. I traced the vine with my fingers and stepped around behind the thing. It was hollow. A box with one side missing. It was hollow, but not empty.

The angel with the pixie-cut blonde hair was in there, arms wrapped around her shins, knees against her chest, her head down, eyes closed, and tongue barely peeking out between her lips, the way of some sleeping cats.

Scared the shit out of me, to be perfectly honest, but only for a moment. It's not every day one finds such a beautiful girl all folded up inside a wooden box. And it wasn't even Christmas.

I looked around to see if anyone was paying attention to me, but they were all still aflutter about this uninvited guest and probably wouldn't have noticed if I set fire to the place. So I squatted behind the podium, put a hand on the girl's shoulder, and gently shook her awake.

Her pupils shrank with the sudden addition of light, and after a groggy couple of seconds she said, "Oh. It's you. Hi."

"Hi. Sorry, but what are you doing in there?"

"Hiding from them," she said. "I didn't mean to fall asleep." She moved nothing but her lips and eyelids. "What are *you* doing up here?"

"Avoiding them."

"Why? They love you."

I peeked out at the guests, who were now beginning to find their way to their seats around the banquet tables. "They love me, eh?"

"You know they do. I saw the way you lit up when you saw them staring at you last time, listening to your story. Why aren't you down there, talking to them?"

"Honestly, I don't really like them."

She cracked her neck, yawned. "Then why are you here?"

"To find out why they're here, I guess." It was difficult to maintain this conversation; I found myself getting lost in her face. "Why are *you* here?"

"Walter's my uncle. He's been bringing me here since I was a kid. He took me in after my parents died. Twelve years." She may have been the saddest girl to ever hide inside a podium.

"He told me he didn't know who you were." I said it without even thinking about how she'd take it, but she seemed fine.

"I knew he would," she said. "He wouldn't want me talking to you. He wouldn't want me to, um, ruin the surprise."

I went from squatting to kneeling. "Oh? And what surprise would that be?"

It was like her eyes had invisible arms that reached out, took hold of either side of my head, and forced me to stare at them until she was sure she had my undivided attention.

"These people," she whispered, "eat other people."

The thing about working in the morgue is you're always around dead people, so the thought of dead people doesn't bother you. The thing about this lovely little girl telling you that you're sitting in a room full of cannibals is that the thought of cannibals doesn't bother you. It doesn't bother you because you're not surprised about it. You've known all along.

There are people who have convinced themselves that the Holocaust never really happened. There are people who get diagnosed with some kind of terminal disease, but then convince themselves that the doctor has made a mistake, or maybe it was all a dream, or anything else that makes it easier to sleep at night. Or maybe they don't convince themselves. Maybe they just don't let themselves think about it at all.

People want to know, but not really.

And now, kneeling behind this grand podium stuffed with this gorgeous girl, in this beautiful room full of suits and dresses and wine and pearls and rich-folk conversation, I really knew.

"What's your name?"

"Angela."

"Are you one of *these people*?"

"No, I'm not. Are you?"

Would you believe I didn't know how to answer this question? You'd think there'd be a pretty clear line on this one. Yes or no. "Um. I don't know. I don't think so." I felt a panic rising in my stomach, like that myth about Pop Rocks and soda. "You want to get out of here? Like, now?"

She reached out for my shoulder. "We can't. If my uncle finds out, he'll get suspicious. He's a little paranoid. I'll get you my number before the end of the night."

All I could do was nod. Her not-so-subtle revelation had me freaking out more than I was willing to show.

"It'll be all right. Just don't start freaking out, ok? We'll talk more later."

I started to say something, but she shushed me with a small, thin, red-tipped index finger to her lips, lined with dark brown and colored the same. She threw her head in the direction of the two-eyed, no-horned, buying, wealthy, people eaters.

I stood up and left her there, in the podium. Under other

circumstances, meeting her could have been a lot of fun. I guess we don't get to choose such things, though.

So I went back to the group. I just took a deep breath and walked up to them like nothing was amiss, like I was perfectly comfortable, like my mind wasn't racing.

Everyone was still talking about either McGovern or financial matters, which was fine by me. I had some serious thinking to do. I couldn't figure out why Synchek had left me out of the loop. If he wanted me join his little club, why wouldn't he have told me everything? Why try to sucker me in? Why was this girl, this wonderful hidden girl, hiding in the podium? Why wasn't she down here with everyone else? Why had I let myself ignore such obvious truths?

It was an exhausting few minutes.

It was almost 9:30. Almost feeding time. People began taking their seats, unfolding their napkins, talking about how excited they were about dinner. Some of them went to the bar and refilled their glasses.

"Why don't you come have a seat, Mr. Eliot." It was Damien, inviting me to his table.

What could I do? I had to sit with him. By this point, my head was so fogged up I'd have said yes to just about anything. "Ok."

"What did you think about the food last time you were here?" It was Damien's wife, Elaine, who was shifting the centerpiece as she talked. "Exquisite, wasn't it?"

In a cartoon, a light bulb would have appeared above my head, glowing bright and maybe exploding. The food. It was some dead guy. Or some dead woman. That was the food. That's what Synchek had given me when I left last time. That's what I'd eaten before taking Virginia home that night.

"I don't know if I'd say exquisite, but it certainly hit the spot." I'd already eaten someone.

Let's think about that a minute. *I'd already eaten someone.*

There was Jason, Erica, pilot guy, and now someone else. Someone I didn't know. Someone who wasn't survival or necessity. Someone who wasn't anything but dinner. I ate this person, and what happened? I didn't get drunk. *Couldn't* get drunk. I took Virginia home and tore her to pieces. For three days, I tore her to pieces. I slept better. I felt more awake, aware, stronger, fitter, happier. For three days I was King of the Fucking Jungle.

And then I wasn't. LT, he failed me. I was back to the tired and the lazy; back to, well, me. Only, not totally me. I was thinking an awful lot about the accident, and the surviving, and the corpses at work. I was becoming addicted.

I'd already eaten someone, and it was really fucking with me.

But let's get back to Mrs. Rogers.

"Well, *I* thought it was exquisite."

Mr. Rogers looked like he was ready to chuck that fucking trolley right at her head. "Oh, shut up, Elaine. It's not a *competition*, for Christ's sake."

And shut up she did.

"Now, Mr. Eliot— "

He was interrupted by Conicella, aheming. "Sorry to interrupt, Damien, but Walter wanted me to ask Travis if he'd join him for supper."

"Well, sure. I'd hate to continue boring him with the stock market. Poor guy." It was a joke. "Enjoy your meal, young man."

And with that, I was moved to the head table. The cool kids' table, if the cool kids were twisted, man-steak eating, well-off gentlemen with law degrees and Rolexes. I thought about that table at a high school prom with all the prom court sitting around it. I couldn't tell much of a difference.

Tony took a seat two seats down from mine, the chair between us like the urinal between two men who respect the rules of the men's room. "Walter and Dick both wanted to talk with you during dinner. I didn't know you worked with Dick."

"Yeah, I work with Dick."

With Dick, that clever bastard who had me delivering bodies the way the Good Humor man delivers ice cream. I could've killed him if he wasn't my boss and related to one of my good friends. I couldn't believe he never told me he was a PEP member, a *founding* member.

"I didn't know he was a member."

"He's one of the oldest. Without him, we'd never have been able to pull this off." Tony would have been able to answer most of my questions, if only I'd thought to ask him. He seemed like the kind of guy who was more than happy to let you know that he knows. He also seemed to think that I knew what was going on, that I hadn't been duped. "You like working with him?"

"I do, actually. He's a pretty cool boss."

"I would imagine so."

And then our conversation was interrupted by the kitchen doors opening to allow Stearns, the asshole, to enter with a cart stacked high with plates covered by metal lids. He wheeled the thing around, stopping at each table, setting a covered dish in front of each person. Nobody removed the lids.

Cansellini, Conicella's other buddy, followed shortly with another cart.

I found myself sitting at a table with six covered plates and four empty seats. I had trouble breathing as I thought about what I'd find under the lid in front of me. I knew what it would be, but was unsure about how I'd be able to handle it. I mean, eating a person when you don't know it's a person is one thing, but if you know, well, it brings up all sorts of interesting moral and ethical questions. It tests your constitution. It is, if nothing else, a defining moment.

The waiters, in their expensive suits and with their slick hair, took their seats across the table from me, offering a "Hello" and a "Nice to see you".

I couldn't speak, so I nodded to each of them. I even tried to force a smile, but I don't think it went over too well, which didn't really matter because they were both distracted by Synchek, Dick, and Gregor, who entered the room like hitting the mute button on the television. Everything went quiet, and everyone watched as they approached my table. Dick sat between me and Conicella. Gregor (or, John Gregory, as I'd figured out by this point) left an open seat between us, to my left.

Synchek didn't sit down. He looked over the room and cleared his throat. "Before we begin this evening's meal, I'm quite sure there are many questions concerning today's uninvited guest. Although we're not certain how this young gentleman learned of our little group, I can assure you that the situation has been handled, and he won't be telling anyone else of our existence. And with that, enjoy the meal."

There was a round of applause, and then the sounds of the stacking of metal lids, the scraping of forks and knives on the china. The sounds of people—rich, classy people—talking through full mouths, mmming and ooohhing over the food. I was beginning to think that everything becomes *exquisite* once you have money.

I looked for Angela but couldn't find her.

I looked at my plate, which Synchek had been kind enough to uncover for me. It did look damn good, steaming and colorful. I knew what it was, of course, but the presentation was so spectacular, so tempting, that even my morals barely managed to get in the way of my drooling. The roasted red potatoes gleamed with butter and were speckled with flecks of parsley. The spears of asparagus were there, poised to pierce taste buds with their earthy flavor and a touch of salt, of garlic. And the meat, covered in a dark, thick sauce, whole peppercorns sprinkled over its top like tiny black snowballs—God, it looked good.

"*Mangia*, Mr. Eliot," Synchek said, as he unrolled my silverware from its napkin nest. "John Gregory made sure to give you a fresh cut. It's quite tender. Succulent."

They call it a moment of truth. "Um. I'm not very hungry," I said, staring at my plate. "I think I may have had too much wine."

Dick slapped a hand to my back, where he left it as he told

me, "Food is what you need. Soak up that alcohol."

I started to sweat. "Is this… uh… is this Mr. McGovern?"

The rest of the table laughed, and Stearns choked on his mouthful of wine, spilling it down his chin and onto his food.

"Of course not." Synchek gave me an assuring look, which went a long way towards calming me down. I had no intention of eating anyone who'd just been murdered.

Gregor spoke up. "We have to bleed him out. He won't be ready for at least a couple days."

They all nodded in agreement, like this was perfectly respectable table conversation. And on the plates? In these peoples' mouths? It was some other poor bled bastard. Right in front of me, they were chewing and swallowing, washing him down with gulps of wine.

Dick, hand still on my shoulder, picked up his glass. "Eat, Travis. This is one of Gregor's best dishes."

"Yes, Travis. Eat." Synchek wasn't making fun like the rest. He was serious. He wasn't insisting I eat, not the way your grandmother might, not out of any desire to see me satisfied. This was a demand. A demand which, somewhere not too far beneath the surface, was a threat.

So I ate a potato. "It's good."

"The meat, Mr. Eliot. Try the meat."

I now had a hand on each shoulder. I now had five sets of eyes focused on my apprehension.

I held the steak in place with my fork and cut into it with my black-handled steak knife. Medium-Rare, I'd guess. Juicy, but not too bloody. Warm, pink center. Exactly the way I like it.

I put it in my mouth, chewed, swallowed. They all watched me. I wanted to vomit. I wanted it to make me sick.

But it was just so fucking good.

Through his own bite of dead-man, Stearns mumbled, "Not too bad, eh?"

"It's delicious," I said, to the whole table as much as to him. I wished I didn't mean it, but a man has to realize when he's been defeated.

By the time I finished soaking up the juices left on the plate with a piece of bread, I'd almost completely tricked myself into thinking it was just another dead cow or chicken, another pile of heated protein. Denial is a hard nut to crack, unless you're sitting at a table with a group of walking, talking nutcrackers.

"We lucked out tonight, Travis," Dick said through his napkin. "Nothing like a quality cut of meat."

The rest of the table agreed, nodding their heads and saying "mm-hmm."

"And nothing like a little murder to add some excitement to dinner, eh?" I'd never have said this if I'd never met Virginia. As soon as I said it, I hated myself for talking to that girl.

Synchek cleared his throat again. "This, Mr. Eliot, will never be spoken of again. It is unfortunate, yes. We do regret any instance in which we must take a person's life, but sometimes it cannot be helped. If we feel we are at risk, we'll do what needs to be done."

It's funny how the threat of death will straighten you out. No more funny business. Some people just have no sense of humor, I suppose.

"I can understand that." I was wearing my best poker face. "You do what you have to do to survive. I know that better than anyone."

"Exactly." He put his soiled napkin on his plate and excused himself. He walked over to one of the other tables and laid a hand on a man's shoulder, leaning down to get his mouth level with the man's ear. With a nod of his head, the man stood up and followed Synchek into the kitchen. The man had a narrow waist and huge, broad shoulders, like a gymnast or a swimmer. Although I only saw him from the back, I thought him at least ten years Synchek's junior.

"Who's that guy?" I directed my inquiry at no one in particular, figuring someone would reach out and snatch it from the air above the table.

People want to know, and they want other people to know they know.

I thought it was going to be Conicella who answered me, but it turned out to be Stearns. Like a frog going after a fly, it was Stearns. "That's Michael Devereaux. Detective, or Lieutenant, I'm not entirely certain. He's been a member for, what, seven years?" He stood up and stretched his belly. I imagined him at home on Thanksgiving, belt loosened, pants unbuttoned, getting ready to watch football after his person leg dinner.

"I imagine," he continued, "that Walter would like him to find out who this McGovern character is."

I couldn't resist. "Or, who he *was*, anyway."

"Well, he'll be a part of us soon enough," Dick said. "That's what a lot of cannibals throughout history have believed, anyway."

"You don't believe that?"

"No, Travis. I don't really believe in much of anything anymore. Too many years of the deceased as my only company. One of the drawbacks of the job, I'm afraid."

By this time, everyone had cleaned their plates and were again standing in their groups, like gnats waiting to get into the eyes and nose and ears of some innocent passerby.

"Come on, son." Dick stood up, dropped his napkin to the table. "Let's mingle with Pittsburgh's elite."

And mingle we did, although I couldn't tell you with whom; it was like meeting clones of the same man, only with different clothing, different hair-colors, different wives. Dinner was the half-time of a game whose only rules seemed to be talking about money, trying to one-up whoever you were talking about money with, and completely avoiding the fact that you just sat down to a nice meal of broiled man-flesh.

This left me with little to say, considering I really had no interest in financial discussion and a great deal of interest in the fact that every single person in this room was a cannibal. They'd made me one of them, and then wouldn't talk to me about what had made me one of them.

It really wouldn't have bothered me, all this boring babble, if I hadn't suddenly felt more energetic and talkative, more restless, antsy, weirded out, afraid for my life, uncomfortable, and more than a little bit concerned about the fact that I'd just eaten someone I didn't even know.

And let's not forget about suddenly needing to fuck. I thought about Virginia. Dirty thoughts. Good thoughts. Well, maybe not so much *good* as *fun*.

It was impossible to pretend I was interested in all this talk about oil prices and the DOW, NASDAQ, whatever. I mean, people are into whatever they're into, and these people just so happened to be into money and power. Good for them. Whatever gets you off, you know? Those things just aren't the tickling of my pickle. What can you do?

You can slip out while nobody's paying attention, that's what you can do. You can mention to the air that you have to use the restroom, and where is the restroom? Then you can start off in that direction, loop around the rest of the crowd, get yourself into that long hallway, and finally out the door.

But once you get out there, you realize that you have no idea where *here* is, and that you'll have to find someone to blindfold you and take you home.

So I slinked back inside and found Dick. "Dick, can I get a ride?"

"Sure, kid. You going home or you going out? I'm sure you have all sorts of energy right now." Dick was full of surprises.

"I need the bar," I said.

"Gonna find a woman there, huh?"

I just looked at him.

He smiled. "It used to do that to me at first, too. Hang on a sec. I'll tell Walter I'm taking you home. I'm about finished with this for the night anyway."

23

"You want to fuck, don't you?"

"I haven't even said hello to you yet."

"You still want to fuck."

"I want to drink."

"You want to fuck."

"Fine, I'll fuck. But can I have a drink first?"

"No."

"God. You need it that bad? Ok. I'll drink afterwards. Let's go in the back."

"Here's your Woodford, you fucking snob. I could tell you wanted to fuck as soon as you walked in the door."

"How's that?"

"I don't know. I can just feel the vibes. I sound like a goddam hippie or something. *Vibes*. It's just a gift I have."

"Good gift."

"Yeah. You'd be amazed at how horny everyone is, though. All the time."

"Everyone?"

She tongued her lips, but only a little. It was subtle, and I like to think she was trying to hold it back, but I'm sure that's just my ego talking. "Yeah," she said. "*Everyone*."

She went off to be a good bartender, flirting with the boys, persuading them to drink whiskey because "no self-respecting woman wants a man who'll drink a key-lime martini".

Virginia and her little bum in those black pants.

"It's been a boring night. I'm glad you came in."

I adjusted my imaginary tie. I'm a big dork. "Glad to see me, eh?"

She rolled her eyes. "Don't flatter yourself. I'd flirt with Hitler if he was here right now. And I'm fucking Jewish."

A man in Dockers and a black t-shirt walked in and all the way to the other end of the bar, Virginia's eyes on him the whole way. She growled as he walked by. "Look at those shoulders. They're so hot it hurts me."

I thought about eating his liver. "Well, go take his money."

"Oh, I'll take more than his money." She raised her eyebrows, shot me a playful smirk, and went bouncing down the bar. (She'd admitted she knew how to get any guy's attention: "If they're too big for me to dance with, I might as well use them for something.") I watched through stolen glances, a flipbook with pages missing. She was down there long enough for a few more patrons to arrive, although not enough of them to make the place busy.

I drank and fantasized about cutting the meat from that guy's shoulders and using the bones as a coat hanger. How dare he waltz in here with his muscles and steal Virginia's attention from me. Sure, I was only after the sex, but there was a bit of pride in there, too. Not to mention a near-rabid libido running wild in my pants. LT was in no mood for this shit. He'd been lying down for too long, and now, again, he was up and ready for some serious fun.

His fun, though, was now at the other end of the bar, running her eyes like naughty hands over this asshole's shoulders, over the ridges of his muscles, and, unknown to him, down the center line of his abs and down his pants.

This last part is merely the speculation of a jealous and sexually frustrated young man at the end of a stressful day. She was probably content with just the shoulders. But she had a dirty mind, that girl, so you never know.

Right or wrong, I was still pissed off, and I've found that when anger is concerned, I'm about as subtle as a Catholic fundamentalist outside an abortion clinic. I might as well carry a placard that says, quite simply and eloquently, "FUCK YOU." Red letters. Big, red, angry letters.

"Hey there, cranky."

I couldn't even look at her.

"Oh, relax. Just because he's hotter than you doesn't mean you're not getting laid tonight." She laughed, which could have been at me, or herself, or anything, really—I couldn't tell—and she poured me another drink. "Where's Adam? Isn't he supposed to be coming in tonight?"

"Why? You want to fuck him tonight, too?" I tried to make it sound like a joke, like I wasn't upset at all.

Although she had a terrible wink that looked completely foreign on her face, the scowl she gave me was something she must have been born with. "Maybe I do." She started to walk away.

"Wait. Don't go." Surprisingly, she didn't. "I'm sorry. I've had sort of a rough night so far. That's all. I don't mean to be a dick."

"And I don't mean to be such a slut. I guess we are what we are, right?"

"Ok, ok. You're right. I had no right to make it sound you were such a slut."

"You just don't want me to stop serving you. I know what you're up to." The tone was still there, but at least the scowl had disappeared. And the tone was almost always there, so I was beginning to learn to pay it no mind.

"Damn right I want you to keep serving me. I'm in the mood to get totally fucked."

"See. I knew you wanted to get fucked." She adjusted her bra, sneaky wench. "So what was so bad about your night?"

People want to know.

"I can't even begin to explain it to you."

"You were at that meeting thing, right? Wasn't that supposed to be tonight?"

"Yeah, but you weren't supposed to remember that."

"I have my moments." She made a quick scan of the bar,

searching for empty tanks. "Hang on a sec. I have to go fuck Shoulders real quick. We'll continue once I get my pants back on." She smiled and took the man another drink.

He was definitely hotter than I was. You may have even called him "chiseled". He had that square jaw thing and a few days' stubble, a solid smile, and, of course, those damned shoulders.

He was making friendly with Virginia, and she was buying it. Smiling and laughing and flaunting. She was good. But she was quick about it this time.

"So, how was it?" I asked when she got back to me.

"Oh, the sex was great. Much better than his looks would lead you to believe."

"What do you mean?"

She went into math tutor mode. "Guys who look that good usually suck in bed. It's because they never have to work for it. Well, that, and because girls nowadays are way too quick to suck a dick. Anyway, guys like you are different. You feel like you have to prove yourselves, which means that, most of the time, you're way better in bed."

"Wow. I assume you've done a lot of research about this."

"I've done enough, yeah. You dick." She stopped a moment, trying to remember something. And she did. "So. That meeting?"

Damnit. "Right. The meeting. The meeting was, well, just as weird as the first one."

"You figure out what they're about yet?"

I thought about what I'd look like carved, grilled, and garnished with a sprig of parsley. And then I thought the same about Virginia. And sure, she would have been great eating, but I didn't want that for her.

"They're just a group of people who have been through things sort of like I have." I lit a cigarette and fooled around with the ash tray, played with the straw in my drink; anything to avoid eye contact. "Lots of plane wrecks and camping accidents and missing limbs. Lots of interesting stories and tailored suits."

"That part doesn't make sense to me. I mean, do only rich people have these accidents?" She was climbing down the ladder, one rung of logic to the next, like she would have with a proof. "And why are they so interested in you?"

I suddenly longed for women with makeup, miniskirts, large breasts, and small brains. The thing about these smart women, these women like Virginia, who pay attention and rely on their brains rather than their bodies, is that they figure too much out on their own. These women, they'll tear you to bits.

"Everyone's interested in me," I said. "It's like when… I mean, when you're single, nobody wants anything to do with you, but once you have a girlfriend, they rub up on you like cats in heat."

"Cats in heat. Good one."

"Thanks."

"What's it got to do with your well-dressed friends?" Like an arrow, this girl.

"Well, now that I have this great story, and since I've told it on television and everything, people are all over me. Nobody gave a shit before." I sipped and thought for a moment. "Well, some people cared, I guess. But then I had to eat them."

"Good thing I don't care, then. I mean, if that's what happens to people who really care about you."

"Yeah. Good thing."

She shook her head at me. "Well, since you obviously aren't going to tell me anything interesting about your little meeting, I'm going to go do some work."

"Thanks for letting me off the hook."

"Sure. But, just out of curiosity, what do you do to people who only care about Tiny Travis?"

"It's *Little* Travis, thank you. And I usually eat them, too. They don't seem to mind much, though." Nothing like a cunnilingus joke to brighten your spirits.

"I know it," she said, and she turned and went back to work.

She went back to work, and it got busy, and I got bored. I

didn't know anyone who came in, although I did get a couple shots from people who knew me. That pseudo-famous thing was all right sometimes. But, shots or not, I was still bored and in no mood to hang around another three hours for closing time.

"What do you mean you're leaving? I thought you were coming back with me." It was sort of flattering. She seemed genuinely disappointed.

I told her not to worry, she could stay and fuck Shoulders one more time tonight, and that I'd leave my window open so she could climb in after work.

"How dare you tell me how many times I can have sex with a man in one night."

I told her how to get onto the fire escape at my place, and I left. I figured I'd spend the rest of my evening with LT. It had been so long since we'd been able to play together.

24

The thing about opening a window is the window has to be closed when you begin. My window was not closed. Nor was it any longer a window. At some point in the evening, the smooth single pane of glass that separated me from the elements had been shattered. At some point in the evening, the lock had been unlocked, and the wooden frame lifted.

As I stood in my kitchen, eyeing the jagged edges of what used to be my window, all I could know for sure was that someone had broken in.

The rest, merely guesses. Someone may have swept the glass from the floor, seeing as it was clean. Someone may have made a pot of coffee, which was still almost full and still steaming. They may have eaten something and washed the dishes, which were now in the drying rack.

Yes, they were only guesses, but they were educated. Logical.

I got the feeling that I would find a little girl with golden locks sleeping in my bed. It really wasn't a bad thought.

It was, however, inaccurate. There was no girl in my bed. As it turns out, she was in my shower, and she hit me in the head with a shampoo bottle when I threw open the curtain.

"Ow, dammit! That hurt!"

"What do you think you're doing? Opening the curtain while someone's taking a shower?" Apparently, I'd startled her.

"You are in *my* shower, Angela."

She didn't close the curtain, didn't cover her chest or her crotch with her hands. She just went on with her shower, and with her rationalization for nailing me in the head with my own bottle of some sort of very expensive French shampoo. "It was just self-defense. I didn't know it was you, or else I wouldn't have hit you."

She lathered her left leg, toes hooked on the edge of the tub. Her inner thigh, fair and delicate and appetizing in an inedible kind of way, dripped with tiny bubbles and shone with its thin coat of water.

"You could have been anyone," she said.

I snapped out of my trance. "*I* could have been anyone? It's my apartment. You're in my shower. I come home to find a broken window, and *I* could have been anyone?"

She shrugged and switched legs. "Well, you never know."

I sat on the toilet. "What are you doing here, anyway?"

"I'm showering. Those people always make me feel so dirty." She rinsed, the water splashing off her clean skin and onto the dirty bathroom floor. She arched her back, her round, small-girl breasts now in the streaming water. It was a gratuitous shower scene from some bad '80's flick. (Ok, maybe not *that* bad...)

"You just gonna sit there and stare at me, or do you want to hand me the shampoo?"

"You mean the shampoo you threw at my head?"

"Yes I do."

I picked the bottle up from the floor and handed to her. "So, why are you here again?"

"Well," she said, spitting water from her lips, "you left before I could get you my number, and I needed to talk to you as soon as I could, and it was a piece of cake finding your address, so there you have it."

"What? That whole celebrity thing?"

"You're in the book, actually. If you're in the phone book, you're not really a celebrity."

"Right." Sometimes, I'm a bit of an ass.

"Are you drunk?"

"No. Just a little dazed. Something's not right in my head."

"Great. Well, we have to talk about my sociopathic uncle. A shower should straighten you out. Get in."

"In the shower?"

"No. In the toilet. Of course in the shower. It'll help."

"I… uh…"

"What?"

"I don't want to make you uncomfortable is all."

She laughed. "Why would I be uncomfortable? Because you're excited? You've been watching me wash myself for like five minutes. And I know what you had for dinner. Of course you're excited. Now come on. We don't have all night."

It was rough, but you know that whole *a man's got to do* thing. And apparently I had to get into the shower with a beautiful and mysterious girl who had broken into my apartment. It was about time for a surprise to turn out to be a good thing.

I took off my shoes and socks. My pants hit the floor, spilling some change onto the black and white tiled floor, a nickel rolling behind the toilet. I pulled my button-down over my head, along with the t-shirt beneath it. I pulled the elastic band of my CK boxers (say what you will—the man makes comfortable underwear) away from my body and let the shorts drop to my feet.

And there was LT, bobbing up and down like a springboard whose diver has just left to find the water.

"Come on," she said. "I'll wash you." She stepped to the end of the tub, the water now only hitting her feet.

I stepped into the shower, facing her, and the slightly hot water fell onto my back, trying to push while LT tried to pull me into her.

I wasn't budging, though.

Angela worked up a lather and told me to turn around, she would start with my back. "Wow. Your butt is so small."

"I haven't showered with anyone else in a long, long time," I told her.

"It's good to get clean when someone can see," she said,

slowly going over my back, half washing, half massaging. "It's almost like confession. It's best when someone else washes you."

I remembered the feeling of being washed very well; someone's clean hands covered with soap, washing off what I couldn't get to. The last few times this happened, I felt like a shoe being polished, a car being waxed. The nurses could very well have been old black men in the subways or teenagers at their first jobs.

This was different. This was not her duty. She was cleaning me because she knew I needed to be cleaned. It was her own personal baptism. She was making me a part of her church.

She finished the back of me and told me to turn around. I did, and she was smiling. "Feels good, doesn't it?" She looked down. "I guess that was a stupid question, huh?"

"They say there's no such thing as a stupid question." I raised my right arm to allow her access to my armpit. "Of course, They fuck things up a lot of the time."

Without another word from either of us, she finished the front of me. She was… thorough… and even when she was washing LT, she was completely non-sexual about it. It's a great feeling to be both excited and soothed.

With the steam of reheated mac-n-cheese rising to my face (*reheated* because these were the leftovers of a B & E) and that wonderful post-shower lightness to my skin and head, I waited for Angela to come out of the bathroom. She'd said I should eat something while she stayed in the shower. "I like to meditate once I've finished all the work of getting clean," she said. "I like the steam and the way it sounds when you cover your ears and listen to the water hitting you, like it's actually inside your head."

So I ate and waited, and she eventually emerged with a towel on her head and another wrapped around her torso. She was so small that the towel covered all of her knees and at least a third of her shins. "What are you thinking?"

"Nothing, actually." I swallowed. "I was just waiting and not thinking." It was a welcomed, if unintentional, break from my head, even if it had only lasted a few minutes.

"I think it's strange how when you have the most to think about, your brain can go completely empty." She stole a bite of my food and said through a full mouth, "I'm sorry to jumpstart your head like this, but there's no time. I have to make you think again."

I wasn't thrilled about it, but I nodded in acceptance of the situation.

"First of all, you should know that my uncle is a suspicious man, and I'm sure he has someone keeping an eye on you. It's the way his mind works. I mean, he doesn't want to end up in jail, you know?"

I nodded again. It was all I could do.

"I broke in because I want to tell you my story, and I want to tell you my plan."

25

"When I was twelve, my parents died. Somehow, my dad managed to run the car off the road and through some trees and eventually off a cliff—not a huge cliff, just a little one on the side of a hill—and they died when the car hit the ground. My uncle told me their bodies were so messed up they needed dental records to make sure it was them. I'm not sure why their licenses weren't good enough, but whatever.

"So we had a closed casket thing for them because my uncle didn't want me to see how awful they looked. At the funeral, I asked him where they wrecked—I hadn't thought about it until then, I was only twelve. He said it was on some road north of the city. Like I would have known any road names or anything anyway, you know? So that was good enough for me.

"Anyway, my parents, before they died, obviously, used to have Uncle Walter babysit me when I was little. It was, I don't know, once a week or so, like when they'd go out to dinner or something. But then they stopped going out. At least, they stopped going out without me. And one day my dad told me to tell them if I saw my uncle, if he stopped by the house or by my school. This was a few weeks before the accident, but I never saw him in those weeks, so I never even thought about it.

"So my parents died and my uncle was my closest living relative, and I always liked him and he always took good care of me whenever he'd watch me, so I went to live with him. And then one day he told me he was going to take me to dinner. A special dinner, he said, at a special place, to show me how happy he was to have me with him.

"He took me to this really fancy place downtown with candles and chandeliers and everything, but he took me really late. There were no waitresses or anything. Just the chef, who was my uncle's friend.

"Uncle Walter told me that his friend made food that tasted better than anything I'd ever eaten, and that it was so good that it actually made you feel better after you ate it. He said it was so good that it would even help me get over what happened to my parents. It would make me feel so good it would be impossible for me to be sad. And he said I was special, because his friend wouldn't cook for just anyone.

"And you know, he was right. After dinner I felt better. It's not like I wasn't sad at all, but I was better. I felt sort of strong, like I'd be able to handle anything a little more easily. It was a pretty intense feeling.

"My uncle told me not to tell anyone about his friend. He said there wasn't enough of his friend's food to spread around, so we had to keep it a secret. It seemed like a fair deal to me. I got to feel stronger and happier and less empty, and all I had to do was keep it to myself. So we would go down there once a month or so for dinner.

"And then, after a while, there were more people there, eating this magical food, so I asked him about it. He said his friend had found a way to make more of it, so now he could help more people feel better. After a few years, there were so many people that we all couldn't eat in the restaurant anymore, so my uncle bought the warehouse, and we started eating there.

"By this time, I was like seventeen. I asked him, for the first time, what the food was. What does Gregor put into it? What kind of meat is it? So he tells me some Native American myth about this guy that eats this food, and he gets stronger and stronger, and he can do things most other people can't, and all this other wonderful stuff, just because he's eating this food. He tells me it's not just a myth, that this food really does this. And he finally tells me that the food is other people. He said the reason it makes you so much better is because you absorb the dead person's spirit, and two spirits are better than one. A person's spirit has all strengths and no weaknesses. The weakness comes from the brain, he said.

"Of course I freaked out and told him I was going to go to the police and he'd go to jail and all that. Then he told me that my parents were going to go to the police too, and look what happened to them. And it wouldn't do any good anyway, since some of the people who ate with us were policemen. He said he only wanted me to be involved because he loved me so much and wanted me to be happy. He said he'd rather not have to have me killed. That was unreal. I mean, when does anyone say that to you and actually mean it?

"So I never told anyone. I stopped eating it, though. God, that was so much harder than quitting smoking. It was awful. I'd get the shakes and everything. I'd vomit. It was bad. I would have left, but they'd have been able to find me—all that money and resources and everything.

"And I kept going down to the meetings with him because I figured I'd have to know what was going on, just in case. I told Uncle Walter that if it made him feel good, I was ok with it, but I wouldn't eat it anymore. He was fine with that, actually, just as long as I never told anyone and he never had to kill me.

"So, for the last, what, nine years or so, I've just been having this fucked up life. And every year they kill and eat more and more people. And it has to stop.

"I was ok—well, not ok, but better with it when they only ate people who were already dead. But this murdering people thing has got to stop. I can't let it happen anymore.

"That's why I need you."

26

The mac-n-cheese was gone and I needed a beer. I knew enough to know I didn't want to think about this, and enough to know that I wouldn't be able to think about it if I drank enough to pass out.

But I had no beer. No whiskey. Nothing. It wouldn't have mattered anyway, considering what I'd had for dinner.

All I had was a hanging jaw and the sudden inability to blink. I couldn't figure out how I'd gotten involved in this, or why Synchek wanted to get me involved. I hadn't thought about it before.

"None of this makes any sense," I said.

Angela put her hand on my head. "No, it doesn't."

"Why did they want me?"

She took the towel off her head, her hair all messed, which looked great. "Believe it or not, my uncle actually means well. He believes that eating the dead is good for the living, and he wants to do well by people. And he knows how addictive it is, so he knows that people who have already had a taste of it will almost always want more. They sucker people in. They don't tell you what they're about, and then they feed you. I mean, why would anyone suspect the food? They get you hooked on it, and you feel so good that you don't want it to stop. It's like a little cult."

"Great. A cult. Next you'll tell me they're going to castrate me or get me to drink that fucking wine laced with arsenic so we can hitch a ride in the tail of a passing comet."

She shook her head and laughed. "No. Nothing like that. They'll just make you stay."

"And how will they do that?"

"Well," she stood up and walked to the sink, "My uncle will

tell you that anyone who leaves only ends up strengthening the souls of those they left behind." She set a glass of water in front of me.

"Oh, so they'll just kill me." I took a sip of the water. "I guess it could be worse."

"Don't forget, after they kill you, they'll eat you."

"Right. They'll kill me and then they'll eat me." I was beginning to feel like a baby cow might feel if it had any idea that it would soon cease to be known as a calf, and henceforth be referred to as veal. "So, what do you have in mind?"

And then she screamed. Imagine a horror movie. Imagine sitting on something sharp. Imagine me choking on my sip of water. It was certainly a get-your-heart-going sort of moment.

I turned around to look at what used to be my window and saw a leg on its way to the floor. Connected to this leg was a small ass in tight black pants.

Once she was all the way in, Virginia looked at me and asked, "Who's the jumpy little girl?"

"This is Angela."

Angela, her face red and breath fast, forced a smile and a hello.

"And you gave me shit about that guy at the bar. Unbelievable."

I couldn't tell if she was actually upset, but figured she was. She slurred a little, and her posture was more rigid than usual. She stared at Angela like maybe she recognized her, and maybe it was because of something bad.

"What happened to your window?" She said it to Angela.

"Someone broke in."

"Oh. I see." She bit her lower lip. She bit her lower lip, and suddenly both of these girls were doing very naughty things in the bedroom of my imagination.

Virginia finally looked back to me. "No way, Travis. Don't even think about it." She may have known me a little too well.

"Think about what?" What else could I have said, you know?

They both looked at me like I was supposed to do something.

"Oh, uh, Angela, this is Virginia. She's a friend of mine." This situation was far too awkward for three in the morning. I found myself longing for a long night in the mountains. One good thing about being stranded and hungry and hurt is that, even though you think you might die, at least you can't get yourself stuck in the middle of two women, looking at you like you're a perverted sonofabitch, looking at each other like, well, two women with a man between them. If only they'd have realized that I was no man.

"So," I said, "how was the rest of work?"

Virginia crossed her arms. "Stupid. Lucrative, but stupid. I did talk to that guy all night, though, so it wasn't a total loss."

She'd swear up and down that she didn't play games, but I know when someone's trying to make me jealous. It would have worked, too, had I not already had so much on my mind.

"That's good," I said.

"Yeah. He's a pretty nice guy. Michael something. He said he's a detective or something. I think he may have only been trying to get some."

Angela kicked me under the cover of the table, raised her eyebrows, and threw a nod in Virginia's direction. I didn't get it. She shook her head. "I'm sorry Virginia, but his last name doesn't happen to be Devereaux, does it?"

I should have picked up on that kick to the shin.

"Maybe. I mean, it sounds right. But the bar's kind of loud, and I try not to know the last names of the guys who come in. Makes things too personal." Another glare at me. "Why? You know him?"

"Yeah. I think I do."

"Oh, that's good." Virginia sat at the table. "Travis, he wanted to meet you. He said he recognized you from TV. I didn't want to just bring him up though, so he's out waiting in his car."

"In his car?" Me and Angela—surround sound. We turned our heads like chihuahuas turning their ears to the sound of a car door slamming outside.

"Yeah, in his car. You mind if he comes up? He's a pretty cool guy. I think you'll like him."

"Oh shit," was all I could muster. It was like she'd given me a shot to the solar plexus.

"What? I just thought we'd hang out and drink a little more, and then he'd go home and we'd, well… He'd really like to meet you, anyway."

Angela stood up. "I'm going to the other room. I think you two should talk." She slid her chair under the table and went to the bedroom.

"What the fuck was that about?"

This was going to be difficult. "Listen, Virginia."

"You fucking that girl? Good for you. She's cute."

"No, I'm not."

"So why can't he come up?"

"This is going to be, well, odd, but you have to trust me, ok?"

She nodded, but I think she was skeptical.

"I can't tell you why he can't come up. It would be bad for you."

"What does that mean?" She crossed her arms and leaned back, away from me.

"Um, I might be in some pretty deep shit. Like, movie-type deep shit. And if I tell you about it, you'll be in it, too. And that guy down there, Michael, he's involved, and he's one of the bad guys."

"What the fuck are you talking about? You expect me to believe this shit?"

This must be what it's like when you try to argue that the lipstick on your collar isn't lipstick at all. It's cranberry juice, or ink, or blood, or whatever. "No, I don't, actually. But you have to. I'm telling you, you have to believe me. It's serious. We could die." I couldn't believe I was saying these things. I couldn't believe these things were true. "I need you to go down and tell him I'm asleep. I don't feel well. I'm fucking some girl. Anything. Tell him anything except that Angela is here. Nothing about Angela. Please. And don't let him think you know anything."

She stood a good, violent stand. "I don't know anything! This is fucking insane!"

"No shit. It's fucking ludicrous. But it's happening, and if he thinks you know *anything*, we'll get murdered, all right? Please just trust me."

"Fine. I'll tell him you found some bitch at the bar. But I'm coming over tomorrow."

"No, don't. I'll call you when everything blows over, I swear. But stay away from me until then. Promise me."

"Fine. I promise."

"And call me when you get home, just to let me know you're ok."

She went back to the window, crawled through, down the fire escape.

I didn't even think to tell her goodbye, be careful.

"Does she know about the meetings?" Angela's voice just about knocked me to the floor. I'd been watching Virginia crawl out the window and had forgotten anyone else was around.

"No, she doesn't." After another moment spent somewhere between thought and lobotomy, I said, "Well, she knows there were meetings, but not what they were about. And she doesn't know Devereaux has anything to do with them."

"I fucking hope not." It was the first I'd heard her cuss. It was hot, but for a different reason than Virginia's dirty mouth was hot. Virginia's language was sexy because she didn't need any help with it. It fit her like those black pants.

Angela's dirty mouth was sexy because it made you feel like she wanted to be dirty, but needed some coaxing. You just wanted to bring out the dirty in this girl.

Angela's dirty mouth was also sexy because it was right there in front of me, and I was in the mood to be dirty, too. Oysters and chocolate got nothin' on human flesh, you know?

"Help me cover this window."

We turned the table on its side. I got my drill and affixed it to the wooden window frame.

"I'm not tired," I told her.

"Neither am I. And I think leaving might be a bad idea. I mean, what if Devereaux's still out there?"

Beautiful and logical. No way to argue with that.

"Yeah, I think you should stay. I'll take the couch, if it'll make you more comfortable."

"You have to stop worrying about my comfort level. You think I invited you into the shower for nothing? You think I've been hanging out in a towel all night just because?"

The thing about meeting a girl like Angela is that you never know what to expect. You might find her sleeping in a podium at a gathering of urban cannibals. You might find her in your shower. You just never know. Maybe it was because of her rather irregular upbringing, or maybe she was just that way. And there's only one thing to do when a girl like Angela says she wants to stay the night: let her stay the night. A few times, if you have it in you.

27

In the morning, the little red light on my phone was flashing. First was Virginia, who wanted me to know she got home just fine. "How dare you fuck that girl when you're supposed to be worried I might die. You're a fucking asshole." I don't know how she knew I was fucking Angela just then, but she was right about the asshole thing. I deserved it.

Then it was Dave, asking if I'd seen Adam. He was supposed to pick up a quarter on the way home last night, which he may have done, except for the part about getting home. Did Adam crash at my place? If he did, tell him to get home with the weed.

"Messages?" Angela stood in the bedroom doorway, an olive green t-shirt hanging an inch too low, the letters NRG stamped across the chest and a picture of a carabiner on the back.

"Yep. Messages." Somehow I was able to tear my eyes from her and look at the clock. "Shit."

"What?"

"I have to be at work. Very soon." I looked at her again, all petite frame and knotted hair. "Fuck it. I'll just have to be a little bit late." Salivating, LT ready to go, I moved towards her.

She stopped me, her hands on my shoulders, arms rigid. "No. You have to go to work."

"I will. Just, late." I kept walking. Even though her arms wouldn't bend, she was too small to stay put.

"Pearson will be there."

And there it was. Nothing kills the mood quite like the thought of a man who is quite possibly out to make sure that you become what you eat.

She was right, of course. If I was going to be on time (or at least close to on time) I had no time to shower, so I got dressed and left. Although I did wash her out of my stubble, I would get to work with the scent of Synchek's niece hiding out in my pants. There's always something exciting about knowing you have sex on you, but this time I was a little worried. It's not like anyone would be sniffing my crotch; even if they would, chances are they wouldn't know it was Angela who'd been down there last night. Even the most potent of them aren't *that* identifiable. But you don't always think straight when you think you might die, so it was on my mind.

I left Angela at my apartment, where she would leave for work at Barnes and Noble in an hour or so, just in case I was being followed. If someone broke in while she was still there, we'd be in trouble, but whoever might be following me wouldn't wait outside the building once they'd seen me leave. They'd follow me. That's what following someone is all about.

I got into the waiting room and saw Eli sitting behind the desk, his coat already covering his pale, thin creepiness. "Figures. The one day I actually make plans around you coming in early, and you show up ten minutes late."

"Sorry, E." Of course, in my head, I was thinking *screw you, you ungrateful weirdo*, but I didn't want to get into that.

"Yeah, well, there's nothing to do. I don't get it. Suddenly, nobody's dying."

I laughed. Right out loud, I laughed. And it wasn't a brief little chuckle or a quick snort of breath from my nostrils. This was a hearty, belly-shaker of a good time.

"What the fuck are you laughing about?" He wasn't pissed or offended or anything. He just couldn't figure out what he could have said to get that reaction, so he asked. People want to know.

Sometimes, you slip up. Sometimes, you tell them.

"Trust me," I said, catching my breath, "people are dying. People are most definitely dying."

Eli, he just stood there, frozen waist deep in an icy lake of befuddlement. "You on something, Eliot?"

"Oh, not really." I laughed again. "Not really."

"Whatever, man. I gotta go. Dick's in his office. He wanted to see you as soon as you got here." He put his bag over his shoulder and bolted.

The last person who would see me alive, and I didn't even get a goodbye.

He did manage to get me to vomit a little in my mouth, though. I guess you take what you can get.

Let's think about that vomit for a moment. I'd never been so scared I puked. Come to think about it, I'd never felt any emotion so intensely that it made me sick. That vomit got me thinking maybe I should just leave, run out the door screaming and waving my hands over my head like a terrified Muppet.

But I didn't. I just lingered there in the waiting area for a minute, the way the acid taste of puke lingered in my mouth.

I couldn't have left anyway. Something had to be done. I wasn't sure what, exactly, because Angela had never gotten around to letting me in on her plan, but *something* would not have included running scared through the streets of the city. There were lives at stake, here. I wasn't sure whose, exactly, because Devereaux had never gotten around to letting himself into my apartment, but more lives than mine, to be sure.

So I went to Dick's office.

"Wasn't sure you'd show up today, Travis," he said, playing with his desk-caddy's luggage, scrawling something onto something else.

I sat on his couch and tried to pin my voice to the mat, to stop its shaking. "Well, it's my job, Dick. Gotta pay the bills somehow, right?"

He put the pen back into the golf bag and looked up. "The way you behaved last night, Walter thought we'd have to put out a search party for you. He gave me an earful for taking you without telling him about it."

"No," I said. "I think a man is only entitled to one search party per lifetime. I don't want to get greedy." I hoped the clever-boy routine would soften him up.

He straightened up to show me it didn't. "I'm not joking, Travis," he said, and he came to stand directly in front of me so I'd have to look up at him, so I'd be reminded that I was smaller than what was going on here. "I just want to make sure you know that Walter means what he says about protecting our interests. You're a good kid." He put his hand on my shoulder and took a breath. "I much prefer seeing you walking into work as opposed to being wheeled in."

I'd watched enough psychological/police dramas to know what was going on here. This was the old *good cannibal, bad cannibal* shtick. Walter the scary tough guy, Dick the compassionate, *I'm here to help you* guy.

I figured I'd go with it. "I feel the same way, Dick. And I didn't mean to make anyone nervous. I just had to leave. This has been a confusing couple of months."

"I can understand that. Sometimes, this is a difficult lifestyle to accept." He meant that. He wasn't a monster.

"If there's anything you need to work out, or to talk out, come to me. I'll listen." He meant that, too.

"We don't want you to stay because it will make us happy. We want you to stay because it will make you happy." Yep, he meant that, too.

"If it doesn't make you happy, talk to me or Walter about leaving. We'll figure something out."

That last one was total bullshit.

"Thanks. I guess maybe having a little support would make this easier for me." Two can play at this game.

"Well, good." He smiled, smug. "It looks like today's going to be an easy day in this place, and I'm done with everything I needed to do, so I'm getting out of here. Here's a snack if you get hungry." He pulled a styrofoam container from his mini-fridge and handed it to me. "Leftovers from last night. I have more at home."

"Oh. Uh, thanks, Dick." I hadn't eaten breakfast, so I was sort of hungry. "Anything in particular you need me to do?"

"Not that I can think of." He got out into the waiting room, almost to the front door, and turned around. "Oh. You haven't seen Angela since last night, have you? Walter's niece? Apparently, she never went home last night."

I would have lied and said no, but it's hard to speak when you're about to choke on your bite of person *au piovre.* I shrugged and shook my head instead.

"Oh, well. I'm sure she'll be around." He lowered his head, almost a bow, and left.

28

Dick was right; coming to terms with the fact that you are, by definition, by diet, a cannibal—it's fucking hard.

I'd been struggling with it since it first crossed my mind, way up on that mountain.

The first time you eat someone is not like the first time you smoke pot, not like the first time you have sex. The first time you eat someone brings up a whole new set of ethical issues you never dreamed you'd have to deal with.

It starts with the separation of body and soul, spirit, aura, whatever. In your head, you may have always thought you knew it—a body is just a vessel, a temporary home for what some would call our greater consciousness.

How very worldly of you.

But try looking at your friend's face right before you have to cut him open. All the things you knew him to be, they all came from that face. That's the face he wore when he did all those great things that were the reasons you loved him. All those great things he said, from that mouth.

It's not as easy as it sounds, separating the absolute truth about who that person was from what that person looked like.

Granted, it's easier if the person is a stranger, but it's still no walk in the park.

Then you start to think about that person's family. You imagine the looks you'll get from his mother. It's a difficult expression to picture because you can't possibly imagine what it must be like to look into the face of the man who *ate your son*.

Survival or not, you ate him. You chewed him up, swallowed

him. He was dissolved by the acid in your stomach, absorbed through your intestines.

Survival or not, you lived because he died.

Survival or not, your crap was, at one point, comprised of this woman's son.

Even if she can possibly bring herself to understand, she's going to hate you until the day she dies. She'll hate you in ways you can't possibly fathom because you'll never have a reason to hate anybody that much.

Of course, this is only if she knows it was you. Unfortunately, I had two mothers to deal with. Exponentially worse, I had to look both of those mothers in the face. And they used to like me so much.

If you're a religious person, you worry that this may be a big no-no. It's not written anywhere in the Bible; there's no commandment that reads "Thou shalt not eat the flesh of another man" but it's got to be somewhere in the bi-laws.

If you're a spiritual person, you worry about the karma, the chi. This has to put the negative way in the lead. If you ever want to recover, you'd better figure out how to bring about world peace, and you'd better do it quick.

If you're neither religious nor spiritual, you start to think that maybe you should be. If anyone can forgive you, it's a benevolent spirit who created the universe.

The first time you eat someone—since you've never researched the laws regarding this type of thing—you worry about the possibility of going to jail for a very, very long time. You don't worry too much because it's not like you killed this person, but the system is a funny place, a house of mirrors, so you can never be too sure.

The thing is, you're so worried about all this other shit that you don't have time to worry about the potential psychological effects this will have on you. If you're this close to eating somebody, chances are your psyche's pretty fucked anyway.

But after the first one, things are different. Everything gets easier with practice.

It's dissociation. It's forgetting your glasses are on your face. You start to get used to not thinking about it. You just chew and swallow. You just eat. You're hungry, and you've already eaten one person, so what the hell? Once you're fucked, you're fucked. And besides, who's counting?

You are, if you're smart.

And you're also keeping track of the circumstances. The first three, they died in a plane crash, and you would have died if you hadn't eaten them. You did what you had to, and that's perfectly forgivable.

The fourth, he was slipped to you like he was a mickey. You didn't know what you were eating, so that wasn't your fault. Also forgivable, but barely.

This fifth guy, though, this guy you're eating while you're at work, is different. Like the first three, if you wouldn't have eaten him, you'd have died, passed on, been murdered, whatever. So, when you rationalize, this guy was a survival thing, too.

And there it is. It was survival cannibalism, and you're protected by the law. It's not like you're some crazy fucker and they're going to find kidneys in your crisper. It's not like they're going to come to where you work and find you noshing on this guy who's missing and presumed dead, murdered.

And that's where it all falls apart. You're sitting at work, eating leftover dead guy and enjoying it.

That's where it all falls apart, and you know that things are wrong that need to be fixed. But not until you're finished with your meal. You did, after all, miss breakfast.

29

"Yeah, right. Whatever you say, man."

I was at Dave's apartment, Adam's apartment, trying to tell Dave what was going on. I told him I hadn't seen Adam in a couple days, so I couldn't help him get his weed. I told him Virginia was more than a little pissed at me because I sent her home with a potential murderer, and I didn't even wait up to see if she got there safely. I told him that the meetings I'd gone to, the meetings Adam and Virginia had told him about, were meetings for people who like to eat people. I told him that his uncle, my boss, was a founding member.

I told Dave everything. Passwords, fancy dinners, unclaimed dead. The possibility of becoming one of those unclaimed dead, one of those fancy dinners.

I told him everything, and all he could say was, "Whatever you say, man."

I could have killed him. I told him he had to believe me. His uncle was a cannibal. I knew. I'd seen him. I'd been there with him.

"So, you're a cannibal, too?"

"No," I said. "I'm not a cannibal."

"Then why were you allowed to go to cannibal meetings?"

"Because they asked me to go. But I'm not one of them. I swear to fucking Christ I'm not."

He ground a butt into the sole of his shoe, tossed the filter into the trash. "So you didn't eat those fancy dinners, then?"

I felt like he was missing the point. "No. I mean, yeah, I ate the dinners. Just the two. The first one, they didn't tell me what it was. And the second they forced on me." I saw no need to tell him about my gift from his uncle at work.

"Oh. Let me see if I got this straight." He took a sip of whatever he was drinking. "A one-armed man sends you a letter inviting you to meet him at the James Street Tavern. So you do, and then he invites you to speak at this meeting. So you do, and they feed you, but they don't tell you what they're feeding you. Then, on your own, you find out about the next meeting, and you go. They feed you again, but this time they tell you you're eating a dead guy. But you don't want to eat a dead guy, so they make you and tell you they'll kill you if you tell anyone. Is that about it?"

I couldn't tell if he was patronizing me or not, but at least he'd been paying attention. "That's about it, yeah. And I think Virginia may have gone home with this guy that the one-armed man had following me."

"Wait. She did a guy you think might kill you?"

"No," I said. "Well, I wouldn't be surprised if she did, but all I know is they left at the same time, in separate cars. She left a message, but didn't say anything about him being there."

"Ok. And this guy wouldn't kill her because she doesn't know anything, right?"

"I hope he's not going to kill her, anyway." I wasn't fully convinced of this, but I was working on it.

"And he's really only after you?"

"Right. Well, I think he *might* be after me, and only *maybe* to kill me. And if he knows about it, this girl that stayed with me last night. She's from there, too."

"So you fucked one of them?"

"She's not one of them, but I did fuck her. She's One-arm's niece."

He looked like his head might explode.

"It's a long story."

Dave, poor Dave, had had enough. "All right. Shut up. That's enough. There's no fucking way you're telling the truth. No fucking way. I mean, come on, you don't really expect me to believe this, do you?"

"I guess not."

"Yeah. That's what I thought."

"But, come on, Dave. Why would I make all this up? Have I ever lied to you before?" I thought for a second. "I mean, other than about that girl in college."

"I think you should go back to the doctor, man. You sound like a fucking lunatic. And you're talking like you're all coked up."

I had to give him that one. "But it's not coke. It's... It's people, man. You get all this energy and you can't..."

"Wait, wait, wait." He stood up. "When's the last time you ate someone?"

"This afternoon."

"They made you do this today?"

"No. Your uncle had some leftovers in his office. He gave them to me." It just slipped out.

"And you ate them?!"

"I, uh..."

He made like he was going to hit me, and I, all folded up in the chair in his living room, went to protect my face. But he didn't hit me. All he said was, "Wouldn't that make you a cannibal by choice?"

I'd have rather he hit me. I knew Dave was right.

People want to know.

I want to know.

But I did not want to know how messed up I'd become. I did not want to know that I was falling off of that fence that separates the crazy from the eccentric, and falling to the wrong side, at that. I did not want to know that I had found a path and taken it, only to find that it was leading me to a place where I'd be hiding human blow-up dolls under my bed and collecting fingers in a coffee can.

It's funny how something so big can change so suddenly. How you can go from being fucked up by force to being fucked up by choice. How you don't even notice the change until someone else points it out for you.

It only takes a little nibble. Just that first bite. Just because you're hungry.

"Shit, Dave." I put my head in my hands. Melodramatic, yes, but not intentionally.

"You're serious, aren't you?"

I nodded.

He tried to rub the skin right off his face, smushing his cheeks and nose, grinding his eyelids with his fists. "Oh shit, Travis."

I lit two cigarettes and hoped he'd take one. He did, and without hesitation, but this does not mean he was ok with all this new information.

"Jesus! You're a fucking cannibal! What the fuck, man! I mean, how… why…what the fuck?!" He was in a healthy pace now, back and forth across his living room, hands gesturing out in front of him. "This is so fucked up, Travis. I mean, shit. Like, I get the whole accident thing. Anyone would've done that. But this is fucking crazy. *You* are fucking crazy."

He was handling it surprisingly well.

"And my uncle?! Shit. My uncle! I swear to God, if I find out you're fucking with me, I'll fucking kill you!"

"You'll have to get in line, buddy. And besides, you should be relieved if you find out I'm lying." For a second, I thought I may have said the wrong thing. This was only because, for that second, Dave's eyes were on fire. I swear it. His irises, brown and plain, actually went reds and oranges. It was really frightening.

But Dave was a pretty sharp guy and usually kept his head about him. "Huh. I guess you're right." He calmed himself the way I imagine Poseidon smoothing out the waves, and he sat. "All right. We're smoking the rest of my pot, and we're playing video games. This has to sink in a little."

Sounded good to me. I needed a break, and if video games are enough to make an entire nation of children utterly retarded, I figured they'd be able to take me out of my head for a bit.

"You're not going to start gnawing on my leg when you get the munchies, are you?" Dave, like most of my friends, was just cynical enough to deal with this situation.

After a few rounds of Tekken and a few games of Madden, Dave wished Adam was around. "I need to smoke more," he said. "That fucker's probably driving around, stoned off my weed."

It wasn't like Adam to up and disappear. He was raised to call his mother if he was going to be late for supper or out later than he'd planned, and this habit stuck with him. We always knew where he was. He'd leave phone messages or notes on dry-erase boards. If he left neither, it meant he was at the bar.

"He didn't leave a note or anything?"

"No, man. Nothing. Yesterday morning, he said he'd be at the bar with you last night. You didn't eat him, did you?"

"Nah, man. I think I've eaten more than my fair share of friends already."

"Good point. I'm glad to hear it, too." He leaned forward, dropping his arms between his knees, getting down and close like he was telling a secret. "Um, you don't know the names of the people you ate, do you? Other than, you know, Jason and Erica?"

People want to know.

I asked why he wanted to know.

"I don't know. I guess… I guess it just seems like one of those things that would be easier the less you knew about it, you know?" He may not have been able to phrase it very well (he was stoned, after all), but it made sense to me (I was stoned, too). I told you, he was sharp.

"That's quite the astute observation, David." Sometimes, when I get high, I like to use big-boy words, just to give myself a breather from the monosyllabic and crass language I usually use. We all have our things. "I know the one guy's name, but I don't think I actually ate him, and I never met him."

Dave raised his eyebrows and opened his hands, inviting

further explanation.

"Thomas J. McGovern."

He went white as the paper on his cigarette, which he dropped on the floor and didn't even think about picking back up.

"What, Dave?"

Nothing.

"Dave! What's the matter?"

He stared at the floor between his Pumas. "You don't want to know."

"Don't want to know what?"

You could tell he didn't want to, but he told me. "Remember your last year at school? There was this kid who started hanging out right before you graduated. Remember? Tall? Red hair? Kind of stupid, but funny?"

I remembered.

"Well, that's him. Only, not really."

"What do you mean, 'not really'?"

"Before the end of our last year—mine and Adam's, I mean—we had this huge party and everyone got completely wasted. This was like the night before everyone moved out. Anyhow, in the morning we found this kid's ID on the porch. No wallet or anything. Just the ID. We tried to find him, but he already left to go home, so we just kept it because the kid looked like Adam, and you never know when you'll need a fake, you know?"

I'd begun this conversation with an unclear head. I was hiding in the fog that makes you feel safe because, even though you can't see anything, nothing can see you. Then Dave came along, and with one gust he blew that fog away, and I was left in the clear, facing a snarling, nasty beast that I'd have been much happier never knowing existed.

"Bullshit," I said. "Fucking bullshit."

Dave said nothing. He just sat there, staring and twitching.

"Bullshit."

30

Once you tell a story often enough, it's almost like it never happened. Like you read about it once, years ago, in National Geographic. Like even if it did happen, it didn't happen to you.

If I'd ever thought about it, I'll bet I'd have thought this transformation would take a long time to occur—years of telling the story at parties and weddings and water coolers and reunions. Turns out that a couple weeks of talk shows and magazine interviews take care of it pretty quickly, like some sort of intense repetition therapy or something.

And you know that thing about stories changing over time? It really happens. But it's not always that the adjectives get bigger or the adverbs more exciting. It's not that the settings get more exotic or the actions more impressive.

There are some stories that are not changed for the audience.

What happens is your mind erases details that remind you what you felt then, so it gets easier to tell the story. The more things change, the less involved you feel.

What's left is fill in the blank.

What's left is a Mad Lib.

I ran out of food after ________ days. ________'s body was about _________ yards from the wreckage. The first thing I ate was his ________, and then his _________. It tasted like _________.

You get the idea.

You separate yourself from the story so you can enjoy yourself while Conan O'Brien messes with his hair and makes a funny face at the camera. This is so Paul Schaffer can play *She Drives Me Crazy* by Fine Young Cannibals as you come on-stage and shake Dave Letterman's hand, take a sip from your coffee mug. This is so Carson Daly can tell you about the time he and Fred Durst toilet-papered that guy from N*Sync's house. This is so Bill Maher can ask what you think about the government using scare-tactics to influence American citizens' views on whether or not to go to war with Iraq, but you can't get a word in edgewise because right across from you is that one slutty bitch from *Sex and the City* who won't shut the fuck up.

The story doesn't change for the audience.

The story changes so the teller doesn't feel like a character. He's just the messenger, the voice-over. James Earl Jones selling you phone service. Queen Latifah pushing pizza.

It turns into an out-of-body experience.

The story changes so you can forget about it, so you can move on.

It happens so you can go out and get drunk off the shots bought by all those people who saw you on Good Morning America, when that girl flashed the camera.

This happens so you can keep going.

This happens so that after some psycho invites you to dinner, murders your best friend, and threatens your life, you don't completely lose it.

If you were still all wrapped up in that plane wreck thing, you'd never be able to handle this new thing. This cannibal debacle.

The story changes because now it's over, and there's nothing you can do about it. It changes now because it couldn't change then.

That story is over, and now you have other shit to worry about.

31

I left Dave's an emotionally overloaded man. There was that relief that comes with getting it all off your chest—*sharing*, if you're a group therapy person. There was the fear/paranoia that I was being followed by the car behind me; that if I stopped, the guy in that car would get out, and I would have to meet my maker all slurred speech and red eyes. There was the guilt about dropping all this crap onto Dave, the Wile E. Coyote to my ACME inventions.

I was also horny, anxious, terrified, confused, determined, and tired.

I was a fucking mess.

But my concern for Virginia outweighed everything else. If she had somehow become involved I this, it was because I'd planted her right in the middle of it. Sure, it was unintentional, but most of the time intentions have surprisingly little to do with outcomes. Even Hitler thought his intentions were good, which means they were, but that's a philosophical debate just itching to get going, and I'm not much one for debate. Besides, that's not the point. The point is that Hitler meant well in his own fucked-up way, and look how that turned out.

The bottom line is I wanted to see Virginia. She deserved to know what I'd gotten her into.

So I drove around until I was sure I wasn't being followed, parked on a side street, and cut through a few courtyards and backyards to get out to Carson St. I did a quick sweep of the bar, looking for Shoulders while trying to stay hidden behind the spiked hair of all the wicked-cool hipsters crowding the place up. As far as I could tell, the coast was clear. I sat at the end of the bar, my face hidden from the crowd by a Megatouch 3000 Emerald touch-screen thing.

Virginia brought me a drink and an incredibly unpleasant look. "You better tell me what's going on right fucking now."

"You're right. That's why I'm here, actually."

"Well fucking start talking, then." God, how I love women with no desire for nonsense.

I lit a cigarette. For some reason, I hoped it would ease the tension, like the act of someone smoking a cigarette somehow made everything more casual. Yeah, it was a fool's hope.

"You're going to have to be pretty open here," I started. "This is going to sound pretty fucked up. Those meetings I've been going to—the people there—they're cannibals."

She straightened up, but not out of any sense of panic. This was most definitely an angry move. "Fuck you. I'm being serious."

"I know you are. So am I." I sipped my shot, just so I could feel the burn of it. "They eat people. I just found out the other night. The night that girl was at my apartment."

"Bullshit," she said. She shook her head and stormed off to pour some drinks. Four shots. Two for a couple guys in baseball hats, two for herself. She took them down like they were full of some magic potion that would fix everything going haywire in her head.

I watched her and wished the whiskey really was magical. I felt horrible knowing it was only booze. She deserved better. I wished I could have given it to her. As it was, I had nothing of any real value.

She came back. "You better be joking."

I shrugged and shook my head no.

"You're a sick fucking bastard." This had no tone. Not even a hint of anger. No lingering scent of her playfully bitter perfume. And she was looking at me, but only because I was what happened to be in front of her. I don't think she was seeing with her eyes just then, anyhow. I think she was envisioning a good-looking man with painfully hot shoulders strangling her as she slept. Or maybe he was stabbing her. Either way, Virginia had just learned something I'd become quite comfortable with by this point: picturing your own death is not a pleasant thing.

"So then, you're fucking a cannibal." The thing about women is you spend your whole life trying to figure out where they're going to go with this, and just as soon as you think you have it figured out, they go the opposite way. We'll never agree on what's important.

"Actually, she's not a cannibal. It's sort of a long story."

"But you are fucking her?" Like an arrow, this girl.

"I fucked her, yes. But that's not the point." I took the rest of my shot. "Did you fuck the guy with the shoulders?"

She leaned in. "Of course I did, you prick. And it was good, too."

"No it wasn't."

"And how would you know?"

"You said he wouldn't be, and I'm willing to bet you're never wrong about these things."

"Well, I..."

"It doesn't matter. You fucking the guy with the shoulders isn't the point, either. The point is that these people killed Adam. And I think they want to kill me. I just wanted you to know because I have a feeling they're keeping an eye on me and the people I know."

She took the empty shot glass and full beer away from me. "I'm never letting you drink in here again, you know. Get out."

"Listen..."

"No. Get the fuck out."

And then it happened. I watched it happen. A look came over her face, and I knew exactly what was happening in her head and in her heart. I've felt the way her face looked. I've always had trouble with empathy, but I understood this one, and I felt for her.

She looked at me, sad and desperate. "That food—that food that you brought in here..."

"I know," I said. "I know. I'm so sorry. I'm so very, very

sorry. I didn't know. I swear. I would never have done that on purpose."

"You," she said. "Fucking," she said. "Asshole!"

"I know. Please under—"

"Please what!? Please understand!?" She grabbed the empty shot glass and chucked it at me, but she missed, and her fury hit the wall, shattering and unfulfilled.

"Hey!" I yelled. "Please! Wait!"

But she picked up my beer. I jumped back, anticipating that she would throw it in my face. This would not have been the first time this has happened to me, and it likely won't be the last. What I did not anticipate, however, was that the glass itself would be flung with its contents. The thing hit me square in the forehead, followed by a shower of beer, like a comet and its trailing debris.

"You fed me a dead person, you son of a bitch! Get the fuck out of my bar!"

I didn't look, but I didn't need to. Heads were most certainly turning.

"Virginia, please. You have to—"

"Anyone who punches this asshole on the way out gets a shot!"

The thing about being famous is that the public has a short memory. And they're fickle. This does not bode well for the celebrity, who is, after all, human, and will inevitably make a mistake big enough to sway public opinion.

Three guys got out of their seats the moment she said it. I knew all of them.

I should have told her it was just another hunk of dead cow.

32

There are two ways I know of to lose track of the days. The first involves a lot of pain, hunger, cold, death, and brief-to-extended periods of unconsciousness. Sometimes you're out for hours, sometimes entire days. You can never really be sure.

The second is almost exactly the opposite, except for the death and hunger. You can have so much going on that it all seems like one unreasonably long day. Even the sleeping seems active. Sure, you'll hear the date on the radio or see it on a calendar, but whatever you hear or see are only numbers. Numbers and blocks of time named after gods or goddesses or seasons. Sometimes our measurements for time just don't cut it. It's all relative. It's like Einstein, only not so scientific.

A day can feel like a year, and a year can feel like a day. There's no defining it. Some things just are.

I knew damn well it was the end of the summer, and I was aware that, whether I was paying attention to it or not, time was moving forward. I just couldn't decide if it was moving too quickly or too slowly.

Either way, the Weather Channel said it was August 14th and to expect rain, lots of rain, this evening. They also did a story about some small town in Kansas that was pretty much destroyed by a tornado. Three dead, a bunch more injured. (Pat Robertson ran a story about it, too, incidentally. He said that God was no longer watching over this town because the schools were teaching intelligent design. So much for *judge not*, I guess.)

I thought about all those people who no longer had homes. No schools, no bars. I thought maybe I should go there, volunteer, offer my help to people with worse luck than my own. It would be perfect. I could get away from everything and do something good, all in one go.

Then someone knocked on my door, and the do-good thought bubble burst in a puff of smoke.

It was Mr. Hanlon.

"Mr. Eliot," he said as he passed by me and into my living room.

"Hi, Hr. Hanlon." I ducked back into the bedroom for a pair of jeans and a t-shirt. "What brings you up here?"

He was inspecting the place, not like tossing a jail cell or anything, but just looking around, trying to find something different, out of place, the way you find differences between two pictures on the back of a cereal box. "Mrs. Greenly, downstairs, said she heard some sort of commotion a couple nights ago. Breaking glass or something like that. I'm just checking to make sure everything's ok."

"Oh. You should check out the kitchen, then. I got home and there was glass everywhere. And a rock. I think someone threw a rock though the window." I felt horrible, lying to an old man. That's the problem with these kids nowadays. No respect for their elders.

"Probably those kids that have been spray-painting their names and cuss words on the dumpster and the wall around back. Little bastards." He took a look in the kitchen, saw the table drilled to the window frame, and turned around with his hands held out in front of him. "What's that all about?"

"Oh. I just wanted to make sure nobody came in. Sorry. I get a little paranoid sometimes. I'll take care of the holes in the wood. Wood putty or something."

"I should probably get the windows replaced, anyway." He walked/hobbled back out of the kitchen and down the hall, then stopped, his head poking into my bedroom. "Mrs. Greenly said she also heard a lot of thumping and crashing and screaming from up here, too. She said it sounded like a fight."

My room looked like that town in Kansas. I hadn't had time

to clean up after the night Angela had stayed, so the fallen bookshelf and its books were still on the floor, the leg that broke off my desk chair was still sitting on my nightstand, the chair on its side, and all sorts of random crap was strewn about the room. Yeah, it was a fun night…

"Looks like there was a fight in here," he said. Then something caught his eye, and he bent over, slowly, to pick it up. "Looks like my kind of fight," he said, holding up a condom wrapper and smiling.

He had to have been the coolest old guy ever.

I actually blushed. "Yeah. She did a number on me."

He dropped the wrapper. "Well, try to keep it down next time, ok? I can't keep walking up those steps just because Greenly hasn't had sex in so long she's forgotten what it sounds like."

"Yeah, sure. Sorry, Mr. Hanlon."

"And I'll get that window fixed tomorrow." He headed for the door. "I almost forgot. You had a visitor last evening, around seven-thirty. Strange fella. Talked kinda funny. Only had one arm." He stopped like he wanted me to tell him who this strange fella was.

No way. "What did he say?"

Hanlon got the point. "He said today's Thursday, and you know where to find him."

Hmm. Thanks.

"You're not doing anything stupid, are you? Or illegal? You're not running drugs in my building, are you?"

If only it were that simple. "No, sir. No drugs."

"If you say so. Get that table off the window tomorrow morning. I'll have someone here in the afternoon." And he left to do battle with the steps.

No, sir. No drugs. Just something incredibly illegal and monumentally stupid.

I was scheduled to work at noon. Angela didn't answer her phone, and it was almost ten, so there was no time to go looking for her. No time to tell her that Walter had stopped by my apartment. No time to ask her what I should do.

So I cleaned my room instead. I re-hung the bookshelf and reorganized its tenants. I drilled the leg back onto the chair and folded my clothes. Made the bed.

I fixed up my room because something had to be fixed. Now. And if I couldn't fix anything important, I'd have to make do.

After the room was back in order, I took a shower and thought about how the bedroom had gotten to be such a mess in the first place. It was a good shower, a long, hot, dirty shower, and when I came out of the bathroom, Pearson was on my voicemail. "Don't come to work today. Walter says you're going to meet him this evening, so I got Eli to cover your shift. Remember what we talked about. See you tomorrow."

It's good to know there are people who can leave clear, concise messages. Too many people just ramble on and on, making no sense. Of course, his directness was the only good thing about that message. I was a little worried about the actual content. If he was giving me the day off, he must have known something was up. I was getting tired of being out of the loop.

On the plus side, now I had time to find Angela. Time is important when you have to find someone based solely on their place of employment. It doesn't sound too difficult, but you have to take into consideration how many Barnes and Noble Booksellers are in the Greater Pittsburgh area. The phone book said six. I called a few of them, but couldn't make any headway.

So I called Virginia and left a message begging her to be careful about who she talked to and not to be alone at night, and I sounded like my mother. I left a nagging message for Virginia, and I began my search.

Three stores and five books later, I found Angela reorganizing picture books in the kids section. This was in the South Hills. This was close to neighborhoods with big houses and Lexus convertibles in the driveways.

She was leafing through Silverstein when I tapped her on the shoulder, picking *The Giving Tree* off the floor when she spoke. "What are you doing here?"

"I have to talk to you."

"You could have just called and asked for me, you know." She did not sound happy to see me.

"I tried. Is there some policy about not being helpful when someone calls this place?"

"There might as well be." She pulled me behind a tall shelf stocked with kids' science books full of experiments to Make Learning Fun!

People want to know.

And they want their kids to know, too.

"You shouldn't have come here," she whispered. "If anyone sees us together, it'll be bad. Very, very bad."

"It's ok. I made sure nobody was following me. I'm not an idiot, you know."

"Oh. Well I guess you've already thought about what would happen if someone was following me, then."

Oops. "Is someone here?"

"I don't know about right now, but those Italian guys, Conicella and Cansellini, they've both been in here today. And one of those rich-bitch wives, but I couldn't tell you which one it was. They all look the same to me."

"Well, at least no one's in here now."

She shook her head. "Yeah. At least, not *inside* the store."

If you've ever realized you're a total idiot, you'll know about how I felt at that moment. "Oh. Right. Sorry."

She rolled her eyes. "Well, there's nothing we can do about it now. What did you need to talk to me about?"

"Your uncle stopped by my apartment and talked to my landlord. He wants me to meet him at James Street tonight." I did a horrible job of hiding my concern.

I could see the wheels turning in that pretty head. "He wanted to take me there for dinner. This can't be good."

"Yeah. That's what I was thinking. What should we do?"

"I don't know."

How could she not know? I needed her to know. I *needed* it. I'd somehow landed myself smack in the middle of the lion's den, and I needed some divine intervention, here. She was my only shot.

"Look," she said. "I said I don't know. This is a new experience for me too, you know." She moved some books around on the shelf next to my head. "Well, the tavern is a public place, so he can't do anything to us there. I guess we just go and see what he has up his sleeve."

"We just go?"

"You have a better idea?"

"No," I said, defeated. "Shit. No, I don't."

"Ok then. I'm thinking he's just, I don't know, feeling us out. Trying to get a sense of whether we know each other. We'll just have to do a good job of acting like we don't." She was calm. I don't know how, but she was.

I, well, let's just say that transcendental meditation has never been my thing. "What if he already knows we do?"

"He doesn't. If he did, he'd have dealt with it by now. I'm sure he's suspicious, though."

"At least the man's consistent."

"Right. Now, you have to go. They've been coming in all day, and if they see you, we're dead. So please, please be careful."

"I will. And just so you know, I got a complaint from the lady who lives beneath me about the other night. Seems we kept her awake." I couldn't resist.

She smiled. She couldn't resist, either. "I should hope so."

33

Uncle Psycho had his martini, his blue suit, his tie, his toe tapping on the floor. He also had his niece, who had a beer.

"Mr. Eliot, so good to see you."

"Walter. How's it going?" I sat across from him, caddy-corner to Angela, and I tried to figure out how I should behave. I mean, how do you speak to a man who just maybe wants you dead? What happens if he knows you know he wants you dead, and he catches you acting like you don't? What happens if he doesn't know you know he wants you dead, and you say something that tips him off?

See how difficult it is to wrap your head around a situation like this?

I ordered a shot and a beer.

"I want you to meet my niece. This is Angela." He put his arm around her, and somehow she didn't shudder. Maybe she was used to being afraid of him. Or maybe she had balls of solid rock.

I smiled. "Hi, Angela. I'm Travis."

She straightened up. "Oh. We've met once before, sort of, when you spoke at PEP."

So, I guessed we'd met once, sort of. News to me. I'd been told we'd never met, didn't know each other. Now that her story had changed, as they all do, I had to completely shift gears. All the stuff I'd gone over in the car, all that crap I'd practiced saying out loud so I could hear myself say it calmly, just to hear myself do it, might as well have been sucked out the window with the smoke from my cigarette.

"Oh. Right," I said. "I don't think we really got to talk

though, right? There were so many people."

She nodded. "Yeah."

"Well, nice to actually meet you, then." The small talk would only take us so far. This was almost like a really bad blind date, only not as blind.

The waitress came back with my booze, and the shot glass never touched the table before it found its way back to her cocktail tray.

"Something on your mind, Travis?" Synchek had a talent for sounding sincere and without agenda. I was glad I knew better.

"Not really. I just had sort of a rough day. Need to loosen up a little."

The fucker smiled at me. "I can certainly understand that."

Five Guys Named Moe went into Brubeck's "Take Five." It's a great song, even if it is a bit overplayed, even on the Weather Channel. Synchek closed his eyes and nodded in approval of the selection, but he didn't say anything. We just sat there and listened to the music. God, it was painful.

I couldn't take it. "So Angela, what do you do?"

"I'm sorry. 'What do I do'?"

"Yeah, you know, for fun? How do you spend your time?" My intention was to make this seem like any other get-to-know-you conversation. I figured we should have been talking. It's what boys do when they meet a cute girl. Either that, or they trip all over themselves and sweat a lot, eventually leaving the room a pathetic, embarrassed shell of a man. Thank God I've gotten over that shit.

"I like to read," she said. I think she realized, like I did, that we hadn't really had a normal conversation since we met. She sounded excited about it. "Easy stuff. Mindless stuff. Like mysteries."

"Oh? Who do you like?" I asked as if I'd ever read a mystery paperback in my life. I mean, I knew some names, but come on, I had a degree in Creative Writing. I'd never lower myself to that crap. I'd been trained to be an arrogant asshole about books.

She blushed. "I really like Patterson. And Sue Grafton."

"I've never read either of them. I've seen a few movies that were Patterson novels, though. They were good."

She sipped her beer. "What do *you* read, then?"

"Literary fiction, poetry, and every now and again I'll get into some sort of religious history."

"Come on. Who do you like?"

I didn't even have to think about it. I was trained. It was all reflex. "I like Hemingway, but not his novels. Just his short stories. Dante I like. Ray Carver's a god, as far as I'm concerned."

"So, you're a snob, then?" She was flirting. Right there in front of Walter, she was flirting.

"I'm not a snob. I'm just not stimulated by mysteries, that's all."

"No, you're a snob."

I couldn't argue. At least not convincingly. "Yeah. Fine. I guess I'm a snob. But, just so you know, I'm not claiming to understand all the stuff I read."

She laughed. "Yeah. Whatever, snob."

Walter chimed in, without opening his eyes. "Nice to see you two are getting along. I was hoping you would." He sat up straight and looked at me. "Angela doesn't really get the chance to meet too many gentlemen her own age."

"Shut up, Uncle Walt."

"Travis understands. Don't you, Travis? I'm sure he can see how it would be difficult for you." He took a sinister sip from his martini glass. Martini glasses are good for that. A rocks glass would have had nowhere near the nastiness.

"Um, sure. I guess I can see that." I hated agreeing with him.

"That's why I wanted you to meet him, Angel. I want you to get to know Travis, here. He's such a fine young man. And honest. And I'm certain he's loyal. Look at him. You can tell he's the kind of guy who would do anything to make sure you didn't get hurt. Isn't that right, Travis?"

This moment convinced me that this man spoke only in death threats. Anything he said—*anything*—could have been translated into "I'll kill you," or some variation of that tiny sentence. Maybe it would be "I'll kill her" or "Any of you fucking pricks move, and I'll execute every motherfucking last one of you".

I tried not to get rattled, to act like I didn't get the hint. "You're gonna make me blush, Walter. You're making me sound like Christ, over here."

"Well, you're certainly not Christ. You certainly cannot raise the dead, can you?" He made sure he got his point across with that one. He was good.

"No. No I can't."

"But you are the kind of man who'd risk his own life to save another's, aren't you?" Dictating conversation is easier than it should be.

"Um. I guess so." I lit a smoke. My head was not meant to handle things like this.

"Good." He stood up and set a Benjamin on the table. "You two stay and get to know each other. Travis, would you be kind enough to bring Angela home tonight?"

I didn't say anything. I just looked at him.

"Thank you," he said, and he kissed Angela on the forehead. "I'll see you in the morning, Angel."

He left, and we watched him all the way to the door. Angela stole my cigarette and hit it deep.

I lit another. "That went well, don't you think?"

She shook her head and flagged the waitress. "You want another drink?"

"What's he up to?"

"I'm not sure. I really wasn't expecting him to leave like that." She drummed her fingernails on the side of her glass and chewed her lower lip. "I can't—I don't know."

Why not? "Well, as long as I have Uncle Walter's blessing, you want to go back to my place?"

She looked tempted at first, but that didn't last long. "I don't know if that's a good idea. I'm afraid he might have someone follow us."

"So what? They're following us already. I mean, we can always just say I was showing you something. My books or a movie or something. Besides, we can actually talk there. You never know, someone in here might be keeping an eye on us right now."

And yes, I was trying to get her to come back with me so I could do it to her. I'd been eating my spinach, remember? And LT knows no fear. He'll risk it all for a little fun.

But let me be clear about something. The sex was only half of my motive. The other half was pure. We needed someplace we could be alone to talk, to figure out what was going on, and I knew my place was safe. I even had a new window.

"Listen," she said.

The way she said it, I knew what was coming. I was a heterosexual male with plenty of relationship experience. I'd had enough conversations with women to know exactly what 'Listen' meant. There was only one place to go, and I really hoped she wasn't going to go there.

"Listen. The other night, that was fun. But I have to tell you… I like you. I do. But my uncle's right. I don't get to meet many guys my own age. And you're a good guy, and I like you, but the other night… there was a lot going on, and I kind of just needed the distraction. And so did you, I think. I don't want you to get the wrong idea. I don't know what I'm saying, exactly. I just don't think we should do that again."

Yep. That was what I thought was going to happen.

"Why shouldn't we? We could both still use the distraction, don't you think?"

"Don't you think we have enough to deal with? And I doubt my uncle would appreciate you sleeping with me. I am his little girl, kind of."

This was totally unacceptable. And totally fucked up.

Unfortunately, she had a good point. The only thing worse than a father figure who wants to kill you for sleeping with his little girl is a father figure who wants to kill you even *before* he knows you're sleeping with his little girl. Sex is good, but not worth dying for. Even if it would be super-mega-knock-down-drag-out sex.

"That's a shame," I said. "The other night was incredible." This was my subtle last-ditch effort.

"It is a shame. Maybe someday when this is all over. If we're still alive, I mean."

"Of course." Dammit. I wanted to get laid. I was actually sort of expecting it. These things happen, I suppose, and at least it left us with time to talk. "So, what's your plan?"

She looked around the room—just a bunch of people, eating, drinking, listening, but not to us. She moved her drink off to one side, and then mine. She rested her elbows on the table, propped herself up on them, and leaned over the table, her face next to mine, her breath in my ear.

"I think," she whispered, "we have to kill them."

34

There's a mantle above what used to be a fireplace that is now bricked-over and hidden by a not-quite-clean fish tank. These people that live here, they're religious. At least the wife. The husband is this Harley Davidson meets ZZ Top drunk. So this mantle is decorated accordingly. A cross, and that fucking "Footprints" poem. A four inch tall Harley with a digital clock on its body. A snow globe, a big crystal ball type snow globe, with some big church inside. Wedding picture in the gold frame. A picture of their daughter, Erica.

This is a few years before I ate her.

This is about a year after I dumped her the week of her prom, and her father swore he would shoot me with the very same shotgun he showed me the first time she brought me home.

This is so you understand why, also on the mantle, in front of Erica's senior picture, is a shell with T-R-A-V-I-S etched up its casing.

"Don't worry," she says, "he doesn't want to shoot you anymore. He only keeps it there to scare any other boys I bring home."

She was my first girlfriend, Erica. It was great. Fucking porn star sex all the time. And the rest of it, all the actual *relationship* stuff, that was all pretty good, too. And when I was finished with it, well, let's just say my first attempt to end a relationship didn't go well. It was effective, but clearly something I'd have to work on.

That's what got that shotgun shell up on the mantle, right between a framed Jesus and a pewter dragon.

"Sometimes I think about..." she picks up the shell and turns it so she can read my name. "He's just such a drunk asshole all the time."

She puts the shell back down. "Sometimes I just want to kill him."

She looks at me and realizes she's just said it, out loud. "I never would, though. I couldn't. He loves me and Mom. It's just, you know, something that pops in there sometimes."

I knew she'd never kill her father.

But this was the first thing that came to my head when I thought about murder. I thought about that little shell with my name. How I would have died if he'd actually shot it at me. How he would have died if Erica had shot it at him. How she'd still be alive if either would have happened.

I was getting used to dead people being around, but I was having trouble with the concept of making people be dead.

"But I think you should get a gun." Angela had her hand on my thigh as I was driving her home. "At least for protection."

"But if I have a gun, I might shoot someone with it."

"Only if they're going to shoot you first."

"They'll definitely shoot me if they know I have a gun."

"Not if you pull yours first."

Imagine chaps and a ten-gallon hat. Imagine tumbleweeds and dust blowing down the streets of Pittsburgh.

"What is this, the OK fucking Corral? Do I look like Doc Holiday to you? I've only ever shot a gun once, and it wasn't a handgun. No gun." I was proud of myself for knowing that me and a gun would not end well.

"Ok, no gun. We'll have to think of another way, then."

I almost ran over a man and his dog. He was not pleased with me. I was not pleased with Angela. "Wait. I thought you said you had a plan."

She took her hand off my leg. "I did have a plan. But now it's different. Now they'll kill us. My own uncle will kill me. He'll kill you. This is a little more serious."

Unbelievable. "I think we should call the police."

"It won't do any good. You know that. These people are rich, Travis. They have connections. Some of them even *are* the connections. They'll find out we called the cops, and they'll kill us."

Women are right more often than I would like.

"See," she said. "We have to think of something."

I agreed, dropped her off, and went home.

35

The thing about working at the morgue is you're always looking at dead people. Always, they're dead. Even the people you work with have a vague sense of finality about them.

But the ones that are really dead—cold, stinking, wretched and pale—they're dead, and that's all. You can forget all that crap about the strength still being there, trapped. You can forget about releasing souls and letting them live forever. You can forget all of it.

And sure, maybe there's some truth to feeling stronger, more virile, better, after you eat a person. But that doesn't make it healthy, and it certainly doesn't make it any less fucked up.

The thing about working at the morgue is you're always looking at dead people. These are people who, just yesterday, maybe flipped you off at an intersection. These are people who were making plans for the weekend. These are people who, unless they were terminally ill, had more to worry about than being dead today.

These people, I'm pretty sure they had no desire for you to see them, every fleshy inch, naked and lying prone on a cold metal table. At the very least, I'm sure they weren't expecting it.

But still, they're here, dead and exposed. And your job is to look at them, to touch them and move them and do all manner of things they'd surely have objected to yesterday. It would be so embarrassing, if they weren't dead.

The thing about working in the morgue is you're always looking at dead people, and every so often you're sure you know this person from somewhere. You could swear she sold you coffee the other day. You rack your brain about it. You stretch it into a map of everywhere you've ever met anybody, and you do it because it's hard to believe that this thing in front of you used to be a person, but no longer. Now, it's just a body.

Death is only final if it's actually the end of something. When all you see are dead bodies with no history, you start to forget that there has to be life before there's death.

You have to know that these people were people before they became someone's dinner. You have to remember that, even though we all die, it's still a sad thing.

You have to remember this because it's quite possible that people want you dead. They want the end of you. You have to remember that once you're dead, that's it.

Even if all this shit about immortality is right, even if someone eats you, absorbs you, they'll eventually crap you back out again.

You have to remember that your friends, whom you've eaten, whom you've crapped back out, were not just dead bodies. You have to remember that they were not just cellophane-packaged protein.

You have to remember that the story changes, but not for them. Their stories are over.

The thing about working at the morgue is you're always looking at dead people, and every now and again you could swear they're looking back at you. You could swear they're looking at you, trying so hard to tell you something. Maybe they knew you, saw you on TV, on the street. Maybe they don't want their story to end the way it's ended.

Of course, if you believe this, you have to believe that they're still in there, trapped. And you can release them. You can let them live forever.

The thing about working at the morgue is you're always looking at dead people, and you're a cannibal, and people want to kill you, and people want to eat you.

The thing about it is, it can really fuck you up. Without you even noticing, you're now really fucked up.

It can get you thinking that a couple years ago you were just some guy doing some things, normal things, boring things that no one would ever remember you for doing. You barely remember, yourself. It doesn't really matter that you don't remember, though, because that story is over. That guy isn't even you.

It can get you thinking that just months ago, you were sort of famous. You were a survivor. *The* survivor. The guy who went through this great and terrible ordeal and no one could believe anyone could be that strong. But that story is over. That guy isn't you, either.

It can get you thinking that now you're an abomination with a twisted addiction to human flesh, no concept of what life is, or what death is, and no desire for your story to end anytime soon.

And right then is when you really start to agree with Angela.

These people have to die.

It gets you thinking that you've never been a murderer, not now, not ever. You've never even had it in you to go hunting.

It gets you thinking that maybe it's time to change the story. This story has to be over, and it has to be over soon.

This guy, he isn't even you.

36

The other thing about working at the morgue is that your boss is one of the people who may want you dead. You have to go to work so he doesn't think you're up to something.

"I hear you and Angela had a nice time together." Dick was doing paperwork, and he looked up at me, raised his eyebrows. "Walter says she got home pretty late. I hope you two were behaving yourselves."

I couldn't tell if he meant sex or if he meant scheming. Goddam double entendres. "Yeah, we had a good time. She's a pretty cool girl."

"Well, I'd be careful if I were you. Walter would probably be a little upset if he found out the two of you were up to no good."

For a moment, I worried that maybe Dick was psychic, maybe he knew what I was thinking. But that's just crazy. "No. Well, someday maybe we'll be up to no good, but I'd like to get to know her a little better first."

"That's probably a good idea." He stacked his papers, put down his pen. "I hope you've been thinking about what we talked about the other day. About settling in to everything."

Oh boy. "Yeah, I have. I don't know. I mean, I feel a little weird about it being, you know, a *lifestyle*. But it does make me feel so good." I can't begin to explain to you how much I wished I was lying. "And it's much better than the alternative. I think I just sort of freaked out about, you know, actually being a cannibal."

He leaned back in his chair and zipped up his fingers. "I know what you mean. There's a certain stigma about it. It's not something you're brought up with. Taboo. It's the word. *Cannibal.* The connotation is very negative. But you have to remember, cultures have been practicing this for thousands of years. There are definite benefits."

I had to go along. Pretend. The way some Soviets would hide their Bibles beneath loose floorboards; the way some Jews would keep an autographed picture of Martin Luther on the mantle table during the Holocaust. Kids, lying is bad. But sometimes it's the only thing you can do to ensure your own survival, kind of like cannibalism.

"You know, Dick, I think you're right. I just have to get used to it. I mean, all those people, at PEP, they all seem pretty happy. And they probably needed some time to adjust, too."

"Exactly. I'm glad you're thinking about it that way. Don't get me wrong, there are people who just take to it naturally, but I think most of those people are a little, well, nuts."

I laughed. "Yeah? Who are those people? I'll keep my distance."

"Oh, I'm sure you'll figure that out soon enough." He stood up, went to the window. "I don't want to lie about it. We were starting to worry that something would have to be done. That would be a shame."

It was good to know that Dick genuinely liked me. Cannibal or not, he was a good guy.

"Yeah, that would be a shame," I said. "I don't want to lie to you, either. That's one of the reasons I'm ok with giving this some time. I don't want anything to have to be done."

"That's a relief." He looked at the bird clock. "I have to run out for a while, take care of some things." He went to his dorm room fridge and tossed me a can of Coke. "You can hold down the fort, right?"

"I don't see any reason why not."

"Ok. Well, there's nobody new, or no new bodies, in the back, so you should just hang out in the front. I'd tell you to clean up or organize something, but you've already done all that. So just read a book or something. I'll be back in a few hours."

I don't know where he went, but he went. And maybe he trusted me, and maybe not. One thing I'd figured out about people in PEP was that I'd never be able to tell what was really going on. As with women, it wasn't really their fault. I just didn't understand.

With no work to do, no book to read, and an abundance of exhaustion, I did the only thing I could think of: put my head down and took a well-deserved nap.

Eli, gentle soul that he was, nudged me awake by means of a three-inch binder slamming against the counter next to my head. "Dammit, Eli! You fucking asshole!"

"I couldn't resist."

"What are you doing here? I thought you requested today off."

He came around behind the counter. "I did. I just forgot my bag here last night, or this morning, or whatever. Came back to get it."

I looked around, but didn't see the bag. "Where'd you leave it?"

"In the back. I put it down to help Dick move the new girl, and I never picked it back up."

Wait a sec… "There's a new girl?"

Eli did that one-eyebrowed, quizzical kind of look. "Yeah. I'm surprised you're not back there, actually. She's just your type."

"My type?"

"Oh, come on, Travis. We all know the way you like the meaty ones. It's ok. Everyone has their type at first, when it's still new. I used to love the really petite ones. Like five feet, ninety pounds. Don't know why, really. It's not like we fuck 'em or anything. Everyone is just sort of fascinated at first. One of those things, you know?"

"I guess." I thought it best to leave that conversation alone.

"How didn't you know she was back there?"

"Dick. I guess he just forgot to tell me." I didn't want to eat Eli. I don't imagine he'd taste good anyway.

"Hmm. That happens, I guess." He went to the back and returned with his bag over his shoulder. "All right, man. I'll see you, when? Tomorrow?"

"Tomorrow."

"Later."

And off went Eli, leaving me there with a dead girl that Dick had obviously wanted me to stay away from. Unless he really did forget. But I doubted it.

The thing about working in the morgue is you're always looking at dead people, and once in a blue moon you pull that sheet off—that blue sheet you always see in cop dramas on TV—and you could swear that you're looking at a big-breasted bartender with a foul mouth and a serious appetite for cock. You could swear you knew this girl.

But her story is over.

This girl, she's not even her.

37

The Pirates are losing badly on the television, and the volume's all the way down. Nobody needs to listen to that crap. Not that anyone would hear it anyway; the bar's empty. Almost. There's one guy, way down at the end, drinking Iron City and playing the touch-screen. And there's me, and there's this guy next to me who's crying a little and drinking a lot. A friend of his died recently, in an accident that was, he says, his fault.

I leave the oxymoron out of it.

This is Jason, still with meat on his bones.

He says his anchor didn't hold, and his friend's repel was suddenly a lot more like a cliff-dive into a sea of rock.

"It's not your fault," I tell him. "You know you were safe." He's always been good about triple-checking all his knots and hitches, all the gates on the carabiners.

But he won't hear it. "No. I set it up. I had to have done something wrong." He finishes his drink.

I wave to the bartender. This is well before Virginia starts working here. This is when nobody I know is dead. This is before all those endings of all those stories of all those people who meet me and then die.

"No matter how you cut it," he says, "if I didn't set it up the way I did, she'd be fine."

And this was what came into my head when it finally registered that this dead girl here, this was Virginia. I knew this was my fault. If I hadn't set it up the way I did…

I looked at her for a while, long enough to think about alive moments with her body. It looked different now. There was no anger, no passion about it. It was just there, that loaf of bread. I looked at her for a while, then I covered her back up, put her back into her drawer.

Then I vomited on my shoes.

By the time Pearson got back, I'd had just enough time to mop up the floor and rinse my kicks, to sit behind the counter and really start to hate myself.

"Hey. You feeling ok, Travis? You look a little green." This moment. This was exactly the reason I told Angela no gun. I'd have killed him, shot him right in the face. And I'd have loved it.

"I thought you said nobody was here."

"What are you talking about?"

"Come on, Dick."

"What?"

I wished I'd found myself a gun. "You don't have anything to do with this?"

"To do with what?" I had to hand it to him; he looked sincerely puzzled.

"I know that girl, Dick. Her name's Virginia."

He put his hand on my shoulder. I could smell it, a sickening blend of formaldehyde and sandalwood hand lotion. "Oh. I see. It's always hard, the first time you know one of them. I guess you two were close? That why you look like you're going to be sick?"

I wanted to break his arm, but held myself to brushing his hand off me. "Fuck you, Pearson. You know I know her."

He took a step back. "I don't know who she is, Travis. I swear to God."

"You fuckers killed her." My face was burning. My voice was getting louder. My stomach collapsed into itself.

"Listen." He knelt in front of me. "I don't know what you're talking about. They brought her in early this morning. Three o'clock or something like that. She fell down her steps and broke her neck. Her BAC was huge." Either he was a damn good actor, or he was telling the truth.

Whichever it was, I realized pretty quickly that I was close to losing it, to blowing everything. If I flew off the handle now, flipping out at Dick and accusing him and his buddies of murdering Virginia, they'd see it as threatening, and I'd be toast.

I composed myself as best I could. "Oh, God. I'm sorry, Dick. I just… I don't know. That was just a really hard moment to handle."

He stood up again. "It's ok. Everyone here breaks down at some point. Nature of the beast, you know. And you've had to deal with a lot more than most. I'm truly sorry about your friend." He went to his office.

I just sat there, listening to his door open, then close. Then open, then close.

He came back in. "Why don't you take the rest of the day off. You don't want to be here right now."

All I could do was nod, give a little whimper.

I didn't believe him, but it didn't much matter. By the time this was over, he'd be dead anyway. I'd eat his heart, and the rest of their hearts. Until I was full. Until I never wanted to eat again. I would devour them the way the Aztecs did their enemies. I would steal everything about them, make it my own.

"Oh, and the next PEP meeting is Wednesday. If you're not up for it, though, I'm sure Walter will understand."

And their brains. I'd eat their brains, too.

38

I was beginning to feel bad about the nature of my recent conversations with Dave. Opening his door to find me standing there could only mean bad news. I could see it in his face. He knew I was going to say things like, “Virginia’s dead. I’m pretty sure your uncle and his friends killed her because she knew about them,” and, “I hate that it’s this way. I’m sorry about it. But if they find out you know, they’ll probably kill you, too,” and, “I think we have to kill your uncle.”

If I were Dave, I wouldn’t even have opened the door. I’d have said, “Fuck you. Go away, and never talk to me again.”

Either he was stoned, or he never imagined he’d have to hear such things coming from my mouth. Whichever it was, he let me in, and I said all those things to him.

“Call the police, Travis. You can’t kill anyone. Call the police.”

I explained to him all the reasons the police were no good to me. Some of these people *were* the police. The rest of them were rich enough to do whatever it is rich people do to keep their hands clean.

I did not, however, explain to him that I had no desire to call the police. I did not want justice. I wanted revenge, vengeance, retribution. I wanted a reckoning of Biblical proportions. If I had the power, I’d rain down sulfur, turn them into pillars of salt, cover them with boils before force-feeding them their own first-born.

He’d have thought I’d gone crazy.

And he’d have been right.

“So now you got me involved, too.”

Yeah. Sorry about that.

"And my uncle's a cannibal. And they're killing and eating, who? Everyone?"

Certainly seems that way.

This was about the point in the conversation where Dave was supposed to flip out. This was about when I expected to get screamed at, maybe hit with something. This was when I expected to get thrown out of his apartment.

But none of that happened.

He stood up and paced around the living room, smoking, presumably trying to make some kind of sense out of all this nonsense his friend was laying on him.

"You're sure Virginia's dead?"

"Yeah. I saw her. She's dead."

"And you're sure they killed her? I mean, her blood alcohol level was really high, right? You sure she just didn't get blitzed and miss the top step or something?"

"Well, I don't have proof, but I'm sure it was them. It's just too coincidental to be a coincidence, you know?" I couldn't stop rubbing my temples.

Dave couldn't stop pacing and smoking. "This would be easier if I wasn't stoned."

"Not really," I said. "Listen, Dave. I know how screwed up this is. I mean, I'm sure you hadn't planned on being involved in murders and conspiracies and everything. And I'll understand if you'd rather me just leave and not get you any deeper into this."

He stopped walking. "Yeah. I'd rather not be involved. But if they really killed Adam and Virginia, and if they're going to kill you, and maybe me, I think I'm already a little too deep to get out, don't you?" Pothead friends rock.

"I guess you're right."

"I don't think I can kill anyone, though. I mean, I'm a pothead, man. Murder isn't really my thing."

I told him I understood. He didn't have to kill anyone.

"And," he said, "I'm not so sure you can kill anyone, either."

"If I can eat people, I can kill them."

To change the story, sometimes you have to change the characters. They have to grow. Sometimes they have to become something totally new. Weak to strong, alive to dead, frightened to courageous.

To change where this story was going, I had to become a killer.

It's funny how something so big can change so suddenly.

I don't think he believed me.

"Dude, why don't we try the police?"

"Dammit, Dave! Listen to me!" I was getting heated, but I didn't think he was listening to me. "If we call the police, these people are going to find out about it, and then we'll be dead. They'll kill us and eat us and get away with it. I'm telling you, the only way to stop them is to kill them."

He listened that time. "And how many of 'them' are there?"

"Somewhere between forty and a thousand."

That caught him off guard. "A fucking thousand?!"

"Not really a thousand, Dave. That was a joke."

"Not funny."

"Sorry. But I don't think we really have to kill many of them. I think just the head guys. Maybe like seven people." Seven, even to me, sounded like too many.

"And of those seven people?"

I hated to say it, but, "Yeah, buddy. Your uncle's one of them."

Poor Dave. "This is not right."

"I know."

"I don't know if I can do this."

"They're going to kill us, Dave. Well, probably me. And maybe you. And maybe Angela."

"Who the hell is Angela?"

"The head guy's niece, remember?"

"That girl you fucked?"

"Yep. She's going to have to kill her uncle, too. You guys should meet. You have a lot in common."

He chuckled at that one. "That's really not funny."

"Sure it is."

"How can you make jokes about this?"

"I'm planning on killing a bunch of people, Dave. I have to laugh about it, or I'll go insane."

"Yeah. You're really in your right mind now." He lit a smoke. "And what if they find you out?"

It was a good point.

"Well, I imagine I get murdered, and they feed me to the fucking pigs."

39

Back in my apartment, I had a new window. It was locked, a note taped right to the middle. *No charge. But be careful. There's been some strange people around. Mr. Hanlon.*

I thought maybe I should warn him. Yeah, there are some strange people around, and you'll never believe who they are or why they're around.

It was beginning to feel like I was stranded again, like my legs were broken and everyone around me was dead. No one to call to. No one to help me. It was unfair that this should happen to me again. I would have given God one hell of a talking to, but I knew better than that. If He existed at all, cursing him out would not have helped my situation. Of course, if He existed at all, why was this happening?

Luckily, this time around I had two friends who were still alive, at least for the moment. Survival is much easier when it's a team effort.

I got back to my apartment and checked my phone. The light flashed. I hated that fucking thing.

It was Angela. She said not to try to get a hold of her. She'd see me at PEP on Wednesday. Don't call. Don't try to find her at the bookstore. Just wait to see her on Wednesday.

She wasn't whispering, but she was quiet, hushed, brief. Maybe it was more like she was rushed. There was a sense of danger in her voice that made me nervous, and I was instantly and acutely aware that I would have to end this, and it would have to be on Wednesday.

I had no plan. I had no help from Angela.

On Wednesday, this would be over, one way or the other.

On Wednesday, stories would change.

On Monday, however, everything would remain the same. I'd get a phone call from Dick before I was ready to leave for work, and he'd tell me to take the morning off—we had a delivery to make that night.

And I knew who that delivery would be. I'd have to load poor dead Virginia onto a truck, drive her to Gregor's "research facility," and carry her into a fucking meat locker. I fucking knew it.

I showered and thought about the Wari in Brazil. I thought about this tribe that ate their deceased loved ones rather than burying them in the ground. It was better, they thought, to eat them than to let their bodies decompose in the cold earth, to be devoured by worms and time. These people, they loved each other so much that it was unthinkable to abandon their dead. It would be disrespectful. It would show the person no honor.

I ate breakfast and thought about the Aztecs. I thought about this tribe in Central America that would eat their enemies. The hearts of their brave warrior enemies, they thought, would give them more courage. They'd be stronger because the heart of this person they were eating, it was a strong heart. It was as much out of respect for the fallen enemy as it was out of the desire better themselves.

I thought about Mama Cass, a cat I'd had when I was growing up. This cat, she ate most of a litter she'd had under the back porch. Mama, she ate her own children because she didn't think she'd be able to care for them well enough, and she didn't want them to suffer. It was better, this cat thought, that they should die now, before things got bad.

I thought about people in China, during the Great Leap Forward, who were so poor and hungry that they'd sell their children to other hungry Chinese, or just eat them themselves.

I thought about Dahmer and Fish. About these fucked up men who got off on eating and fucking and doing God knows what else to the bodies of the men, women, and children they'd killed.

I thought about transubstantiation. About all these Catholics chewing and swallowing the body of their Savior. These righteous, pious believers who wanted to achieve divinity through the absorption of the honest to god flesh of Jesus Christ.

I thought about the Donner Party. The Franklin Expedition. That damned rugby team in the Andes. These people, they'd have died if they hadn't done what they'd done. If they hadn't eaten those who were already dead.

I thought about myself. I'd have died, too.

I thought about all those crazy, greedy bastards, obsessed with power and money, who would kill me and eat me for little more than a decent high.

This is some heavy thinking for first thing in the morning. But if you're going to change what the story is going to become, you have to give some serious consideration to where it's been. If you're going to change where the characters are going, you have to think long and hard about where they've been. And if you happen to be one of those characters, you'd better be damn sure about what you believe and why you believe it.

Sometimes the changes are for the audience, sometimes for the storyteller, sometimes for the characters, and sometimes, just sometimes, they're for everyone involved.

The only problem is, when you're in the middle of the story, you can't be sure how it's going to turn out. Before you set out to change things, you have to accept that the results often have relatively little to do with the intentions.

After my pensive morning, I'd come to the conclusion that my intentions were good enough to risk my life for. In fact, I'd decided that my intentions were good enough to risk Dave and Angela's lives for, as well.

This guy here, he was the new me. And the new me had a plan.

I called Dave and told him what I needed him to do.

He sounded skeptical. "You sure about this? I don't want to

end up in some rich guy's fat belly."

"I'm sure," I said, almost completely honestly. "You'll be fine. Just make sure you don't mention me, Adam, Virginia, or Angela. You'll be fine."

He sighed one of those sighs that are unmistakably of resignation. "Ok. Where do I go, and what time do I need to be there?"

The fear of death will drive people to do some crazy shit.

40

That night I got to the morgue about ten minutes before seven and found Eli at the front desk, filing things, doing more work than I'd ever seen him do before.

"You know," he said, huffing and puffing for effect, "I hate when you get to come in late just to help Dick drop those bodies off. It always means more work for me." Poor guy.

I made my way behind the counter. "Well, if it's any consolation, I don't really like delivering the bodies. If I wanted to be a delivery boy, I'd just get a job with FedEx or UPS or something."

He laughed. "You would look damn sexy in those little brown shorts."

"Right. What's with all the work?"

He told me that afternoon an elevator cable snapped, and something was wrong with the emergency brakes, so the thing just dropped. Fourteen people died. "You lucky bastard," he said. "I've been doing paperwork for these fat, non-stair-taking assholes all day. I'll be here at least another three hours, and you'll be riding around in a fucking truck."

I didn't care. Not at all. Not about his extra work. Not about those fourteen people who probably had enough time during their fall to realize that they were about to die very painful deaths. I just didn't care.

"Bummer," I said.

He shook his head and glared at me, kind of. "Right. Dick's in the back. I think he's already started loading up the truck."

I thanked him, took a breath, and went back into the human

filing cabinet room. The back door, the pseudo-garage door, was open, and Dick was in the back of the truck, heaving a bagged body onto a shelf about waist-high. This was the second body on the truck. The first was resting comfortably on the shelf at his knees.

"Hey, Travis." He was breathing heavily. "I figured I'd get started a little early, you know, to make up for not helping load it up last time."

"That's nice of you." I couldn't take my eyes off that first body bag. I knew who was inside. "How many more we got?"

He came out of the truck. "Just two." He shook my hand. "Apparently, Wednesday's going to be a smaller group."

"Why's that?"

He shrugged. "I'm not sure. Walter just wanted a smaller group this week. He did mention the other day that he sort of missed the way it was in the beginning. It was more intimate. It felt like we had more of a bond with one another."

It's still amazing to me that all these people thought this was a normal thing, like getting together to smoke cigars and talk about the stock market, or maybe a potluck at church some Sunday afternoon.

"And who's in this smaller group?"

"The older guys, mostly." He wiped his forehead with his sleeve. "Me, Walter, Conicella, Cansellini, Stearns, and their wives. Gregor, of course. And a few others. It'll be nice, I think."

I tried not to, but I smiled. I couldn't help myself. This smaller group of psychos would make things infinitely easier on Wednesday, my day of reckoning. Still, it made me suspicious.

"Wow. How'd I manage to get into such an elite group?"

He didn't answer right away. In fact, he hesitated long enough to convince me that something was up. Finally, he said, "I think Walter thinks a smaller group will help you acclimate yourself. And Angela will be there. She asked if you could be there, too. I guess she likes you."

Sneaky sonofabitch, working a sweet, cute little girl into the conversation that way. They say flattery will get you everywhere, and I guess they're usually right about that. Unfortunately for Dick, he wasn't exactly sly.

"That's good to know," I said. "I do like her. And a smaller group will be less intimidating, I guess."

"I hope so."

I asked him who we still needed to put on the truck, and he pointed me to a couple of shorter guys, both a good bit heavier than they appeared. And that was that. We loaded them up and headed for the South Side, this time remembering the gurney.

Dick drove, and on the way we again listened to jazz. "This must be a little more pleasant when you're sober, eh?"

I laughed and nodded. It was a shame that Dick had to die. I really did like him. But I'm sure even Dahmer had a friend or two. And, when you think about it, Dick was exactly the kind of guy who, if other people ever found out he was a cannibal, they would say, "He was such a nice, quiet guy. I can't believe he'd do something like that." It's always the quiet ones.

We got to the old meat locker, and everything went exactly like last time. We wheeled the corpses into the big fridge, lifted them onto the tables, and talked to Gregor for a while.

This time, though, I had a plan. During a lull in the conversation, I turned to Dick. "Hey Dick, I have a question to ask you."

"Go ahead."

"Is Virginia in one of these bags?"

That caught him off guard. He stammered in his normal Dick way. "Why do you ask?"

I wanted to hit him. I knew damn well she was in one of those bags, and I was in no mood to play games. But I had to play it cool. "Well, she doesn't have any family, so I figured no one would have claimed her body. And since we bring the unclaimed bodies here, I figured she'd be one of them."

"You sure you want to know?" I told you, he was a decent

guy.

I nodded.

"Yeah, she is." He lowered his eyes. "I thought it might make you uncomfortable to know."

Here it was. My plan. If I was really going to pull it off, I had to start right here. And so I did. "It would have," I told him, "but I've been doing some research about cannibalism, and I came across this tribe in the Amazon that eats their dead loved ones. They feel that it helps the mourning process. They believe it's a way to keep them alive forever."

Gregor smiled and nodded. "You mean the Wari. It's good to see a young man who knows the importance of knowing about what he's getting into."

I didn't bother to tell him the reason I was in this mess in the first place was because I didn't look into what I was getting into. At least I learned from my mistake. I did, however, tell him, "Yeah, the Wari. Anyway, they have this whole ritual of dismembering the deceased themselves, and then cooking and eating them. And, I don't know, I guess it just sort of makes sense to me. I feel like maybe it would help me with everything."

Dick looked at me as though my head had just fallen off. Gregor, though, seemed to understand what I was saying, even if he didn't know I was lying about it.

I went on. "I was kind of hoping I could, you know, do that. With Virginia's body, I mean, if I'm going to end up eating her anyway." I was proud of myself for not backing out. I don't know if you've ever tried to convince someone to let you dismember, cook, and eat one of your friends, but I can assure you that it's not as easy as it sounds.

Dick didn't say anything. I think it was because he simply couldn't find anything to say. He had to have been surprised by my request. It was all he could do to look over at Gregor and wait for the hairy chef to answer me.

"It sounds like an ok idea to me," he said. "I'm going to

carve her up anyway. I don't think Walter would be ok with you having the whole body, though."

"I don't think I could eat her whole body anyhow. She's not exactly a small girl."

Gregor put a hand on Dick's shoulder. "What do you think, Pearson?"

Dick said it sounded fine, if that's what I wanted to do.

"I think it would be good for me, Dick." And you know, right then, I kind of thought it would be.

So it was settled. I would come by the next night, Tuesday, the day before I would become a murderer, and perform my own little ritual. Gregor would teach me. "We'll take the bodies to the warehouse tomorrow. But tonight," he said, "I have to bleed the bodies, the way you would with a deer. It makes the butchering a much less messy job."

41

I was late to work again on Tuesday. I was bloodshot and a little wobbly because I couldn't get to sleep the night before. I couldn't sleep because I had a cousin who'd been a hunter. One day he had me go into his garage to get something (a rake or a baseball bat or something, it's not really important), and when I turned on the light I was met with a buck, spread eagle and hanging from the rafters. It was bleeding drops like a leaky faucet onto a tarp spread over the floor. The head was just hanging there, the way I imagine a dead guy on an inverted cross, only with a really long neck.

That's what I saw. Darkness, the sound of dripping liquid, and then BAM! out of nowhere, a big-ass dead animal suspended from the ceiling, its cold juice pooling on the floor.

I could have killed my cousin.

I couldn't sleep that night because I was stuck on this vision of Virginia hanging there like that, only with bigger breasts and significantly less fur.

You might think I couldn't sleep because I was freaked out about carving her up the next day, but I was actually pretty cool with that. It was the idea of her being bled that kept me up.

We've already talked about this. Eating people, for any reason, really fucks with your head. I mean, shit, I was planning to murder people. More than a handful of them, even. But sometimes it's not about being crazy. Sometimes it's about survival.

Then again, sometimes being a little crazy helps.

I couldn't sleep because after returning home from work, I opened my mail to find another envelope with a letter and polaroids inside. A few months ago, these were always the most exciting letters. Who doesn't want to get dirty pictures in the mail, right?

These pictures were, without a doubt, dirty, but not in that wonderfully arousing way. These pictures were of Adam. Or part of Adam, anyway. They were shots of his head with its long hair and 70's sideburns. They were shots of his head, and that's it.

No body. No Zeppelin t-shirt. No jeans. No cowboy boots. Just his head, alone and on its ear on a shiny table.

And the letter wasn't much of a letter, either. All it said was, "I wouldn't tell anyone else the password."

I couldn't sleep Monday night because this was some cold, twisted shit.

I couldn't sleep because who can sleep after that? You can forget about counting sheep. Forget about warm milk, NyQuil, a bottle of wine.

Forget about sleeping. It won't happen.

But let's get back to being late for work.

Like always, Eli was there with Dick. Creepy little Eli with his albino-pale skin and his tics. Creepy little Eli with his lack of conversational skills. Creepy little Eli was there because he'd worked the graveyard shift, like always.

He just sort of stared at me for a minute. "You're late," he said.

"No shit?"

"Forty-five minutes late." He kept staring, like the first time I met him. "And you look like shit."

"No shit?"

"What's your problem? I'm the one who's been stuck at work." He was right. I may have been a little fucked up in the head, but I knew I was being an asshole.

"Sorry," I said. "I just couldn't get to sleep last night."

"It was a rhetorical question, Travis. I really don't care."

"Asshole."

He cocked his head and smirked. "Eat me," he said. "You obviously haven't had your power breakfast this morning."

I desperately wanted to say something back. Anything. But I was either too stupid, too tired, or too shocked. It took longer than it should have for me to find my voice. "Huh?"

"Oh, come on. You drool like Pavlov's dogs anytime you get near one of them." He thumbed towards the back. "It's easy to tell who does it."

"You're kidding, right?"

He swung his bag over his shoulder and went for the door. "It's ok. I've tried it, too. Just didn't like it much."

"What didn't you like about it?"

"I don't know. I guess I'm just not as fucked up as you." He wasn't trying to insult me. At least, I don't think he was. He said it matter-of-factly. And then he left, without a smile.

I sat behind the counter and worried about Eli ratting me out to, well, someone. I didn't get too caught up in it, though. I didn't have the time. I had a plan, or most of a plan, at any rate. I had to focus. I'd have to cross that Eli bridge when I got to it, if he cared to build that bridge in the first place.

But let's get back to my plan. Well, it wasn't much of a plan, really. It was more of a play it by ear kind of thing. Choose your own adventure. Mad Lib.

__________ decided he had to __________ a bunch of people. He figured that __________ would be his best option.

The best option that came to my mind was poison.

The thing about working in a morgue is you're surrounded by a shit-ton of chemicals.

Something in this place had to be lethal. I had about an hour and a half to find out what it was and figure a way to smuggle it out before Dick got to work.

Most people steal a stapler from work, maybe some pens or an ink cartridge for their printer at home. I used to take shit like that all the time.

But not anymore. That guy wasn't even me. This was the new Travis, the transformed character. Changer of stories, slayer of cannibals. This was the new Travis, mass-murderer extraordinaire, but with a hint of Robin Hood in there somewhere.

PEP was the enemy, the roaches that scatter when the lights go on, the rats that dig into your cereal—and I was the exterminator.

Of course, even exterminators need some sort of pest-killing agent, so I had to do some quick research, and there's no better time to research the potential hazards of chemicals than when your boss is off somewhere, doing whatever it is he does when he's not at work.

I had only a short time, but I wasn't worried about it. We had internet access there at the front desk, and trust me, if you want a crash course in Murder 101, there's nowhere else to go. God bless the web.

I don't want to bore anyone with a lot of details about all the chemicals we had, which of them were poisonous, and at what levels they became lethal, but I will tell you that I could have taken out most of the city if I thought it was necessary.

In the end I decided on hydrogen cyanide, which, as coincidence would have it, is used to kill rats. It's remarkably versatile stuff. It can kill you if you ingest it or inhale it. It can kill you if you get enough of it on your skin. In liquid form, it's called hydrocyanic acid, and it's colorless or very light blue. As a gas, it's clear as the air.

It's some wicked shit and can kill you in minutes. I fell in love with it instantly.

Apparently, some people are of the belief that Adolf Hitler and Eva Braun swallowed cyanide salts rather than let themselves be captured by the Allies. This has nothing to do with my story. I just thought it was interesting.

Anyway, all this learning only took about forty-five minutes, so I had plenty of time to get into Dick's office to find the key that unlocked the cabinet with all the chemicals, find a full bottle of the stuff, throw it into my bag, return the key to Dick's office, tape the key to Dick's office back up under the front desk, and sit there, checking my email and feeling hopeful about my next twenty-four hours.

I was looking forward to this, like going to a baseball game or waiting for the hooker to show up at your door.

As it was, I had no hooker. It was only Dick who showed up. "How we doing today, Travis?"

"Oh, we're good. Slow, easy day so far."

"What have you been doing, then?"

"Checking my email. You interested in any sort of penis enlarging drug? I can get you any kind you want. Pills, powders, creams. And every one of them is the only one that actually works."

He chuckled. "No thanks. I'm a little too old to worry about the size of my dick. At this point, a bigger pecker would only make it that much harder to get it up."

For a second, I thought maybe there was some way I could do this without having to kill him. I mean, I couldn't picture Dick actually killing anybody. I couldn't even see him hurting anybody. If everyone else was gone, he'd really have no reason to kill me, either.

"So," he said, "are you excited about tonight? With Gregor?"

I sort of gasped, sort of laughed. "I don't know if I'd say excited. Anxious, maybe. I'm not really looking forward to it, but I'm not running and screaming from it, either. So I guess I'm saying I'm not sure how I feel about it." The truth is I wasn't sure, and I was beginning to think that this whole ritual thing might just have some merit. I'd have loved to go deeper into it with Dick, but knew it would have been a bad idea.

"Yeah, I can understand that. It's kind of like the first time you have to kill someone, and—" He cut himself off, and his eyes got fucking huge. He'd let it slip. He was a murderer. "I mean, uh..."

"No, it's cool, Dick. Sometimes you just have to do certain things, you know? Survival. I understand." And I did.

I also understood that Dick would have to die whether I liked him or not. Pity.

42

If you've ever spent any time high in the mountains of some almost-but-not-quite charted area of Canada, you've learned to hate Canada and everything Canadian. All of it. Fuck it. Fuck Dudley Do Right and the Barenaked Ladies. Fuck Rush. Fuck the almost-but-not-quite French. Fuck hockey, except for Mario Lemieux. Even free health care. Fuck free health care. If you've spent any time in those mountains, you've learned that even free health care has been sent by the Devil as a plague upon this Earth.

But a hatred for Canada is only the tip of the iceberg that carved out those mountains in the first place. You've learned much more than that, unless you died there. If you died there, you lucked out.

If you died, you didn't have to learn that blood does not wash off with snow. You didn't have to learn that a person's thigh, although plentiful, is tough and almost gamey, while the bicep is tender and succulent and tastes a lot like filet mignon. You didn't have to learn that you can only eat so much at one sitting before you vomit, and not because you're too full.

If you died, you didn't have to learn how to crawl without causing too much pain to your already broken legs. You didn't learn that six heavy jackets, three pairs of long johns, four pairs of heavy pants, and five and one half pairs of socks are just enough that you don't freeze to death at night, but not nearly enough to keep you warm.

If you died, you didn't learn that you can, and will, do whatever you need to so you don't. You didn't learn that you're capable of surviving some pretty brutal shit.

If you died, you're dead. If you didn't, you're alive.

And that's all it comes down to, really. Alive or dead. Predator or prey.

If you died, you didn't learn how to mix a cocktail of water and hydrogen cyanide. You didn't learn that its given name is hydrocyanic acid. You didn't learn that you can do this in the privacy of your own home. All you need is a big fucking pot and the proper ingredients.

It's amazing what you can learn if you're not dead.

43

We loaded the bloodless bodies back into their bags and then into a white conversion van. No shelves in this one, bodies just stacked haplessly atop one another. We drove from the city to the warehouse, and again I was blindfolded.

We unloaded our cargo, unzipped those black bags, and placed the bodies on their own respective stainless steel tables, the surfaces scarred from countless meetings with professionally sharp cutlery.

Virginia's lips were the same blue as the acid in my backpack. She looked as cold as her sarcasm had been and was lying on her back, which was never her favorite position, although I'm sure she preferred it to being dead.

"Wow, Gregor," I said, taking it all in. "Much nicer than that little meat locker in the South Side."

"You sure you want to do this?" Gregor was petting his face, his beard poking through the gaps between his fingers. He was already in his apron, the same kind of thick, rubbery apron we had at the morgue. His gloves lay across the legs of one of the other corpses.

"I guess." I couldn't take my eyes off this blue girl I used to fuck. This was going to be hard.

Gregor tossed me an apron and a pair of gloves, but I wasn't paying attention, so they hit me in the chest and fell to the floor. I picked them up and stared at them a moment. They make clothes for every occasion, I suppose.

"Well, let's get started," he said. "I'll coach you through it."

"Actually, Gregor, I was kind of hoping to be able to do this privately."

"Privately?"

"Yeah. I was hoping maybe you could show me on the other bodies, and I could do her by myself. Alone, I mean."

He stroked his beard and bit the inside of his cheek. "I'm not sure Walter would be ok with me leaving you alone in here."

This would not do. I got my lip quivering. "It's just… We were really close, and I think it'll help me deal with it, you know?" A pretend sniffle. "Please?"

"Well, I guess it couldn't hurt. This is basically just a big prep kitchen anyway." Not all cannibals are heartless bastards. Like Dick said, it's the stigma.

I wiped my eyes and nose with the back of my hand. "Thanks."

"Let's start on this tubby bastard, then." He slapped the cold belly of the man with the gloves over his legs, put the gloves on, and grabbed a cartoon-sized meat cleaver.

It was an awful lot like carving a chicken, pulling appendages away from the body and severing them between the joints. And that cleaver, it was fucking sharp, separating the meat from the bones like peeling an overripe banana.

"Some people," he said, "prefer boiling the entire appendage before carving it because it's easier to get the meat off the bone. But I've found that the boiling tends to toughen the meat. I'm a much bigger fan of doing it like a butcher." He said it like this was any old conversation. We could have been talking about baseball or *American Idol.*

I didn't say much of anything. I tried to make it look like I was paying too close attention to what he was doing to bother with what he was saying.

He noticed my silence and the lack of disgust on my face, and he asked why I seemed so calm about this, why I wasn't turning green.

"I've done this before, sort of. Remember?"

"Then why do you need me to teach you?" It didn't sound like he was suspicious of anything, but one can never be too careful about such matters.

"Well, all I had was my pocket knife, so I couldn't really do much more than cut off a little chunk at a time."

That satisfied him, and he moved on to showing me how to go about getting to a person's liver. "It's really the only organ that tastes any good, assuming the person wasn't a heavy drinker. Well, and the brain, of course."

Of course.

The first body took about an hour but would have been quicker without all the explanation. It would have taken about half an hour, judging by how long it took Gregor to finish the next body, a prettyish blond woman, just this side of chunky and about thirty-five, I'd say. He didn't talk me through this one. He just let me watch.

The next would be mine, and he would talk me through it if I needed it. But I didn't want to start yet. I needed a cigarette. This was sort of a stressful situation, you understand, and I kept getting flashbacks of Erica and Jason, the way I cried the first few days of it, the way I didn't after that.

So we lost the aprons and gloves and stepped out for a smoke, me with my Camel Lights, Gregor with his Djarum Blacks.

I asked him how he was planning to prepare dinner tomorrow. "Unless you're one of those chefs who prefers to keep his methods a secret, of course."

"If you're going to keep things secret, they should be much more important than whether you braise or broil a steak." It was a great answer. "Besides, people ought to be able to eat a good meal even if they're cooking it themselves."

He told me that the secret to cooking a good steak is to sear both sides so the natural juices are trapped inside, keeping the meat tender. "Of course, everyone here likes it rare, so it's pretty juicy anyway." He listed the ingredients he was planning to use, and what he was going to prepare as sides (mashed potatoes with garlic and green onion, and sautéed yellow and green squash, if you're interested.), and then he told me about one of his personal favorite tricks. "Most people just season the surface, but I like to season it from the inside out. You could always just marinate it, but that takes a while and gets a little messy. I like to inject it with whatever I'm in the mood for. Soy sauce or worcestershire or whatever. It doesn't make a huge difference, really. It's just a little faster. It's just the way I like to do it."

And there it was, Gregor filling in my Mad Lib for me. Tonight, he would inject all this flesh with mostly Worcestershire sauce before putting it in the fridge, allowing the meat to soak it all up.

And before he did that, I would pour hydrocyanic acid into the bottle in the fridge.

I dropped the butt of my smoke and stamped it out. "Do you mind if I stick around to give you a hand? I love to cook, and I'm sure you could teach me some new tricks."

People want to know.

They want to know that other people want to know what they know.

"Sure, kid. You can help out. I can teach you some."

We went inside, and he watched me carve up the last body before Virginia.

He patted me on the back. "All right. I think you ought to be able to handle this on your own now. But here's the deal. I'm going to lock you in here because if you decided to snoop around the rest of the building—and I'm not saying I don't trust you—but Walter would kill me. And you have to swear that nobody ever hears about this, that I let you stay in here alone. If you tell anyone, we'll both be in a lot trouble."

I pretended to think it over. "Sounds reasonable."

"Good. I'll be back in around an hour. You ought to be finished by then." He locked the door to the loading dock and walked out the double doors to the banquet room, locking them behind him.

I went straight for the refrigerator—enormous, silver, industrial—and found the biggest bottle of worcestershire I'd ever seen. It had already been used and was about two-thirds full, which led me to believe I was one lucky bastard. A full, new, still-sealed bottle would have meant I'd have to find a new plan. It was a little late in the game for that. I dumped a bit of it into the sink, went for my bag, and poured the poison into the bottle, making sure not to alter the color of the sauce too much. To make sure, I also went after the soy sauce, hot sauce, lemon juice, and the bottle of marsala wine sitting on the counter next to the fridge.

Then I put a towel over Virginia's face and went to work, making sure to wrap a few chunks in some foil and stash them in my bag. I wasn't about to go into this without taking my vitamins first.

Gregor returned to find me covered in blood (apparently bleeding a person doesn't quite get it all out of there) and tossing the last of Virginia's flesh into a bowl I'd found in the cupboard.

"Not bad," he said. "You feel better?"

I didn't say anything, but nodded. The less often you open your mouth, the less often it can get you into trouble.

"Well then, let's get cleaned up and get this food prepped."

I didn't help quite as much as I watched. Gregor took a bowl out of the cupboard and emptied the worcestercyanic sauce into it, added a few spices that he took from unmarked glass jars, and stirred it up. Then he took his index finger and dipped it in the sauce. He touched his tongue to his finger and smiled. "This is going to be good."

I waited for him to fall over, dead. I waited for him to start vomiting or choking on his blood or gasping for air. But he didn't. I guessed it took more than just a drop on your tongue. Or, I hoped so.

He opened a drawer and removed a syringe. "Here's how you do it." He stuck the needle into the bowl of death and pulled on the plunger, sucking up the black liquid. "You insert the needle about a quarter-inch into the meat, push down on the plunger a little, stick the needle into another spot, and do it again. You have to try to spread it around so the flavor's in every bite."

He handed the syringe to me, told me to finish the rest, and cleaned up the kitchen behind me, throwing bones and other miscellaneous body parts into Hefty bags. I don't know what he planned on doing with those bags, and didn't care to ask.

We covered the poisoned meat with plastic wrap and moved it into the fridge to marinate overnight. Then we cleaned the rest of the kitchen and went out for a smoke, Gregor locking the door behind us.

"Not a bad night's work," he said, looking at his watch. "I thought we'd be at least another hour."

I looked him straight in the eyes, extended my hand, and said, "Thanks for all the help, Gregor. You have no idea how much better I feel."

"You're welcome. And tomorrow," he put his hand on my shoulder, gave it a little shake, "tomorrow you'll eat the meal to end all meals."

"I hope so," I said. "I really can't wait."

44

I've never been much of a dreamer, unless you count starving- and loss-of-blood-induced hallucinations. When we first met, Erica for some reason thought I would enjoy a dream dictionary. "There's interesting stuff in there," she'd told me, trying to defend her gift. "A creative writing major ought to be interested in what his subconscious is trying to tell him when he's asleep."

This was before she'd known me for too long. This was before she'd realized I'm not as deep as all that.

I kept the book, of course, but only flipped through it every now and again in search of archetypes I could use in some shitty poem or short story. This was when I was still writing. This was before I had more serious things to dedicate my time to.

This was when I was still the old Travis. This was when I was still worried about getting my dick wet. This was when I'd research sports statistics and the weight limit of dynamic nylon ropes as opposed to serial killers and poisonous chemicals. This was when the only people who knew who I was were my friends. This was before I ate my friends, but not too long before.

But let's get back to the dream book.

It was three-hundred pages of pure rubbish. Water had something to do with cleansing, with purity. A locked door meant you felt trapped. A chicken with a lion's head meant your desire to get pregnant, or some other happy horse shit like that. The book was crap.

So, let's get back to me not dreaming. Or, as the shrinks had corrected me when I told them I didn't dream, not *remembering* my dreams. They said everybody dreams, and if you don't remember them it just means that you're subconsciously blocking out your subconscious. Whatever.

Anyway, I remembered my dream Wednesday morning. Part of it, at least. It was Angela, prettier and more like porcelain than she is in real life (although I don't know how that's possible, even in a dream), sitting on a deep red sofa, holding a glass of deep red wine, swirling it around the glass and smiling at me, who I couldn't see, but could feel.

And that's it. That's all I remembered, but it was vivid as I awoke, like it was happening in the space between my face and the ceiling.

And that feeling—the way I couldn't see myself but could still feel that I was there—that feeling hung around a while, too. Longer than the vision of Angela and the couch and the wine.

I think it's pretty clear that I put no stock whatsoever in dream definitions or meanings, but I'd have loved to see what that stupid "dictionary" would have had to say about all this. Of course, I'm pretty sure that just about anyone could make a fairly accurate guess.

I thought about it over my over-easy eggs with toast and pan-seared Virginia on the side, and some more while I sat at the kitchen window, blowing smoke out into the city. I thought about it, this snippet of a dream, while I was in the shower. I started to think about it after I brushed my teeth, but realized this might be the last day that LT and I would have together, so I spent some quality time with him. (My recent diet had brought him out of his latest funk, and I apologized for ignoring him this past week.) And I thought about this dream as I got dressed.

I decided that it's not the images in the dream that are important, it's the lingering feeling in the morning. It's like a hangover. It's like the sore hip and ass muscles you get after having sex for the first time in what seems like an eternity. Those feelings will stick with you the rest of the day. The dream is usually gone after an hour or so.

And the feeling I had that morning was surprisingly empty considering how much shit I'd been filling myself with recently. I should have been anxious or scared or excited or, at the very least, a little confused.

But I was calm and well-rested. And really, I wasn't even calm. I wasn't anything. Just some sort of vague presence. The afternoon smell of bread baked in the morning. The itch of an amputated limb.

I imagine it's something like what they mean when they say an "out of body" experience, only without watching yourself.

Hell, I don't know. I guess I just felt a little weird.

All day, I felt weird. Something about where I was, what I was doing—none of it seemed real. Like I was in a movie or something. Or I was broken, malfunctioning. I was talking to the stars again, even though I couldn't see them through the blue of the atmosphere.

One of the ways hydrogen cyanide can kill you is if you absorb it through your skin. It can actually kill you more quickly this way than if you inhale or ingest it. Fascinating stuff.

As I spent the late morning hours dissolving my stolen goods in boiling water, a fan in the window set to exhaust, a fine particle mask over my mouth and nose, I was a bit dazed, daydreaming, thinking about things from the past that happened to somebody else, but were somehow still floating around in *my* head.

It was pleasant, this reel of short films. Days at the pool before you cared what was under all those bikinis. Getting stoned in college, munching on Reese's Pieces and guzzling a can of generic grape soda. Sex in the hot tub while the girl's parents were inside, watching *Stargate* on the Sci-Fi channel.

The person in all these scenes, he looks a lot like you, but maybe you're just projecting yourself into them. Maybe you just wish those things had happened to you. Maybe you just envy this person his sense of invulnerability and the way he knows the future is going to be a great place to be. You envy the way he's so into everything, so involved, instead of just observing.

You envy him. As you're cooking up a pot of death, you envy him. He'd never have to do what you're doing now, and he knows it, this doppelganger inside your head. That lucky bastard. And what happened to that lucky bastard, anyway?

You can't let yourself think about that for too long because if you start to remember who you used to be, who you are now becomes jeopardized, and you need to be this new guy. You need to.

You're a new man.

That kid you think about while you're preparing to do very, very bad things, he's not real. He doesn't exist.

He never existed. And still you envy him.

45

"I should have been a pair of ragged claws scuttling across the floors of silent seas."

In college I was thrown out of class by a professor, who'd obviously only gone to college to avoid the Vietnam War, for arguing that Eliot was saying he wished his life had been different, that a crab at the bottom of the ocean would have had a better life than his own. This professor, he wouldn't hear it, and I wouldn't shut up about it, so I got tossed.

North of the city, I was allowed admittance into a secret group of cannibals merely for reciting this line that got me booted from class all those years ago. And the thing is, I don't know if I was right in college, but that's what I got out of it. Walking down that long hall now, preparing myself for what would undoubtedly be a life-defining evening, I wished I was that pair of ragged claws.

Dick had given me directions to the warehouse. "Walter says you've obviously learned enough to know not to cause problems," he'd said. Turns out the place was in Butler County, about twenty minutes from the summer camp I used to work for. Or, the summer camp that one of my past selves used to work for, anyway.

I was late, but not by much, and I looked excellent in my black suit, the only suit I'd ever owned, a beautiful tailored black thing my parents had bought for me three months before their funeral. It had been the only time I'd worn it. I looked excellent in my suit and red silk tie, in my jacket that concealed a camelback filled with highly concentrated hydrocyanic acid, its hose running down the inside of the right sleeve.

I used to wear this camelback on long hikes to gigantic

climbs in Arizona or West Virginia. I used to drink water from its hose.

Or, someone used to.

Tonight, instead of carrying water to rehydrate my tired body, it carried a weapon I hoped I wouldn't have to use. It was dangerous, you see. Sure, if I needed to, I could pour some of it into a wine glass or, if I got desperate, I could spray it all over the face of some asshole who was trying to kill me. But if I got it on myself, well, that would be the end of my story. I didn't want my story to end. I just wanted it to change.

"Well, well. You clean up quite well, Mr. Eliot." Synchek offered that weak hand of his, and I shook it, looking him straight in the eye.

"I figured I should dress the part," I said as I scanned the room for Angela.

"Looking for Angela?" He smiled. "She's around here somewhere. Check the podium. It's become one of her favorite hideouts."

"She hides in the podium?" Actors would call this commitment to a role. I call it being a damned liar.

Synchek laughed. "She's a unique girl, what can I say?"

"I guess she is. I'm going to go say hello to her, if you don't mind." I started walking, but he caught me by the shoulder.

"You'll have plenty of time to talk to her tonight." He steered me toward the bar. "For now, let's get you a glass of wine."

After a brief encounter with Conicella and Cansellini concluded with the shaking of hands and two business cards going into my wallet, we made it to the bar, where Devereaux—with his shoulders that made me hate him almost as much as my suspicion that he'd killed Virginia—was pouring himself a drink.

Synchek began to play the good host. "Travis, I'd like you to meet—"

"Michael Devereaux," I cut him off.

He eyed me, but he wasn't confused. He knew I knew who

he was. "I'm sorry. Have we met?"

"No. But I think you knew a friend of mine. Virginia?"

"Virginia. Hmmm."

"Bartender at the Lava Lounge. I think she told me you were a detective or something." I knew he wasn't going to deny it, but just to make sure, I added, "She went on and on about your shoulders." Flattery, as they say, will get you everywhere.

"Oh, right. Virginia. Of course." He shot a glance to Synchek. "She was, um, friendly."

I slapped him on the shoulder. "Oh, come on now. No need to be euphemistic about it. We're all grown men here. You can say 'easy'. I won't be offended."

He gave me an uneasy smile. "Oh. Well, um. I guess she was."

"I hope you were safe. She's been with a lot of guys. Come to think of it, I think she was waiting for results from a blood test. I guess some guy she slept with called her, I don't know, a week or two ago, and told her he was HIV positive." I couldn't help myself.

And man, did he go pale. It took everything I had not to laugh at him, maybe even throw in a point of the finger and a slap of the knee.

After a moment of standing there, jaw dropped and eyes wide, he shook my hand and excused himself.

Synchek stood there, looking every bit as worried as I'd hoped he would, so I asked if he was all right.

"Is that true about your friend? Is she HIV positive?"

"Why do you ask?" I poured a glass of wine.

"This might be difficult for you," he started, and I could tell he wanted to wring his hands, "but she's, well, she's dead, unless I'm mistaken."

I stayed cool, but gave it a hint of sadness. "I know. I work for Dick, remember?"

"Of course. Of course." He still seemed nervous. "Well I think you should know that she's… I believe you and Dick…"

I was impressed by his honesty about it. "Yeah, Walter. It's ok. I know. And no, there's nothing to worry about. I was just fucking with Devereaux. See, I sorta had this thing for Virginia, and, well, I guess that was an immature thing to do, but it was just a revenge thing, you know? Just to get back at him for sleeping with her."

He didn't say anything, but I could tell he was relieved by the way he dropped his shoulders and sighed. "You seem to be handling the death of your friend quite well. I suppose everything went well last night?"

That was a slip-up on his part, the usually pitch-perfect sonofabitch. Maybe he had something on his mind, something that wouldn't allow him to keep his lies straight, something that had him spinning a little. Whatever it was, he wasn't supposed to know about last night. "It went pretty well, I guess."

"What exactly was it you were doing with Gregor? Dick mentioned something about it, but we had no time to go into detail. Some type of tribal ritual, I believe?" Now, I could be wrong about this, but the man sounded genuinely interested in, perhaps even concerned with, how my butchering of Virginia had helped me cope. It didn't sound like he thought I had anything up my sleeve, as it were.

I told him about the Wari's funerary ceremony thing. "And I took a little bit home so I could, uh, honor her there. Hope you don't mind."

"Of course I don't mind, Mr. Eliot. There's always plenty to spare, which is why we have those styrofoam takeout containers." He laughed like he thought this was much funnier than it really was.

I started to laugh, but decided it was not at all funny and that Walter and I were well beyond the point in our relationship where I had to pretend such things. We were, after all, planning to kill each other.

Of course, I didn't know if he knew what was on my mind. So I decided to find out. "So Walter, unless I'm mistaken, I think

I've seen Mr. Devereaux around quite a bit lately."

His eyebrows went up—not much, but enough. "Oh?"

"You wouldn't happen to know why, would you?"

"Are you certain it was him?"

"Come on, Walter. He's enormous. He's kind of hard to miss, don't you think?"

He blinked a few times.

I felt like a parent trying to get his kid to fess up to taking twenty dollars from the nightstand. "Walter…"

"You have to understand, Travis," he set his wine glass on the bar so he could use his hand to help him speak, "I had to make sure you weren't trying to go to the authorities or the press."

I never thought about going to the press, and I was pissed at myself about it. I'd always thought I was a pretty sharp guy.

"I had Mr. Devereaux follow you to make sure our secret was safe. You have to understand, Travis, that you didn't exactly take to us right away. We were tremendously concerned that you might try something to expose us."

I liked knowing that I already knew this, but that he was telling me like it was some huge revelation, though I was slightly offended that he thought I wouldn't be able to understand his motives.

"I guess that makes sense," I said, doing my best to let a weight fall from my shoulders, or to show the pieces snapping together in my head—some visible sign that I was thinking about it this way for the first time, and it was only now making sense. I should have been an actor.

"I hope you aren't offended. We were merely being cautious. Also, I feel I should let you know that I am truly sorry about your friend, the gentleman with the long hair. Again, we were merely looking out for ourselves." He meant it, I think.

I refilled both our glasses. "So, if you're so sorry about Adam—the long haired kid—what was with the polaroids and the letter?"

He cocked his head. "Excuse me? Polaroids?"

"Yeah. Pictures. Of Adam's decapitated head." I really wanted to call him an asshole.

"And a letter?"

"More of a warning, I guess, not to let anyone else know the password."

He sighed and shook his head. "That would have been Mr. Devereaux. I believe he found out from your friend—Virginia?—that he was a friend of yours. I'm afraid he's a little, well, irrational sometimes. He was never asked to do that. I hope you believe me."

I believed him. "Irrational? Seems a little more like psychotic to me."

"Yes, well…"

He was cut off by Dick, who seemed to have some sort of problem. His face was red, and he was sweating.

Synchek and I both noticed that Dick was, well, out of sorts. I opened a fresh bottle while Synchek reached his arm behind the bar, grabbed a glass for the panting man.

"Are you all right, Dick?" It may have been Synchek who said it, or maybe it was me. I couldn't tell. I was still stuck in that bizarre, out of body type thing.

Dick sipped the wine, caught his breath, but still said nothing.

"Dick?" I snapped my fingers at him.

He looked at me, then Synchek, then me, then Synchek. "Sorry. I just sort of choked. On a breath mint."

Dick was a lousy liar.

Walter was surprisingly gullible.

I was, well, I guess it doesn't really matter.

Synchek raised his glass that inch or two that is almost a toast, but really just an acknowledgement, like nodding at someone instead of actually saying hello. "Oh. Well, it's good to see you, Richard."

"Yeah, boss. How was the shop?" I tilted my glass as well.

"Busy. And we seem to be missing a jar of hydrogen cyanide." He was definitely talking to me.

"Missing a jar of what?" I think I had a problem with my tone on that one. I meant it to sound like I didn't even know what hydrogen cyanide was, but I think it came out a little too much like I was really concerned about it.

"I'm sure I had Eli order two jars, but there's only one. We're almost out after today." He still didn't even look at Synchek.

I tried my best. "Well, you know Eli. He was probably too busy being creepy to pay much attention."

"Maybe. But boy, were we busy today. A lot of old folks. Heart attacks, mostly. One cancer. Two car accidents. And we're still dealing with the bodies from that elevator accident." He never looked at Synchek.

But that didn't matter to the president. "Well, you know, people are just *dying* to work with you." He, and only he, laughed at his joke. He noticed as Dick and I rolled our eyes and sipped our wine. "Well, if you'll excuse me, I'm going to talk to Mr. Devereaux about those pictures." And he left.

Dick took his spot, leaning against the bar. "Pictures? Did that jack-ass send you a threatening letter, too?"

"I guess you could call it that."

"That guy's crazy. We should have kicked him out a long time ago."

"And by 'kicked him out', you mean?"

"Don't get smart with me about that, Travis."

"Sorry."

Dick cleared his throat. "The strangest thing happened on my way here."

"Oh? What's that?"

"I ran into David at the diner down the road."

"David?"

"My nephew."

It took everything in me, but I managed to swallow my wine

without choking on it. "Dave's around? I wonder what he's doing out this way."

Dick wasn't fooled, exactly. I think he was just giving me the benefit of the doubt. Still, I suppose he had to make sure. Dave was, after all, this man's kin. "He said he stopped for a milkshake on his way to some waterfall."

"Oh, right." I searched for something. Anything. "McConnell's Mill is out this way. There's this waterfall you can go behind. We smoke there with Tommy sometimes." I was lying, of course. I didn't know anyone named Tommy, and I don't think Dave did, either.

"Promise me he's not—this has nothing to do with you, does it?"

"No, Dick. Nothing to do with me. I swear. Although it is a hell of a coincidence."

"Yes," he said. "It is."

Time to change the conversation. "So that thing with Gregor went well last night. I feel much better about things."

Dick nodded. "That's good." He sipped. "You better not have gotten Dave involved in this."

I suppose there are those conversations you just can't change.

"If you got him involved in this," but he stopped short of a complete sentence, just short of furious. I think he wanted to threaten me, but realized if I did happen to get Dave involved, threatening me would do nothing to help the situation. Dave would probably die.

And you know Dick. He was really a great guy. He loved his nephew.

I could see it all going through his head. He was putting it together, albeit slowly. And then it registered. You could almost see what was happening slap him in the face.

"What are you up to, Travis?" He was panicked, starting to sweat again.

"Dick. Relax, Dick."

He looked close to tears. "What are you up to?" This wasn't

really a question.

"Listen." But I couldn't think quickly enough to diffuse the situation. My hesitation, I knew, was all the reason Dick needed to know something was about to go down. He wasn't a total idiot, you know. So what could I do? Choose my own adventure. Mad Lib. I made sure no one could hear. "Listen. Adam and Virginia were Dave's friends, too. And Dave—I know he smokes a lot of pot, but he's not stupid. He knew something was up."

You know how he'd stopped short of furious last time? Well, not this time. "How dare you—I'll—I'll—" But he still couldn't get the threat out.

"Dick, this all has to stop. It's wrong, and it's totally fucked up. I mean, eating people that just happen to already be dead is one thing, but people are being murdered. Murdered, Dick."

There was a commotion. People were seating themselves. I was running behind schedule. I still had to talk to Angela, to get her out of the building. And this thing with Dick, it was dangerous.

"They're going to kill Dave if they find out about this. He's going to knock on the door, tell the guy the password, and his name won't be on the list. Then, they'll kill him."

Dick couldn't take his eyes off the crowd as he tried to figure out what to do. I'd put him in a tight spot, and he knew it. "What are you up to, Travis? What are you up to?" It was all he could get out of his mouth, the poor guy.

I had no choice. I had to tell him. It was either tell him or squirt some of the acid into his wine glass while he was too distracted to notice. Killing him now would be far too detrimental to the rest of my plan. This would only work if I could get everybody at once. So, like I said, I had no choice.

"Ok, Dick, here's the deal. That missing hydrogen cyanide, it's in the food. I poisoned it last night while Gregor wasn't paying attention. Supposedly, it's really potent stuff, so I'm hoping it will, well, kill everyone in just a few minutes." A few weeks before, I'd have never believed that anything like this could ever come out of my mouth. Of course, a few weeks ago, I wasn't the same person. "So don't eat the meat, ok?"

He snapped out of it. "You stole hydrogen cyanide from work, and you poisoned the food with it? And what does David have to do with any of this?" He was staying calm, but it was taking a lot out of him.

I tried to make it seem like Dave would be safe. "Dave. He's sort of a backup plan. He's supposed to get here at twenty till ten. Hopefully, everything will be finished by then."

"What, exactly, is he supposed to do once he gets here?"

I wasn't winning him over. He was losing the cool he was working so hard to maintain, and I pulled my hand up into my sleeve to get my fingers on the nozzle of the hose. My plan, it seemed, really sucked.

"Listen, Dick. It's just a distraction."

"What's a distraction?" It was Walter, who had appeared out of nowhere and had his arm over Dick's shoulders.

I froze, nozzle in my hand. This wasn't the plan. This was not what I meant at all. I knew I'd never get out alive if I did it, but I was about to squirt them in the face with the acid. Dick was about to squeal. I fucking knew it.

But he didn't. I don't know why he didn't. Maybe my story wasn't the only one that was changing. He just looked at me, waiting for me to get out of this.

And then, salvation. Angela emerged from her spot in the podium, and I had my way out. "Your niece, Walter. I can't get her out of my head."

Synchek turned to see Angela as she strode calmly toward us, wearing a long black dress, tight at the hips, slit to her left thigh. "Oh," he said. "I see. She is beautiful, isn't she?"

"Yeah. Yeah, she is," I said, taking my fingers off the hose. "She's all I've been able to think about, Walter." And, for good measure, "Has she mentioned me at all?"

He smiled and put his hand on my shoulder. "Once or twice,

young man. Once or twice."

"Well, what did she say?"

But she was already at the bar. "What did who say about what?"

"Mr. Eliot here was just asking if you'd mentioned—"

I stepped between them. "Hi, Angela. It's uh… It's nothing. Right, Walter?"

He laughed. "Of course it's nothing. Now, sit down. It's almost time to eat. I believe I just saw Michael poke his head in. I must speak with him, if you'll excuse me, please."

I was nervous. Nothing good had ever come of Devereaux's presence, and I was sure this trend would continue. At the moment though, I had something more important to worry about.

Angela and I had found ourselves seated and alone, and we talked in hurried whispers.

"Don't eat the food. Any of it."

"What are you going to do?"

"I already did it. Just don't eat, ok?"

"I never do."

"You look fucking phenomenal in that dress, by the way."

"Nice suit."

"Thanks. Now here's the plan. In about fifteen minutes—"

A hand fell on my shoulder like a guillotine's blade falling on a wrongfully-sentenced prisoner's neck. How could I have possibly been in the wrong here?

It was Walter. Always Walter. "In about fifteen minutes… what, Mr. Eliot?"

Oh shit.

Another hand, Devereaux's, found its way to my other shoulder as Walter cleared his throat. "Excuse me, everyone, please. I would like everyone to take a moment to welcome back Travis Eliot. Mr. Eliot has come to accept our invitation and strengthen our group, and I do believe that he will."

There was a round of applause. They were all very excited.

They didn't know what I knew. They didn't know that I'd be strengthening the group the way Synchek meant it. They didn't know they'd soon be eating me.

But I did. The jig, as they say, was up.

"Now," he continued, "everyone enjoy your meals."

They wheeled out the carts and passed out the food as Synchek and Devereaux led Angela and me towards the kitchen. As certain as I may have been about our impending doom, I couldn't help but smile. Twenty-two cannibals in one go. Not a bad start for the new me. Not bad at all.

46

If you've ever spent any time in the mountains of Canada, you know that everything can go to hell in an incredibly short amount of time. You've learned that even the best laid plans can come crashing down around you in a heap of metal and fire and pain. You've learned that intentions, no matter how good in theory, amount to jack fucking shit.

If you've ever spent any time in those mountains, you've learned that it's important to remain calm, even when (especially when) there is a good chance that your story is about to come to an end.

This is an important lesson to remember should you ever find yourself in the kitchen of a cannibal's banquet hall, an enormous man's 9mm aimed at your head, and there, on the table where you butchered Virginia, your friend Dave, unconscious, but tied down just in case.

It's important to remain calm should you ever find Walter pacing the floor of the kitchen, big-ass meat cleaver in his hand, saying something you can't quite hear because you're just coming to, and there's this awful ringing in your ears, but you can tell by the look of him that he is more than a little miffed.

Remain calm if you see Angela, bound and gagged on the floor in the corner. Calm if you see Dick, standing near the door, silent and staring at his shoes.

It's important to remain calm.

As the ringing fades and Walter's increasingly angry voice comes into focus, remain calm. As you hear him screaming things like "poisoned the food" and "treated you like a son" and "treachery the likes of which I've never imagined", remain calm.

Lose it now, and you're dead. Just like that. And nobody will ever know. And a story is only a story if you can tell it to someone.

So it's important to remain calm when you finally realize exactly what's going on here. Remain calm when you remember Walter opening the door of a thousand locks, only to find Gregor dead on the floor, his own personal plate spilled all over. And when you remember Walter running into the banquet room, only to find a good twenty people dead, some sprawled over the tables, some on the floor, some just sitting there. At least they were already dressed for their funerals.

Remain calm when you remember Walter's face, the way he looked at you when he put it all together.

It's important to remain calm when you remember yelling at Angela to get the fuck out of here, now, and then pushing Walter to the floor. It's important to remain calm because you weren't calm when you did this, and it got you a pistol-whipping from a very large man who'd fucked and killed a friend of yours, decapitated another.

If you're alive, you've learned that getting knocked out by the handle of a gun is unpleasant, and the hangover is even worse. You've learned it'll fuck with your short term memory, and you might need a few minutes to figure out what's going on.

It's amazing what you can learn.

I, for one, learned that my plan was almost a total success. Almost. All that was left was the cool kids' table, the prom court, the royalty. All that was left was to figure out what to do from here. All that was left was one last Mad Lib.

47

Sitting there on the floor, I finally got back to normal, if you could really call it that. Let's just say I returned to this current state of reality.

Walter noticed that I was finally coherent enough to comprehend the situation, and he made his way towards me with that gigantic knife. He was determined to do, well, something, and he looked really pissed off, but clear-headed.

It's important to remain calm because when you don't, when you start flailing around in an effort to get to your feet before Walter can get to you with that knife, Devereaux will shoot you in the right arm, and you'll end up exactly where you started, only with more blood. It's not always easy, following your own advice.

"Don't worry about that arm, Mr. Eliot. It's really quite amazing what you can do with only one." He waved hello with the cleaver. "You can, for instance, decapitate a young man who helped another young man, a Judas, a Brutus, murder two dozen people." He turned around and walked slowly towards Dave, saying, over his shoulder, "I'll show you. Pay attention."

I looked over at Dick, whose eyes were no longer on his laces, but now huge and almost connected to this man who was about to kill his nephew, my friend, Dave. Poor Dave. I'd totally fucked him over, and now he was about to be headless.

I looked over at Angela, and she looked sadder than she did in the podium. I suppose the circumstances were a bit more severe now than they were back then, when life in a secret cannibalistic society was all nice, cozy routine. I understood where she was coming from. I also made a mental note of her in those ropes, for later, just in case.

I looked up at Devereaux, his gun still pointed at my face. He was watching Synchek, watching the mammoth blade in the man's hand, and he was grinning. Big. Man, it was sinister, that crazy bastard. Unfortunately, he could still see me with his peripheral vision, so I was stuck on the floor, about to watch the beheading of my friend.

And then the most wonderful thing—the banquet room door, across from the hall door where Dick stood with clenched jaw and everything else, directly behind where Devereaux stood with his gun on me, the banquet room door opened with Conicella in tears, wailing, "She's dead! She's dead! All of them! I went to take a shit, and shit! What fucking happened?!"

Devereaux turned to see. Synchek turned to see.

It's important to remain calm because when God's not opening a window, as they say, He's opening a big fucking door, and you'd better be ready for it.

I wasn't ready for it.

But Dick was. He lunged after Synchek and knocked him to the floor, the cleaver sent sliding across the tile and spinning to a stop right in front of Angela.

Devereaux, with those policeman instincts of his, spun and took aim, but the scuffle left him no shot, as he might have accidentally hit Synchek.

I don't really remember getting to my feet, but there I was, standing behind Mr. I'm Gonna Fuck Your Girl And Then Kill Her, opening the nozzle of my little acid cannon and squirting him in the face when he turned back around.

If you've ever sprayed hydrocyanic acid into a person's eyes, you've learned that first he'll scream and try to shoot you. He'll miss, of course, and by a happy twist of fate catch Conicella right in the eye. Then he'll drop his gun, drop to the floor and convulse like an epileptic at a rave, and die. You've learned that this all happens almost immediately.

If you've ever researched the dangers of hydrocyanic acid, you've learned that it's bad, very, very bad, to get it on your skin. You've learned that it will kill you, but thankfully not nearly as quickly as it has that poor bastard who just took a shot in the eye.

If you've ever woken up and had the distinct feeling that you're not really a part of what's happening, that you're only an observer, you've learned that it's no big deal to dive to the floor after that meat cleaver and lop off your own hand before the poison gets into your bloodstream. You've also learned that this involves an awful lot of blood.

I lay there on the floor, bleeding but relieved, and a big black shoe appeared in front of me, it's reflection upside-down in my blood. I looked up to see Walter. He was a grinning, sweaty-toothed madman, and he had picked up Devereaux's gun.

"I'm going to kill you all. And then I'm going to eat you."

I was getting weak. I couldn't stand. But I could speak. "You're going to kill your own niece? And your best friend? What are you?"

"I am everyone who's become a part of me. And soon I will become you as well, my young friend. This is what happens to those who betray me. You can say goodbye to Angela, if you'd like."

I turned my head, but she was no longer in her corner. Synchek noticed.

"Pity when a man dies alone. I honestly thought she liked you, too."

And then I saw it. That cleaver. The one I'd used to hack up my friend. It was next to his head, stump-side, and then it was under his chin. And then there was Walter, on his knees, hand over his slit throat, choking on his own blood as he looked up to see his niece, holding the blade that cut him.

"So much for living forever, you sick fuck," she said. And then she looked at me and took a step to help me up.

"Come on," she said. "I need to get some air."

There was a voice saying softly, calmly, "Don't get it on you.

Don't get any of it on you. Get out before you get any of it on you."

I knew this voice.

"Don't get it on you."

I was tired, so tired, but I knew my voice.

"Stay calm," I said, mostly to myself. "Stay calm."

The story isn't over yet. The story has time to change.

If you're alive, you're not dead.

48

There were days of well-balanced meals; chicken, peas, rice, milk, juice, Jell-o. There were days of sponge baths. There were nurses and orderlies, feeding and bathing me, asking me questions. They were telling me I was so brave. They couldn't believe it, I was so brave.

There were the doctors and shrinks, another ton of questions. "How did you feel when you decided you had to kill them? When you poisoned them? When you saw them there, dead? When you awoke to discover you were missing a hand?"

Those, of course, are only a few of the questions. But my answers were—oh, fuck it. My answers weren't honest. They were just a way to keep me out of the nut house, or out of prison (plea bargains and probation are two of my favorite things about this country). My real answer is I didn't feel a thing. Not a thing. That wasn't me, who did all those things. That guy, he doesn't really exist.

There were visits from Dave, who'd quit the pot cold turkey. Dave, whose last memory of that night was meeting a "really big dude" in the parking lot of the diner and asking him if he'd seen a warehouse somewhere around here. He quit smoking weed because he knew that guy, but he didn't remember it at the time. It affects the memory, you know.

There were visits from Dick, who'd managed to get some sort of immunity deal in return for turning in the surviving members of PEP. He lost his job, but was fine with it. "No more dead people," he said. "I'm going cold turkey. I think I'll write a book."

If you've ever spent any time stranded and maybe dying in the mountains of Somewhere Near Alaska, Canada, you've learned that you can survive this, but only mostly. You're not dead, you're alive. But you're not the same. Your story has changed because your story has changed you. That guy from before, you can forget about him. He's gone.

If you've ever spent any time with an underground group of murderous cannibals, feasting on unclaimed bodies, sipping fine wine, pretending to be interested in mergers and acquisitions, being afraid for your life and the lives of those close to you, and plotting mass murders, you've learned you can survive this, too. But only mostly. Again, you're not dead, but you're not you. That guy, ancient history.

If you've ever spent any time touring the talk show circuit, the magazines, the newspapers, you've learned that these people, they don't really care that you survived, even if it is only mostly. You've learned that you can make jokes like, "Oh, come on. Give me a hand here," and you can wave your stump in the air, and everyone in the audience will laugh. The hosts will laugh. And then they'll hand you a basket full of useless shit and send you on your way.

They'll send you on your way, home to your little blonde angel, the only person in the world who doesn't need to hear about what happened. The one who understands best who you are now, because she's someone different now, too.

If you've ever done any of this, you've learned to remain calm. The story changes, you change, the other characters change. You've learned to remain calm because it either all goes on, or it doesn't.

You're either dead, or you're alive. And it's amazing the way the story keeps changing when you're not dead.

42392256R00143

Made in the USA
Charleston, SC
24 May 2015